DRAWING A BLANK

OR

HOW I TRIED TO SOLVE A MYSTERY, END A FEUD, AND LAND THE GIRL OF MY DREAMS

DANIEL EHRENHAFT

ILLUSTRATIONS BY TREVOR RISTOW

HarperCollins*Publishers*

Drawing a Blank
Text copyright © 2006 by Daniel Ehrenhaft
Illustrations copyright © 2006 by Trevor Ristow
All rights reserved. Printed in the United States of America.
No part of this book may be used or reproduced in any manner
whatsoever without written permission except in the case of brief
quotations embodied in critical articles and reviews. For information
address HarperCollins Children's Books, a division of HarperCollins
Publishers, 1350 Avenue of the Americas, New York, NY 10019.
www.harperteen.com

Library of Congress Cataloging-in-Publication Data
Ehrenhaft, Daniel.
  Drawing a blank, or, How I tried to solve a mystery, end a feud,
and land the girl of my dreams / Dan Ehrenhaft ; illustrations by
Trevor Ristow.— 1st ed.
    p. cm.
  Summary: Carlton Dunne IV, an outcast boarding school stu-
dent with a secret identity as a graphic novelist, teams up with a
beautiful Scottish girl who yearns to be an American police officer to
resolve an ancient feud and rescue Carlton's kidnapped father.
  ISBN-13: 978-0-06-075252-1 (trade bdg.)
  ISBN-10: 0-06-075252-1 (trade bdg.)
  ISBN-13: 978-0-06-075253-8 (lib. bdg.)
  ISBN-10: 0-06-075253-X (lib. bdg.)
  [1. Cartoons and comics—Fiction. 2. Vendetta—Fiction.
3. Kidnapping—Fiction. 4. Boarding schools—Fiction. 5. Schools—
Fiction. 6. Scotland—Fiction.]   I. Ristow, Trevor, ill. II. Title.
III. Title: Drawing a blank. IV. Title: How I tried to solve a mystery,
end a feud, and land the girl of my dreams.
PZ7.E3235Dra 2004
[Fic]—dc22
                                                              2005020997

Typography by R. Hult
1 2 3 4 5 6 7 8 9 10
❖
First Edition

First and foremost, Dan would like to thank Trevor, without whom this book would not exist. He would also like to thank his brilliant and all-around cool editor Clarissa Hutton for the same reason—as well as her brilliant and all-around cool assistant Erica Sussman, particularly for Erica's final stroke of genius. He would like to thank his amazing agents, Jennifer Unter and Edward Necarsulmer IV. He would like to thank (or perhaps curse) Andy Ball for opening the world of comic books to him. He would like to thank his brother Jim Ehrenhaft, and Jim's freshman fall 2004 English class at St. Albans, for graciously inviting this book into their classroom and for their extraordinary insight, humor, and criticism. He would like to thank his in-laws for choosing to vacation at the home of a Scotsman. And last, but never least, he would like to thank his wife, Jessica, for no particular reason, except that she rocks.

Trevor would like to thank Dan for more than a decade of fruitful collaboration in many different media. He would also like to thank his wife, Sarah, for constructive criticism and modeling as Signy, his brothers Christian and Cles for being grella, and all the comic book artists who have inspired him, especially (in his teens) Frank Miller and (in his twenties) Mike Mignola. He would also like to mention that these drawings were done entirely to the accompaniment of the album *Ectopia* by Steroid Maximus.

For **Mike Sullivan** *(1971–1999)*,
the cornerstone of ENR,
forever and always

Note About This Book

Dear Reader,
Just so you know, this book is about how my life went completely berserk.

Mainly, it's about how my dad was kidnapped—and how I tried to rescue him and how I met this girl along the way, and how I had to solve various freakish mysteries and figure out the truth behind an ancient feud I didn't even believe in—and so on.

Before I get to all that, though, I should warn you: There's a lot of ground I need to cover up front, so it all makes sense later. Plus, there are a bunch of seeds I need to plant for the end. So please hang in there at the beginning if you can. Some exciting things do happen pretty early on. For instance, I get my head shoved in a toilet.

I don't want to spoil it by revealing any more.

So you know, too: Everything described in this book is true. I changed the names of a few of the people and places, but that's pretty much it. I didn't even want to do *that*, but my dad's lawyer said that I had to.

Sincerely,
Carlton Dunne IV

PART I

1

THE HOBGOBLINS
OF GUILT AND FEAR

"The key to telling an epic tale," my creative writing teacher announced on the very first day of fall semester, "is to treat your opening line like a prison break: You bust out in one bold move, and you never look back—not unless you're gonna kill somebody or take 'em with you. Dig?"

Yikes, I thought.

This was important, dramatic stuff. It should have kept me engrossed for hours on end, or at least until the end of the period. Unfortunately, it just wound up as further proof of a certain crucial failing of mine: Copying it down word for word represented the sum total of all the notes I took the first week of fifth form[1] year—in *any* class, biology and precalculus included.

I have a little trouble listening.

Actually, I have a little trouble with a lot of things, but listening is definitely way up there. There's no excuse, either. Not a decent one, anyway. Not like I *couldn't* listen because over the summer a band of

[1] At certain New England boarding schools, the grades you're in are called "forms." (Third form means ninth grade, fourth form means tenth grade, et cetera.) I have no idea why. Maybe it goes back to Old England somehow. Schools like mine generally love to make a big deal of how stodgy and traditionalist they are.

vicious hobgoblins invaded, and they chewed off my ears in an orgiastic frenzy of flesh eating so I went deaf, yet ultimately I prevailed . . . no, nothing like that. And I'd *wanted* to listen. Right before I moved back to campus, I'd even purchased six new Mead™ brand 5-Subject Organizers complete with, as advertised:

- **STORAGE POCKETS!**
- **DURABLE COVERS!**
- **PERFORATED PAGES THAT TEAR OUT TO FULL-SIZE 8 1/2 x 11 - INCH SHEETS!**

The problem was that these notebooks were geared toward kids who, in fact, took notes. They were geared toward the Ivy League bound. Not toward "degenerate comic-book addicts who should take some [#@%&*] responsibility for the money it costs to send a seventeen-year-old to the most expensive [#@%&*] boarding school in the country." (Or something along these lines. I'm paraphrasing my dad.)

I'd planned to change, though.

The smell of the new notebooks alone would be enough to scare me into taking some responsibility. Yes, that antiseptic, papery stink . . . *that* would transform me into a real student, someone who deserved six separate Mead™ brand 5-Subject Organizers. I was counting on that stink. I was counting on those pristine college-ruled pages, too, just begging to be filled with schoolwork and nothing else. I'd gone so far as to label each section: **PRECALCULUS. BIOLOGY. CREATIVE WRITING.** And underneath the labels: **PROPERTY OF CARLTON DUNNE IV.** I'd used all caps, the way a graffiti artist or anonymous stalker might, praying that the class names would inspire guilt and fear every time I saw them, especially above *my* name.

They didn't.

Well, okay, they did—pretty much everything around me inspired guilt and fear on some level—but the labels weren't quite enough.

As usual, by the end of the first week, all my notebooks were full of wacked-out sketches: grotesque villains and alien landscapes, terrible creatures and accursed artifacts. And, as usual, I'd hardly heard a word any of my teachers had said.

2

AN UNCONTROLLABLE COMPULSION

The ironic part is that creative writing meant a lot to me. Mr. Herzog was teaching. As anyone who goes to the Carnegie Mansion School can tell you, this was a huge deal. He was the reason I'd bought all those notebooks in the first place.

Mr. Herzog is the only teacher who can work the enigmatic lingo of a sixties radical into a discussion of *The Iliad* ("Greek gods are more human than *humans*, dig?"); plus, he's worn the same green tweed jacket for the past thirty years, and he pulls it off, with style. He's legitimately groovy, a CM legend, a phenomenon. Everyone—from the skinniest, most invisible-except-when-people-want-to-borrow-stuff (guess who?) to the most perfect, blond, blue-eyed, genetically-engineered-by-a-conspiracy-of-evil-troll-scientists (Bryce Perry)—everyone loves Mr. Herzog and wants to take his creative writing class, and I'd finally lucked out.

Some other interesting facts about Mr. Herzog:

- AS A YOUNG MAN, HE SERVED IN VIETNAM. RUMOR HAS IT THAT HE ENGINEERED A PRISON CAMP BREAK AND BUSTED OUT HIS FELLOW PRISONERS AND NEVER LOOKED BACK.
- AT FIVE-FOOT-FOUR AND NEARLY SIXTY, HE SWAGGERS AROUND CAMPUS LIKE A MAN TWICE HIS HEIGHT AND HALF HIS AGE. RUMOR HAS IT HE'S SLEPT WITH ALL THE HOTTEST TEACHERS.
- HE REFUSES TO CONFIRM OR DENY ANY RUMORS ABOUT HIMSELF. HE ONCE SAID: "RUMORS ARE TO BOARDING SCHOOLS WHAT FLOWER BOXES ARE TO TENEMENT BUILDINGS. THEY ADD THAT SHOCK OF COLOR TO A DRAB FAÇADE—BUT EVEN AT THEIR MOST OUTRAGEOUS, THEY'RE ONLY SEASONAL. DIG?"
- I HAVE NO IDEA WHAT THIS MEANS.
- WITH HIS THINNING HAIR, SQUAT PHYSIQUE, AND PENCHANT FOR TWEED, HE BEARS AN UNCANNY RESEMBLANCE TO MY DAD, CARLTON DUNNE III. EXCEPT HE'S BLACK.
- I DON'T KNOW WHAT THIS MEANS, EITHER, IF ANYTHING. IT'S JUST SORT OF WEIRD.

The point being: If I were compelled to draw comics instead of listen to a man like Mr. Herzog, then I had a problem. Of course, the real problem was that even though I *knew* I had a problem, I still couldn't solve it. I didn't even know where to start.

3

THE DEFINITION OF MISANTHROPE

At the end of first period that very first day, Mr. Herzog flashed a mellow smile and signaled me to approach his desk. I panicked. Everyone else was already filing into the hall. I needed to be alone. This had nothing to do with Mr. Herzog; I always needed to be alone. There's even a word for it:

> **Mis-an-thrope** \misĕnthrop\ n (also mis-an-thro-pist) **1.** A person who hates mankind. **2.** A person who avoids human society.

Just to clarify: I do not hate mankind. I never have. On the contrary, I've always been fascinated and baffled by mankind. (And by womankind as well, even more so.) But basically, my whole life, I've had the same relationship with mankind that a toddler has with the ocean: It's this massive, dangerous, noisy *thing*, and I'd love to jump in and splash around. I'm just not sure how—plus the tides keep shifting and the waves keep coming, and infinity on that level is sort of tough to deal with.

Definition number two, though, fits me about as perfectly as any set of words I've ever seen. Except maybe that I would add one little caveat: *Because that person is frightened of other humans.*

That pretty much sums it up.

Incidentally, I learned the various meanings of "misanthrope" over the summer, when my father bawled me out for staying inside on a gorgeous afternoon.

"What sort of misanthrope sits inside reading comic books when the [#@%&*] sun is shining?" he demanded, even though he'd spent all day in his study, too.

I shrugged. Honestly, I didn't know. But after he slammed the door and stalked off, leaving me alone to look up a word I'd never heard before, I had a fairly good hunch as to the answer.

4

GOOD VERSUS EVIL

"Carlton, would you mind if I took a look at your notebook?" Mr. Herzog asked, once the classroom was empty.

"Uh . . . well." I gripped my knapsack. The rest of my Mead™ brand 5-Subject Organizers hadn't been defaced yet. I was half tempted to pull one out and show him that instead. On the other hand, a blank notebook would be just as much of an indication of a listening problem as a notebook full of wacked-out sketches. Also, it probably wouldn't help if the cover were labeled BIOLOGY or PRECAL-CULUS, seeing as this was creative writing.

Mr. Herzog grinned, absently plucking some lint from his tweed lapel. "Don't sweat it. I know you weren't paying attention. I just want to see what you were drawing."

"Oh," I said. So, junior year was off to the exact same shameful start as the past two years: caught for drawing comics. At least I hadn't drawn any anatomically enhanced portraits of random females in class.

Mr. Herzog took the notebook and flipped through the pages; his brows knit.

My face began to get hot. It's one thing when a teacher catches you doing something in your notebook that you shouldn't be doing. Especially a teacher you admire. Then again, most illicit notebook activity revolves around spreading rumors or sharing secrets. (Not that I have much direct experience with either.) But that kind of sneaky, gossipy stuff rarely says much about you, other than the obvious. For instance, in trigonometry last spring, when Bryce Perry got caught writing a note to Kyle Moffat, and Miss Krebs snatched it up and read it aloud to the class—"*Dude I want to bang that freshman Cindy Henderson so bad cuz she is so TASTY!!*"—there was nothing really embarrassing or revealing about it.[2] The intimate details of Bryce's personality were already well known: He is a moron. But what did a crude rendering of slime-covered, cape-wearing gnomes say about *me*?

"These drawings are far-out," Mr. Herzog said after a while.

"Thanks." I chewed my lip. "Listen, Mr. Herzog, I really do plan on paying attention this semester. It's just the first day of school and all."

"They remind me of your father's work," he said.

"Excuse me?"

He arched an eyebrow. "I know about your father, Carlton," he said.

"You know about him?"

"Yes. He draws a cartoon for the *New England Sentinel* . . . *Signy the Superbad*. I know your father's editor. A cat named Roger Lovejoy."

A cat?

Mr. Herzog smiled and leaned back in his chair. "Carlton, look. Your father is a talented man. And I see you've inherited that talent.

---

[2] Miss Krebs is famous for snatching up notes and reading them aloud. She is heinous that way.

This summer, I spoke to some of the other teachers about you. They all told me the same thing: that in spite of your tendency to skip classes, you have a wonderful artistic eye, in certain contexts. What I want is for you to *expand* those contexts."

"Um . . . oh," I said.

"Carlton, I mean it," he said firmly. "I want you to free your mind. I want you to apply your artistic aesthetic to prose, to the written word. I'm sure you can do it. You see, there's a certain way cartoonists look at the world. I'm guessing it's the way *you* look at the world."

"The way I look at the world?" I echoed, bewildered.

"Yes. Cartoonists tend to view the world as a two-dimensional conflict. They see Good, and they see Evil. Capital G, capital E. Now, it's true a lot of famous cartoon superheroes present two faces. Take Superman. Clark Kent could be a real tortured soul, you know? He has these amazing powers, and he has to keep them secret, and he gets angry sometimes—but still, he doesn't have much of a true *inner* conflict, because he's a good guy at heart. And Signy . . . well, I'm a fan of your dad's . . . but she's flat, and so are her nemeses. Your dad's last strip was a prime example. He could have done a lot with that architect villain, but he didn't. That showdown was the same old showdown between Good and Evil. None of the characters had an enemy *within*. You see what I'm saying?"

Enemy within? I felt a familiar prickle of anxiety. "I think so," I lied.

He chuckled. "Good. And I know you'll do fine, as long as you pay attention and come to class. I don't mean to criticize your father, either. I truly do dig his work. But, listen, before you go, I want to make a confession." He lowered his voice and glanced toward the door, then leaned forward. "This linguistic technique I pull—you know, the beatnik jargon, the way I play fast and loose with grammar . . . it's a gimmick, but there's a point. I am trying to free your mind. I'm trying to break you out of your own mental prison. Hence the semester's opening metaphor . . ."

Hence?

That was it. He'd lost me. It wasn't his fault; even if I'd understood him, he would have lost me. My eyes had already wandered down to my open notebook, sitting on his desk. All I caught were a few snippets of his final observations:

- CARTOONISTS ALSO HAVE ANOTHER PROBLEM: THEY TEND TO THINK SEQUENTIALLY, FRAME BY FRAME, EVEN WHEN THEY'RE NOT DRAWING.
- THIS IS CALLED "BULLET-POINT THINKING."
- BULLET-POINT THINKING CAN LOCK A PERSON IN THAT DANGEROUS MENTAL PRISON.
- IF A PERSON STAYS LOCKED IN THAT MENTAL PRISON FOR TOO LONG, ONLY A MASSIVE EPIPHANY OR A TRAUMATIC EVENT CAN BREAK A PERSON FREE . . .
- ONLY *THAT* CAN STOP A PERSON FROM SEEING THE WORLD AS A TWO-DIMENSIONAL CONFLICT OF GOOD VERSUS EVIL . . .
- OR SOMETHING.

The longer I stared at my notebook, the less I heard. Its blank pages were calling to me. My fingers hungered for them. I know it sounds ridiculous and melodramatic, but it's true. Those 8 1/2 x 11-inch perforated sheets called to me the way a crate full of Snickers might call to a hopeless chocolate junky, the way a big fat scuba diver might call to a bloodthirsty shark—and before Mr. Herzog could finish, I snatched up the notebook and bolted out the door, intent on gobbling it up in a frenzy of misanthropy and two-dimensional bullet-point thinking.

5

WHAT MR. HERZOG DIDN'T KNOW

Actually, I had an excuse.

This time, I had a real, legitimate, honest-to-goodness excuse for avoiding human society, and it had nothing to do with my comic-drawing addiction. Well, it did, but the way I saw it, I *had* to skip my next two classes (biology and precalculus), because I had to be alone to fill all my notebooks with more sketches. Because what Mr. Herzog didn't know was (insert proverbial drumroll here, please):

My dad did NOT draw *Signy the Superbad* for the *New England Sentinel.*

I did.

That's right. Me! Carlton Dunne IV!

You probably saw that one coming. Still, nobody had a clue. Not that they would have cared even if they did. But that's beside the point.

The point is that Mr. Herzog didn't know a lot of other stuff, either. Like that drawing comics was an actual job that I got paid for. Or that I was on a tight deadline, because I had to e-mail the next installment of *Signy the Superbad* to the *New England Sentinel* by 4 P.M. the following afternoon. Or that I knew very well who Roger Lovejoy was, because he was *my* editor. Or that I deliberately hadn't met him in person yet, because he was also under the impression that my dad drew *Signy the Superbad*.

Or that he was *not* "a cat."

When someone as cool as Mr. Herzog describes a person as "a cat," you form a certain mental image. You see a grown-up as cool as Mr. Herzog himself. You see a groovy, tweed-wearing Good Guy.

You don't see a runny-nosed slimeball.

The Roger Lovejoy I knew, though admittedly only over the phone and via e-mail, was Evil. He was constantly distracted by terrible allergies (or maybe a terrible drug habit? I still can't tell) and by the steady barrage of ideas popping into his own head. "Note to self!" he would interrupt when we spoke. "Invent villain whose cape doubles as ultra-absorbent hanky!" (*Satisfied sniffle.*) "Sorry, Carlton. What were you saying?"

I should have hung up on him the very first time I called him.

Come to think of it, I never should have called him in the first place.

But this was eleven months earlier. The Dark Time, as I refer to it: a time when I felt even gloomier than usual—but insightful, too, so my thoughts were deep and poetic and actually sort of annoying, even to myself.

I was sixteen. It was October of my fourth form year. A bright fall dawn. The leaves had just begun to turn outside my dormitory window, casting fiery collages of yellow and red against a crisp Connecticut sky. Yet I hardly noticed. In my mind, I was as gray as a rain cloud. I *couldn't* appreciate beauty. I needed validation for my terrible secret, my curse . . . my comic-drawing habit. I needed proof that it had some kind of meaning. Plus, Bryce Perry had just plunged my head into a toilet for no reason whatsoever. It was the swirlie,[3] his favorite M.O.[4]

After drying off alone in my room, my desperation reached a fever pitch. A wild impulse took hold. I scoured the Internet for the name of a local newspaper and found the *New England Sentinel*, circulation twenty thousand. I searched their site, and I discovered the name of the entertainment editor, Roger Lovejoy. My heart thumped; my adrenaline surged, and somehow, *somehow*, I managed to suppress my misanthropy for a brief instant and called a complete stranger out of the blue:

ROGER: Hello?

ME: Yes, um, hi. Is this Roger Lovejoy of the *New England Sentinel*?

ROGER: *(sniff)* Yeah?

ME: Uh, this is Carlton Dunne. I'm a graphic novelist, and I'd like to talk to you about a comic strip idea I have—

ROGER: Whoa. hold your horses. How old are you?

ME: Why?

ROGER: You sound like a kid. I don't have time to talk to some teenage dork who thinks he can draw comics.

ME: I'm forty-eight.

ROGER: *(sniff)*

ME: Hello?

ROGER: Yeah?

ME: My name is Carlton Dunne, the Third. I am forty-eight, and I am an architect who lives

---

[3] The toilet must be flushing in order for this form of torture to classify as a true swirlie.

[4] M.O. is short for *modus operandi*, which basically means the particular way in which a person performs his signature task, such as the swirlie.

> in New York City and weekends in Fenwick, Connecticut.
>
> ROGER: That's a good one. Have you heard the one about the one-legged dwarf?
>
> ME: Excuse me?
>
> ROGER: What's your point, Carl?
>
> ME: Carlton. I'd like to pitch you my comic strip.
>
> ROGER: Pitch? Who says "pitch"? Or "weekends"? A teenage dork?
>
> ME: No, a forty-eight-year-old architect and graphic novelist.

That's pretty much it. In a moment of existential panic, I lied to a grown man over the phone and pretended to be my dad. And the twisted part is that once I convinced this grown man to take a look at *Signy the Superbad* (chalk it up to irritating persistence), he decided to believe me. Or he hired me, anyway. He called me back a few weeks later, offering $60 a week to produce a strip for each weekend edition of his small newspaper, circulation twenty thousand. I arranged for the money to be electronically deposited into my checking account, so I would never have to see him face-to-face.[5]

Honestly, I hadn't wanted to lie to the guy. I'd just been feeling deep and poetic and annoying. It just sort of happened. Plus, I started making sixty bucks a week. True, my allowance was nearly twice that, but this was *my* money. It was money I could spend however I wanted (i.e., on comic books) without worrying about Dad's decree: "Don't spend your allowance on [#@%&*] you know what."

Anyway, Signy may have been two-dimensional, but I wasn't. I *had* an inner conflict. I had an alter ego, too. I was Carlton Dunne IV, the misanthrope of CM, and I was Carlton Dunne III, the graphic

---

[5] My dad set up this account for me when he shipped me off to boarding school—so he could electronically deposit money, too, and never have to see me face-to-face, either.

novelist of the *New England Sentinel*. I wasn't exactly my own super-hero, but I was definitely my own Enemy Within—the enemy who wanted to please the *real* Carlton Dunne III, who wanted to fill my brand-new notebooks with real-life schoolwork, who wanted to make friends with abusive morons like Bryce Perry . . . the enemy I battled daily.

And there's one more thing Mr. Herzog didn't know.

A graphic novelist hates being called a cartoonist. Comics are not cartoons. Comics are deep and personal. They're *art*. Cartoons, on the other hand, are one-liners. They're cheap gags with illustrations. They're the joke about the one-legged dwarf.

I don't blame Mr. Herzog for not knowing the difference, though. Either you care about comics, or you don't.

6

A VITAL ANGRY RANT, MOSTLY ABOUT A STUPID NONEXISTENT FEUD

An important fact: I never would have cared about comics if it weren't for Dad.

Another important fact: I often shouted this aloud to myself. *"I never would have cared about comics if it weren't for YOU, Dad!"* Because I swear: It's his fault, completely. He is and always has been the driving force behind this freakish obsession of mine—in ways he could never begin to guess. Nor would he want to, I imagine.

It started on my sixth birthday.

Interestingly, this birthday is one of my first clear memories. My mother had died of cancer a few months earlier, so for reasons I'm sure a shrink could explain very well, everything gets a little foggy before then. Anyway, Dad gave me a single present: a coffee-table book about Norse mythology. It was called *The Illustrious Myths of Scandinavia*. I remember thinking it weighed as much as I did. I could barely read, but it didn't matter. Once I started flipping through the enormous glossy pages, the book cast its spell. Those paintings and etchings of Viking gods and monsters were the strangest, most exotic, most savage and beautiful images I'd ever seen.

So I hugged Dad. "Thank you, Dad!" I cried. Naturally. And it's funny, because I used to hug Dad a lot. Ha. (It really is funny.) See, he was my ally back then, as opposed to the foul-mouthed creep who would ship me off to boarding school eight years later, "for my own good." Yes, that was the phrase he used. You can't make this kind of clichéd garbage up. His reason: He was worried I would become "one of those weird loners who spends too much time reading comic books." (Another direct quote.) He said I needed to be in "an environment where a person is forced to form meaningful social attachments."

Talk about funny.

Because if there were ever a case of the pot calling the kettle black, it's *Dad* telling *me* that I should be forced to learn to form meaningful social attachments.

Yes, I may spend more time with comics than I do with people. I admit it. But that's only because I'm scared of people. Starting with Dad himself. He wonders why I hang out alone so much. Why doesn't he look in the mirror? I'm a chip off the old block! Look at what he *does*. He's a *lonely, insane, self-employed architect!* He spends all day drafting so he never has to deal with other human beings except his own clients! He treats everyone else like sewage! EVERYONE!

Take his ex-wife, Martha. The one who walked out on him last winter, because she couldn't stand to be ignored anymore. And who also happens to be one of the coolest, funniest, smartest grown-ups I've ever met—the woman who *loved* Dad and who could have made a really great second wife if he had just paid attention to her.

Then there's their daughter, Olivia. My half sister. Martha's mirror image, in blond pigtails. The four-year-old who just wants some affection from Dad—just the tiniest, littlest bit—and who (oh, yeah) also happens to be one of THE BRIGHTEST, SWEETEST, CUTEST KIDS ON THE PLANET!

I'm not the only Dunne who doesn't know how to form attachments.

But that's not the worst of it.

Well, it is—but I'm talking about a certain little family secret Dad would never admit to anyone *outside* our family, because if he did, he'd be institutionalized. You see, *I'm* not the one obsessed with a crazy legend! *I'm* not the one who believes in a stupid nonexistent feud with some nonexistent rival in Scotland! I may be screwed up, but at least I know the difference between fantasy and reality!

Oops. Maybe I shouldn't have let Dad's crazy secret out.

7

DAD'S CRAZY SECRET

But before I get to all that: Dad has a right to be a little crazy. After all, he was a lonely rich kid who decided to become an insane, self-employed architect because he loved to draw. (*Hmm. Sound familiar? Substitute "graphic novelist" for "architect."*) And, yes, I can do the whole pop psychology thing: Dad inherited a huge fortune from his father—a fortune *his* father inherited and that dates all the way back to medieval Scotland—so maybe he felt he could use an ancient feud to prove that he wasn't just another rich trust-fund lunatic with his own tartan[6] and coat-of-arms.

And, really, in the grand scheme of things, who am I to complain? That huge inheritance fund will be mine someday. Lots of kids have it worse. Most do. Most kids don't have either an inheritance *or* a stupid nonexistent feud (much less a tartan). What are my problems compared to their problems? More to the point, lots of other dads are real psychopaths. Some sell drugs. Some torture puppies. AND YET . . . *and yet* . . . What kind of maniac spends what little free time he has

---

[6] A tartan is a stupid plaid pattern that's supposed to be a big deal for old Scottish clans. It's a form of identification—unique, like a fingerprint or fart smell. You see it a lot on drunken men in kilts.

with his only son obsessing about some supposed fight that started in the Middle Ages? In a tiny town, on a tiny island, in a tiny country most people only associate with the bagpipe?

I'm not exaggerating.

I can't remember a single holiday or family dinner (the few we've shared) where Dad didn't regale me with the same old nonsense. For example: how the "head of Clan Forba" just sent him another threatening letter. And why? Well, it all dates back to what happened in 1214, in the town of Birsay, on the isle of Orkney in Scotland.

According to Dad: Angus Forba stole all our family treasure from our heroic patriarch Malcolm Dunne. Then Malcolm stole it back and everyone in town rejoiced until Angus burned Birsay down—not just as retribution for the stolen treasure but because he was jealous that everybody liked Malcolm better, seeing as Malcolm didn't have a tendency to steal treasure from people he didn't like . . . and that's how the feud started and blah, blah, blah . . . and so on and so on . . . throughout the ages, in glorious insanity and stupidity, for the past eight hundred years—and probably until the End of Time. (Or at least until Dad becomes sane. I'm not placing any bets.)

I wish Mr. Herzog could take a peek inside Dad's mental prison.

But I guess if you spend so much time locked in your *own* mental prison, your imagination ends up being your only ally. You can look at it scientifically, even.

Say for the sake of argument that you're young and clueless and you worship your surviving parent. So you start copying the illustrations from a gift he gave you, a certain coffee table book. You want to show him that you can draw, too.

You want to be just like him.

At first, he seems happy. But in time, he grows distant. You don't get it, but he's not your ally anymore. Something has changed. Then one day he tells you about an ancient feud with some Scottish guy who writes him threatening letters (which he can't show you) and swears you to secrecy. Now you really don't get it. *This* is what's making him so mean and depressed? It doesn't even make *sense*.

So you retreat further into his gift. You find solace in the rage and vengeance of the Viking epics. And you discover the myth of Signy, a wily heroine who was betrayed by her husband . . . and in a weird way, you identify with her. You identify with how the person she loved most went nuts and turned on her.[7]

In the meantime, you also discover other illustrated books about heroes and sadness and betrayal. You discover them on your own, at bookstores, while your father is off looking for meaningless crap about ancient Scottish feuds. These books aren't nearly as troubling. These books are cool. These books are your salvation, and before you know it, you are a full-fledged addict: *MAD*, Marvel, DC, it doesn't matter—even an Asterix anthology will do in a jam. They speak to you. And as the years go by, you take the illustrations of Signy you copied after your sixth birthday, and you spin them into your own comics . . . and suddenly you're seventeen. It's the summer before fifth form year, and you're alone with your drawings in your opulent Manhattan apartment. And Dad is down the hall alone with *his* drawings, plus with that stupid antique letter opener he cares so much about, that oh-so-special Dunne clan heirloom, inscribed in Gaelic *Michts no aye richt*, whatever the hell that means—which leads you to your final question: What kind of demented nut job gives a six-year-old boy a coffee table book about Norse mythology?

[7] For more on the actual Norse myth of Signy, consult your local library or refer to my pitiful explanation in Chapter 14. Not that the real myth plays a big part in my comic. The way I conceived of Signy, she is clever and sensitive, but she also has the supernatural strength of Thor, because she's been reincarnated as a seventeen-year-old badass from the USA. She's more beautiful, too. She has returned to rescue the helpless (most of whom look like me or my half sister, Olivia) and to fight Evil in all forms (most of whom are variations on Dad and Bryce Perry). In short, my Signy represents not only everything I want in a girlfriend but also everything I want in a friend—or, let's face it, anyone who'd just take five minutes to talk to me.

8

SURPRISE INVITATION

But enough about Dad.

Back at school that very first day, I had more important things to worry about. I had to finish the next installment of *Signy the Superbad* and e-mail it to Roger Lovejoy by the next afternoon.

Unfortunately, I couldn't quite get the job done. What with all the classes I was skipping and the mankind I was avoiding . . . Okay: I admit, I didn't have an excuse. I was just sort of unhappy and uninspired. At 4:45 P.M. Wednesday, a full twenty-four hours and forty-five minutes past my deadline, I sent Roger Lovejoy the following e-mail:

> hi roger. sorry. things have been especially hectic at work with all the new architectural projects i've been designing. plus i just had to say good-bye to my only son who is off to boarding school again and it always breaks my heart to see him go ☹ so i'm a little distracted. Anyway, i was just wondering if you could

run an old comic strip and give me another week to finish a new one?

To which Roger Lovejoy replied, twelve minutes later:

Hi, Carlton! That's totally unacceptable and normally I would fire you but I've got good news and bad news! The bad news is that the newspaper is going through tough times and our editor in chief thinks we should run ads and coupons in the space currently devoted to SIGNY! The good news is that we're finally going to meet in person! I just scored us a booth at COMIC EXPO at the Meriden Ramada! All the major comic industry players will be there! (See attachment). I know tomorrow night is short notice but I'm thinking we can get syndication for Signy if we meet the right people! If we don't, you're screwed! Capiche?

All best, Roger! ☺

p.s. I used ☺ to show that ☹ is gay. Please don't ever use it again.

Yikes, I thought.

I knew I faced a stark choice.

Well, three stark choices. The first was telling Roger Lovejoy that using so many inappropriate exclamation points in that e-mail was far more "gay" than using a ☹. The second was telling him that the way he used the word "gay" was pretty offensive, even to someone as un-PC as me.[8] The third was accepting the runny-nosed slimeball's invitation.

I ruled out the first two pretty quickly. But the third . . .

[8] Maybe he was overcompensating, because *he's* gay? Which is fine. Just speculating.

This was hard. I needed *Signy the Superbad*. It wasn't glamorous or anything, but still, I needed it about as badly as I needed anything in the whole world.

So I knew I had to accept.

The problem was, in order to accept, I had to sneak out—because there was no way the CM faculty would give me permission to attend some B-level comic book convention in a hotel twenty miles away on a Thursday night.

Which brings me to the *real* problem: I'd never snuck out before. I'd been too afraid (big shocker). Sneaking out is punishable first by five days' suspension and then by a parent-faculty conference—both of which would probably cause Dad to disown me, if only for the inconvenience of having to spend so much time away from his rigorous schedule of obsessing about the Forba feud.

Also, I'd never had anywhere to sneak out *to*.

Usually, when a guy sneaks out at CM, it's to visit his girlfriend. Sadly, I'd never had a girlfriend. Sadder than that, I'd never had a friend who was a girl. Saddest of all, no girl knew I existed. No shy third-former had slipped me a note proclaiming her love; no brazen fourth-former had requested that I meet her in the woods after dark; no nymphomaniac fifth-former was pining for me in the dorm across the quad . . . and the sixth-formers? Forget about it. No sixth-form girl had ever looked in my direction, except to borrow a pen.[9]

These things happened to guys at CM. They happened to guys like Bryce Perry. Girls flirted and passed notes and sent provocative pictures on the Web and even sometimes made outrageous overtures in public. Just not to me.

But maybe . . . *maybe* . . . not to sound like a total dork . . .

See: Right after Roger Lovejoy hired me, he set up a *Signy the Superbad* fan site. He swore I would get dozens of e-mails a day from

---

[9] Once.

thousands of loyal fans. It didn't quite pan out that way, unfortunately. I received a grand total of thirteen e-mails in eleven months, all from a girl who called herself Night Mare.

To be honest, Night Mare kind of gave me the creeps. She never revealed her true name, and she was just as misanthropic and comic obsessed as I was. As awful as it sounds, I couldn't help but envision a plump and acne-ridden goth, hunched over a computer for most of the day. She was no Signy clone. At least, not in my head.

Yet . . .

If I were in a different environment, if I were someplace where people wouldn't be judged for a comic-book obsession—where they would be respected for it, where they would be REVERED for it— maybe I would meet Night Mare, and she *would* be a Signy clone. More than that, she would be my kindred spirit, and we would run away together to begin a lifelong romance and I would finally lose my virginity.

A long shot, sure. But still. If I wanted to bust out of the mental prison and dive into that symbolic ocean of womankind, then Roger Lovejoy's invitation to COMIC EXPO was a step in that direction, right?

Right.

The invitation was a gift. It was a sign.

One final issue remained, though.

How would I explain to Roger Lovejoy that I was, in fact, a teenage dork?

COMIC EXPO IS...
not comic con !!
COMIC EXPO IS...
everything comic-con should be !!

Meet **Bee A. Vixen** !!!!

The "Sauciest" Model in all of Comic Book History!!!

The Face and Body that made such comics as:

DWARVEN DEATH SQUAD

-and-

Tales of the Post Apocalypse FAMOUS!!!

COMIC EXPO FAQ:
where: The Meriden Ramada, Route 5, Meriden, CT.
when: Thursday, September 9th
Comic Book "Meet & Greet" : 6-9 p.m. in the Ramada Elk Room
Price $60.00 per person

This is "NOT" comic con!!! There will be NO:
Bloated Advertising, Annoying Press Booths, Video Game Salesmen,
Self-Congratulatory Award Ceremonies, Movie Star Appearances,
Product Placement opportunities, Auctions, Masquerades,
Film Clips, Child Care, Transportation, Catering.

JUST PLENTY OF COOL COMIC BOOKS, WRITERS, ARTISTS, & MODELS !!!

9

BRYCE PERRY AND ME

I didn't have to explain much to Roger Lovejoy.

I hadn't even planned on *going* to COMIC EXPO, which is the ridiculous part. I'd fully intended to wimp out at the last minute.

Thursday evening, after wolfing down some sort of gray meat product in the dining hall (alone), I returned to my dorm room (alone). I then settled in with my sketch pad (alone) thereby achieving my goal: to wallow in loneliness. To add a little extra misery to my lonely one-man soiree, I began to doodle little sketches and fantasize about everything I would miss at the Meriden Ramada. Among them:

* GLORY FOR MY COMICS HABIT.
* ABSOLUTION FOR MY COMICS HABIT.
* MEETING BEE A. VIXEN.
* MEETING ROGER LOVEJOY (PERHAPS SMASHING HIS HEAD IN

WITH SOME KIND OF ANCIENT NORDIC WEAPON I'D PURCHASE ON THE WAY OVER).
* SEDUCING EITHER BEE A. VIXEN OR NIGHT MARE OR A SIGNY CLONE WHO'D WORSHIPPED ME EVER SINCE SHE'D LAID EYES ON THE FIRST SIGNY STRIP.

But at 7:15, Bryce Perry started pounding on my door.

"Carlton, dude! I need to borrow your iPod again, okay, bro?"

I opened my mouth to answer him. Then I stopped. He'd broken my iPod. I'd lent it to him Tuesday, and when he returned it, the only song it would play was "The Rose" by Bette Midler—which I'd never loaded nor would ever think to. But there was no point in mentioning this.

"Carlton, come on!" Bryce demanded. The door rattled under his fist. "Open up! At least let me borrow your Discman."

My Discman? I wasn't even sure if I still owned one. Hadn't he broken that, too?

I took a long look at my various belongings. It occurred to me: Even though I'd basically lived alone for my entire CM career, Bryce Perry might as well have been my roommate the whole time.[10] He had damaged or destroyed almost everything. There was my stereo: Thanks to him, the CD player was permanently stuck on Eject. There was my laptop: He'd cracked the screen. And finally, there was that goddamn coffee table book, *The Illustrious Myths of Scandinavia*. Several pages were now shriveled and mashed together, for reasons I didn't even want to think about.

Maybe I should have treated my stuff more like Dad treated his

---

[10] Every freshman at CM is assigned a roommate, no matter what. Mine was Todd Stevens: a mullet-haired drug fiend who was expelled in less than two weeks for publicly snorting a mound of mysterious white powder off a CD case right in the middle of the quad. (Later, the substance was determined to be Sweet 'N Low.) I guess the CM administration took pity on me after that, because they let me live alone for the rest of the year and for every year thereafter. It was nice, but it didn't do much to cure my misanthropy.

prized letter opener: hidden from everyone at all costs.

"What are you doing in there, anyway?" Bryce howled. "Doodling?"

I opened my mouth again . . . but a funny thing happened. I remembered Mr. Herzog's admonition to bust out of my mental prison. I felt a rush of that same fevered desperation I'd felt eleven months ago, when I'd called Roger Lovejoy. And I thought: *There's no reason why I shouldn't hop out my window and go to COMIC EXPO right now.* I was on the first floor. I wouldn't hurt myself. Plus, it was a beautiful evening.

So I said silently: *Good-bye, Bryce.* And miracle of miracles, I managed to put my neuroses on hold for once. I scooped up my sketch pad and bolted.

10

A MAD, MAD, MAD DASH

Sad to say, this triumphant escape didn't rate very high on the old Thrill-O-Meter. It was no Herzog-style breakout. I simply climbed out my window and ran across the quad, then out the campus gates—with Bryce Perry still pounding away and howling. Nobody saw me. Even if anybody had, they wouldn't have stopped me. Half of CM probably didn't even know I was enrolled. Besides, check in and lights-out were still a good three hours off. All in all, it was pretty lackluster and undramatic stuff.

Still, this was what was going on in my brain:

The leaves are crunching under my feet and I am focusing ONLY ON MY FEET because I have to make it to the cabstand before I lose my nerve! But the cabstand is twelve long blocks away, PLUS it's right smack in the middle of town![11] *Teachers might see me! So I make my feet move faster . . . and I try to ignore the sights and smells like the lawns and the children playing on the lawns, because fear is surging . . . FEAR! Fear of getting caught, fear of Dad, fear of Bryce*

---

[11] CM is located in the sleepy, picturesque town of Brookfield, Connecticut. To get a feel for what Brookfield looks like, just imagine a small town in one of those political commercials that talk about "moral values." There's even a church steeple and an old-fashioned clock tower over the bank.

Perry, fear of COMIC EXPO, *fear of Roger Lovejoy, fear of meeting Night Mare, fear of being afraid—and by the time I dash into the cab-stand ten minutes later, I am about to barf!*

Not that I would ever admit this to anyone.

11

HOMECOMING

The ride to Meriden went pretty fast.

Maybe it just felt fast, because I was fidgeting so much. Before I knew it, the cab was pulling up to a squat concrete building the color of old cheese.

From the highway, the Meriden Ramada looks like a cozy oasis, nestled in a forest. When you're right in front of it, you realize that all but a few strategic trees have been cleared and it's actually nestled in a grim parking lot, packed with rental cars.

I probably should have taken this as a bad omen. But I was far too anxious to pay attention to anything except my own sweat. (Did I smell? *Uh-oh.*) It was eight o'clock. I still had an hour to put in an appearance at the convention "meet-and-greet."

The cab fare was pretty steep, thirty-five bucks, but the amount hardly registered. I handed over a wad of crumpled cash—and after a quick sniff of the armpits, I hurried through the big glass doors into the air-conditioned lobby.

The ambient temperature was only slightly warmer than that of a meat locker. This was a good thing. Maybe I'd stop sweating. Another good thing: I had absolutely no trouble finding the convention hall. Every few feet, I passed another cheap placard or banner, proudly announcing: The Elk Room: HOME TO COMIC EXPO!!!

My excitement grew as I rounded the corners. It grew as I passed the friendly smiles of hotel service people. By the time I burst through the doors of the Elk Room[12], I was smiling, too.

I felt like shouting: "People, I made it! I'm finally where I belong! I'm *home*!"

---

[12] The Elk Room was about the size of a gym, with lower ceilings and chandeliers and wall-to-wall carpet.

12

THE PSAT WORD FOR "BIG CHUMP"

The feeling wouldn't last long.

A three-hundred-pound man lurking near the door squinted at me. He was wearing a pink Izod shirt with the collar turned up, a Lone Ranger mask, and a long black cape. "What are *you* staring at?" he asked.

"I'm not sure?" I offered hopefully.

He didn't answer.

I ran inside. Within twenty seconds, I began to sweat again. Within two minutes—after snaking my way through the booths and the throng of convention goers, desperately searching for *my* booth—fear gained the upper hand once more.

COMIC EXPO was a freak show.

Obviously, I expected to rub shoulders with a bunch of oddballs, kooks, and nerds. This was a comic book convention, after all. But from what I could see, COMIC EXPO was something darker, something more sinister. It was a living testament to several major psychological disorders. There were plenty of fellow misanthropes, for starters; and any number of them could have been Night Mare, at least in terms of the mental image I'd formed. Judging from the dirty looks I received, they were definitely more of the person-who-hates-mankind variety, too. Lots were dressed like their favorite comic book characters. I counted six separate Hellboys[13], three of whom were women. There were dopeheads (I smelled marijuana) and kleptomaniacs (I witnessed four separate acts of theft from various booths). There were people with Tourette's syndrome, and Munchausen's syndrome, and whatever other syndrome.[14] There were people in need of anger management, and people in need of anger-response management.

The mental-hospital vibe didn't really upset me so much, though.

No, what really upset me was that I didn't have a booth. Everybody else had a booth. *Everybody.* (The *Peanuts* estate had a booth. Charles M. Schulz has been dead for how many years?) What was I thinking, trusting Roger Lovejoy, anyway? Did I really assume he'd drag me out to someplace where I'd feel safe or welcome? Even after his e-mails? Even knowing he was a piggish slimeball?

A word leaped to mind, one I'd learned while studying for the PSAT: "guileless." Roughly translated, it means "naïve" or "a big chump." I knew then that this experience was teaching me a valuable lesson. Yes. Being guileless was another big problem of mine. It was right up there with being afraid all the time and not being able to listen. Because the shadier the person, the more I *wanted* to believe

---

[13] *Hellboy* is an amazingly popular, ultraviolent comic about the spawn of Satan. He's big and red and has a pointy tail, but he's a Good Guy, in the two-dimensional Herzogian Good-versus-Evil sense.

[14] I'm not sure if these people actually had Tourette's or Munchausen's. I was just lonely and scared, so my imagination went wild. On the other hand, they did exhibit a lot of the same symptoms. Tourette's is a form of obsessive-compulsive disorder; those afflicted suffer from tics, twitching, and inappropriate verbal outbursts. For instance, they might yell: "Get away from my booth, ass munch!" when nobody is near their booth. People with Munchausen's pretend to be sick in order to attract attention to themselves. For instance, they might wander around alone at a comic book convention, rubbing their belly and wailing, "Somebody poisoned the catering!" when there is no catering.

him. As much as other human beings frightened me, I always ended up trusting them. Trusting them made me feel better. In short, I was a poster boy for scams. *Can't look me in the eye, Bryce? No problem; I'll loan you the iPod! Now when's that swirlie!*

I really had no business being around these people at all. But just as this familiar revelation struck—owing to fate or cruel cosmic humor—I found it.

My "booth."

It was a little hard to spot.

It didn't have walls or a display case, as one might expect a booth would. It wasn't much more than a tiny bit of floor space between the Elk Room's emergency exit and the back of a discarded *Mary Worth* billboard.[15] It wasn't labeled, either. Truth be told, I never would have stumbled upon it if it weren't for the heap of *New England Sentinels* all opened to *Signy the Superbad,* sloppily stacked on the carpet. There was no desk. There wasn't even a chair . . . just a stepladder, which I assumed was supposed to serve as a stool.

I had to laugh. Honestly. In the grand scheme of things, what did the booth matter? I'd made it to COMIC EXPO, in and of itself a pretty massive feat.

Plus, I'd snookered Roger, too. He was expecting to meet my father.

Or was he? Had he figured out the truth? Was this payback for lying to him for so long?

Whatever. I couldn't flee now. I'd have to elbow my way back through that crowd. With a big resigned sigh, I turned the *Mary Worth* billboard completely around, so that the back was facing the Elk Room.

[15] *Mary Worth* is actually a really smart comic strip (in my opinion) about a sixty-year-old widow and former schoolteacher who dispenses funny little tidbits of wisdom. The problem is, it's not sexy or violent. Plus, it dates back to the fifties and has gone out of syndication in almost every newspaper across the country, so it's always used as an example (by wannabe hipsters) of everything *wrong* with old-fashioned comics. These wannabes seem to think that light humor is obsolete and that it needs to be quashed in favor of graphic sex and violence, like *Hellboy.* Which is too bad, because most new comics suck compared to *Mary Worth.* (In my opinion.) Then again, I like sex and violence as much as the next guy.

Then I scrawled in huge letters: SIGNY THE SUPERBAD.

Then I pasted a big smile on my face.

I sat down on the hard little stepladder.

As if on cue, a short rotund man in a black suit and green turtle-neck waddled over and glared at me. He had pointy ears and greasy hair the color of ash. He was clutching a purple handkerchief emblazoned with an amateurish yellow skull. It looked as if someone Olivia's age had stitched it. In a room full of scary freaks, he was definitely among the scariest—even scarier than the other rotund man in the Lone Ranger mask who had first accosted me at the door. Gazing into his angry beady eyes, I had the unsettling premonition that he was going to be much, much ruder as well.

13

AIR QUOTE SYNDROME

"So it's true," the man began cryptically. "You are . . . ?"

My ears perked up. I recognized that voice. "Roger Lovejoy?" I asked.

"*I'm* Roger Lovejoy," he said.

"I know. I'm—"

"Let me guess. You're 'Night Mare.'" He made dismissive air quotes.

"I thought Night Mare was a girl," I said.

"I'm busting your chops, kid."

"Oh." I gave him a weak grin. "See, I'm Carlton Dunne's son, and . . . uh, he couldn't make it. My name is also Carlton Dunne. Something came up—and since I go to school so close to Meriden, my dad told me to come here in his place . . ." I offered another weak grin, having run out of stammering lies. "Nice to meet you."

He sniffed and blew his nose in the purple handkerchief. "It all makes sense."

"What?"

"The various communications. All the e-mails your dad sent tonight."

"All the e-mails?"

"Asking me to keep an eye on you," Roger Lovejoy mumbled. "And when your dad 'pitched' me this strip"—he made air quotes again to emphasize his contempt for the word "pitch"—"he asked you to make all the calls, because he thought I'd be looking for the next Jim Shooter.[16] Right?"

"I guess." I replied. He'd lost me. He wasn't making any sense at all. I'd never asked him to keep an eye on me. If anything, I'd wanted him to *avoid* me.

Roger Lovejoy laughed, then sniffed and blew his nose again into the purple handkerchief. "Hey, I really don't care that much. But so your dad knows, the *Sentinel*'s editor in chief did grant us '*armistizio*'"—a third time with the wriggling fingers—"so it's in your dad's interest to cook up a cape for his next strip. *Capiche*? I've told him a million times I want the villain to have a cape. That way, we can start to market these hankies." He waved the snot-covered cloth in front of me and then turned back toward the mad swirl of convention goers. "And remind him that I own all the merchandising rights! Now, remember, I have to babysit you, all right? Don't wander off! *Ciao!*"

"Hey, wait!" I called after him.

I watched him disappear.

Jeez. Of all the foolish fantasies I'd had about meeting Night Mare or just meeting anyone (Bee A. Vixen?) . . . They didn't just seem foolish; they seemed deranged. The only person I'd met was a slimeball who I hadn't wanted to meet anyway. To top it off, he'd abandoned me without offering any explanation as to why the *Signy* booth

---

[16] Jim Shooter was born in 1951. He is one of the most infamous players in the comic book industry. A child prodigy who began selling his own comics to DC at the age of thirteen, he became the editor in chief of Marvel in the 1980s, then worked with Valiant and Nintendo—then started a bunch of magazines, most of which went under. He often insults those he's worked with, and he is always on the verge of a comeback. He's sort of like many child prodigy rock stars that way.

was equipped with a stepladder instead of a real chair—or why he was suddenly using a lot of Italian words, or where he got the idea that I'd sent him a bunch of e-mails.

Plus, if he felt obliged to "babysit" me, then why didn't he stay?

Screw it. I was tired. I was lonely. I was far from school. And this place definitely wasn't my home. I couldn't say what place *was* home. Fenwick? Manhattan? Nowhere?

I glanced at the clock. It wasn't even 8:20. If I bolted this very instant, I could still make it back to CM for check-in and lights-out, with almost an hour to spare. But I also knew deep down that there was no rush. I could spend all night here, and I'd never get caught. My dorm adviser—Mr. Watts, a snooty, sour math teacher with an ugly bow tie fetish—had never bothered to make sure I was in my room by 10 P.M. Not once. He'd barely introduced himself to me. I wasn't offended; he had much bigger worries, *real* worries. He had Bryce Perry to tend to. Bryce Perry might actually sneak out. Bryce Perry was on the faculty's "list."

I supposed I could take some comfort in that. Given the circumstances, though, it was a little hard. At least Bryce Perry had a real chair, where he was.

14

MY BEE A. VIXEN MOMENT

At nine o'clock, my luck began to change.

Everyone was starting to drift toward the lobby when a mousy twenty-something woman with dyed black hair ran up to my stepladder. She wore tortoiseshell glasses and a black dress. She was cute in an angry-at-the-world kind of way.

"Are you Carlton Dunne?" she whispered.

"No, he's my dad," I heard myself answer like a dope. I should have lied. But I smiled. My mood soared. *This could be her! This could be Night Mare!* My solitude was over. I was abruptly filled with a desire to flirt, with a sense of the impossible. *Fear, schmear! Misanthropy, schmisanthropy!* Sure, this woman was several years older than me. But she had asked me my name. That was a start. It was the best I'd ever gotten. I wanted to tell her *everything*: that I'd been sitting on my ass on a ladder for nearly an hour and that it was so nice to finally talk to somebody . . . and that I was also wondering where the bathroom was, as I sort of had to pee.

"He is, huh? Well tell me this: Is he damaged goods?"

I blinked at her. I must have misunderstood. "What?"

"Well, like, his comics used to be smart and funny, but now they're retarded!" she said with a shrill laugh. "What was up with the last strip with that evil architect villain? *Hello*? Can you think of anything *less* sexy than architecture?"

"Less sexy?"

The woman laughed again. "And Signy ends up rescuing a little girl instead of some stud? What's sexy about *that*? I mean, her outfits are always hot, but that's about it." Then she laughed some more for what seemed like a very long time. "Sorry. I'm obsessed with sex. Do you know who I *am*?"

I shook my head.

"I'm Jessica James," she said. "Ring any bells?"

Aha. It did ring some bells. She was one of my idols. Or she used to be, up until about three seconds ago. She wrote a so-called "literary" comic strip called *Horny & Single* for edgy urban magazines. I'd always loved *Horny & Single*. It was one of the few smart new comics out there, sort of like *Sex and the City* for the comic-book set. From what I'd seen, it actually managed to blend the graphic content with the funny, everyday humor. But now I had a question: Was an obsession with sex what made a person literary? If that were the case, then logically, Bryce Perry should be the next William Shakespeare. So should I, for that matter. Not that I wanted to share any of this with her.

"So what did you think of this whole COMIC EXPO shindig?" Jessica James asked, waving a hand around the Elk Room at the mass exodus of lunatics.

I shrugged. "It was okay."

"It sure wasn't Comic-Con, was it?" she said.

"I've never been to Comic-Con."

"Comic-Con rocked," she said. "Let me ask you something. How did your father come up with Signy? She's a Norse goddess, right?"

My mood soared again inexplicably. "Yeah! How'd you know? She was the daughter of Volsung, who was one of the direct descendants of Odin. And she married this supposedly great guy, Siggeir. But he turned out to be a real jerk, and he betrayed her by killing Volsung. So Signy and her brother Sigmund arranged this incredible scam where she ended up having to sacrifice herself. She lured Siggeir into an ambush, but, see, the only way she could do it was by poisoning herself, but she still avenged Volsung because her brother killed Siggeir *and* salvaged her family honor . . ." I took a deep breath. There wasn't much point in going on. Jessica James had turned her back on me.

"Bee!" she was shouting, waving her hand at a ghoulish woman lurching out of the crowd. "Bee! Over here! Damn, you look *good*, girl! I could eat you alive!"

Bee A. Vixen? My jaw dropped. There she was! Or was she? This person staggering toward us did *look* like Bee A. Vixen. But the closer she came, the more I began to wonder if it were some haggish comic book fan dressed *up* like Bee A. Vixen. She was wearing those same vinyl shorts, several sizes too small, and those same garters, but her face was a little wan. There were huge black circles under her black eyes. That might have been because of makeup, I guess. I couldn't really tell.

"Cheers!" she croaked, stumbling up to us. Her voice was husky. She hiccuped, waving a glass full of some toxic brown liquor toward my face. "Who's the squirt?"

"I uh . . ." I had no idea what to say.

"He's the son of Carlton Dunne," said Jessica James.

"You mean that pervert who does *Signy?*" Bee A. Vixen cackled, weaving in her high heels. (And I knew right then it really *was* Bee A.

Vixen, because I'd heard that same fiendish laugh on a Web inter-
view.) She hiccuped again. "Look, son of Dunne. Tell your daddy-o
that if he's gonna draw my boobs every week, he needs to do a sub-
tler job. You know, I oughtta get these trademarked." She glanced
down at her chest, then up at Jessica James. "So whaddaya say?" She
burped. "You wanna get out of here?"

15

RATIONALIZATION

When Dad first shipped me off to boarding school, he gave me a Platinum Visa card. It came with a lone rule—"THE RULE," as he put it—and it needed to be followed at all costs: *I was only supposed to use it in emergencies.* He hammered home the point by droning on and on about how "[&*#@*] credit cards rack up exorbitant hidden charges," and how the "[&*#@*] interest rates are always at least four times that of current mortgage rates," and a load of other garbage I didn't understand.

But tonight, for the first time in my life, I didn't care about THE RULE. No. As I watched Jessica James and Bee A. Vixen scamper off together, arm in arm, I didn't much care about anything. Tonight, I was that bull in a china shop; I was that kid in a candy store. I was full of anger and fire. I'd been set *free.* I owed it to myself to break a thousand rules. (Incidentally, rationalization is one of my strongest skills. I can pretty much rationalize anything. This is especially true in the middle of the night in the middle of nowhere.)

So I skulked out of the Elk Room. I trudged back through the halls and straight to the concierge's desk. I slapped down that forbidden plastic, and I charged the most expensive room available—a luxury suite, "last used by Laura Dern[17]!" according to the concierge—which came fully loaded with a deluxe king-sized bed, Internet access, and Jacuzzi jets in the bathtub. It cost $423.27 a night, pretax and before gratuity. I wasn't even sure what "gratuity" meant.

In my heady, dejected state, I took the elevator up to my luxury suite and immediately logged on to the *Signy* fan site—a sure symptom of severe misery and loneliness, because I hardly ever checked it. What was the point?

Sure enough, there was just one e-mail waiting for me:

> hey carlton dude are you at comic expo right now? I wish I could have gone. is bee a vixen really there? your last strip ruled! LOL! i loved it when signy kicked that evil architect's ass by using that letter opener against him. that was so dope!!! and when signy saved the little girl . . . i don't want to sound sappy but my eyes got red and I'm not even allergic to anything. do you know any architects or did you just make that stuff up? you're like a genius!!! ok gotta run
> ☺—Night Mare

To which I replied:

> Thanks as always for your kind words, Night Mare . . . and yes actually I do know an evil architect. Don't

---

[17] Laura Dern was born in 1967. She is the daughter of Bruce Dern and the star of such films as *Jurassic Park III*. Her great grandfather was the governor of Utah.

worry . . . You didn't miss much at Comic Expo. I'm
not sure if Bee A. Vixen was here or not.

☹—CD

After that, I crawled into bed. The sheets were fresh and cool. I
lay there for a while. I was tired, but I couldn't sleep. I stared at the
dark ceiling, ruminating over the day's events. It was ridiculous: Both
Jessica James and Bee A. Vixen had ragged on Dad, and they didn't
even know him. True, they were really ragging on me, but for some
reason, I felt offended for Dad.[18] He was *not* a pervert. He was delusional and negligent, yes, but not a pervert. Besides, who was Bee A.
Vixen to talk about perversion, anyway?

All of a sudden, I felt a lump in my throat.

Maybe I should call Dad. Just to check in.

Less than a week ago, when he'd shoved me into the town car that
would whisk me off to boarding school, he'd asked me to call to let
him know how fifth form was going. "When you're ready," he'd said.
"No rush."

I'd planned on delaying the call for as long as possible. But I
needed to talk to *someone*. I snatched up the phone on the night table
and punched in his number.

---

[18] The psychological term for this is "transference."

16

INSPIRATION

After four eternal rings, Dad picked up.

"Who is this?"

"It's Carlton, Dad."

"Carlton?" He spoke in a gravelly whisper. "What's wrong? It's one in the morning. Why are you calling?"

"Nothing's wrong. I just . . . wanted to see how you were."

"I haven't had a bowel movement in three days."

"I'm sorry to hear that."

"It's the feud," he muttered. "It's getting worse. It's stressing me out. You know how I get when I'm stressed. The goddamn train won't leave the station."

"Maybe you should take a laxative."

"I took a [#&%*] laxative," he said.

"Maybe you should see a therapist."

"Therapy is for whiners, Carlton. Besides, there are some secrets you can't share with anyone but your own clan. I just got another letter from you know who. That old bastard has sunken to a new low. He claims he's going broke. Here, let me find it . . ."

There was a rustle of papers.

"Actually, Dad, I should go. I'm sorry I called."

"'To the head of Clan Dunne,'" Dad began, as if he hadn't heard me. "'There's an old saying: *Ye never heard a cadger cry stinking fish.* You continue to sell me lies. I see straight through them. I am watching you. I am watching your family. Hand over what is rightfully mine! The time is at hand! I will strike nigh, when—'"

"Dad? It's too late for a phone call. You were right. Bye."

I placed the phone back on the nightstand.

Miraculously, the lump in my throat began to subside. So did any lingering guilt over sneaking out and charging $400+ on Dad's credit card. So did pretty much any lingering guilt over anything. More miraculously, I was struck with the long-awaited bolt of inspiration I'd needed to complete the next installment of *Signy the Superbad*— so the strip could stay in business, so Roger Lovejoy could use his merchandising rights and make a butt load of cash, and so everyone would be overjoyed, except Dad!

The time was at hand!

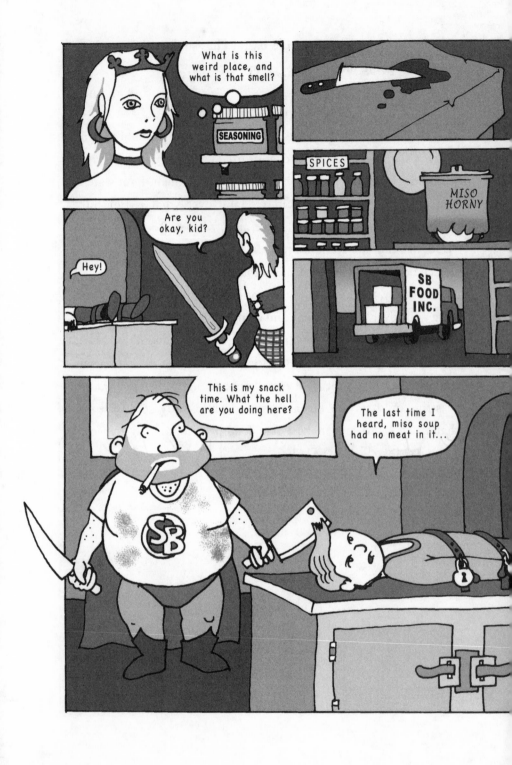

17

KARMIC PENDULUM

The most depressing part?

The most depressing part of the whole COMIC EXPO debacle didn't even occur until after I *left*. Because when I took a cab back to CM at dawn the next morning, and slithered back to my dorm room— exhausted, dejected, four hundred bucks in the hole, etcetera . . . My window was still open, just as I'd left it. My door was still locked.

Which meant I'd been absolutely right.

Nobody had noticed I was gone.

Bryce Perry must have simply given up knocking. Mr. Watts clearly hadn't knocked at all. And the thing is (this is a little hard for me to admit, even now) . . .

My Enemy Within had been hoping for something else.

My Enemy Within had been hoping to find the entire campus crawling with cops, and Dad and the whole entire school all awake and frantic in their pajamas!!! One of Carnegie Mansion's prized students had disappeared!!! And where was he??? And we never told him how much we needed him, but we love him!!! *Come back, Carlton, come back!!!*

And the other thing is . . .

This sort of thinking made me sick to my stomach. So I knew I needed to destroy my Enemy Within. Immediately.

I knew how to start, too. I could start by rationalizing. Which is exactly what I did. True, I was invisible. True, I was a ghost. True, I was nothing—but for a misanthrope, that was good, right? Yes! I could spin this. I could be an *optimist*. Invisibility had its perks. I could sneak out whenever I wanted. (Not that I had any intention of doing so ever again.) I could stop checking in with Dad. (This, I definitely intended to do.) I could act however the hell I pleased!

Yes, as of that sleepless Friday morning, the Enemy Within was no more!

And the plan worked. I swear; it worked for the next week, anyway, because I truly did become invisible. When Bryce Perry knocked on my door the following night? I didn't hear him. How could I? I didn't exist! When he ragged on me in class on Monday? He was talking to vapor! I was unblinking, impassive! Nothing could touch me. I roamed the CM campus as if I were walking on air a thousand feet aboveground.

Had anyone bothered to look up, they might have seen a tiny speck in the sky. They *might* have. But nobody did. And with my silent rage keeping me afloat, the karmic pendulum began to swing back in my direction.

For example:

On Wednesday, Roger Lovejoy called to say that he LOVED my latest strip, especially Chef Slimeball and Miso Horny.

On Thursday, Bryce Perry almost choked to death on split pea and ham soup in the dining hall.

On Friday, Night Mare e-mailed at 8 A.M. to say that she'd bought the earliest possible weekend edition of the *New England Sentinel*.

carlton! du-u-ude! that was like mind-blowing, the best one ever. the next time i eat soup i'm gonna barf . . . you are tha bomb!!! . . . ☺—Night Mare

And that very same Friday morning, in creative writing, Mr. Herzog told our class that he wanted to talk about inspiration. He said that inspiration could come from any number of unexpected places. He told us to think about our required summer reading: *1984* by George Orwell, and *Brave New World* by Aldous- Huxley.[19] He said that Orwell and Huxley—two of history's most famous authors—were both inspired by something none us had probably ever heard of.

That something was Bentham's Panopticon.

So help me God, I'd heard of it plenty.

---

[19] Both of these novels are about futuristic repressive regimes that spy on their citizens and quash individuality—so I suppose it makes sense that they're required reading at a boarding school.

18

BUSTING OUT OF
THE PRISON MENTALITY

"Isn't that a brand of adult diaper?" Bryce Perry cracked.

Everybody in class snickered but me.

I was in a state of shock.

The universe seemed to shrink. I felt like I was watching a TV quiz show and the host had just asked some obscure trivia question and only *I* knew the answer—so I called in for the multimillion-dollar jackpot and a smile spread across my face and I laughed out loud . . . and just like that: *poof!* The week-long spell was broken. People actually turned in my direction. They actually *saw* me. I was no longer invisible. I raised my hand.

"Yes, Carlton?" Mr. Herzog asked with a grin.

"Bentham's Panopticon is a prison," I said.

19

THE ONLY TWO PEOPLE IN THE CLASSROOM

"That's right! Very good." Mr. Herzog cast a quick stony glare at Bryce, and then turned back to me. "Thank *you*, Carlton. Can you tell us anything more about it?"

"Yeah. I guess so." *Hmm.* I wasn't expecting to have to follow up. I nervously cleared my throat. "It was designed by this eighteenth-century English philosopher named Jeremy Bentham.[20] He wanted to solve the problem of prison uprisings."

"Good," Mr. Herzog said. He glanced around the classroom. It was dead silent. Fifteen kids stared at me: fifteen pairs of eyes, including Bryce Perry's.

I swallowed. "Well . . . see, back then, in the seventeen and eighteen hundreds, prisons were really unsanitary and disgusting, so prisoners rebelled a lot. Plus, there was no way to guard every single prisoner individually all the time. So Bentham's . . . well, like—his *genius*, I guess— was to design a prison that would make all the prisoners *believe* that they were all being guarded individually all the time."

[20] Jeremy Bentham lived from 1748 to 1832. He was one of the founders of Utilitarianism, although I'm not really sure what this means. In fact, I don't know that much more about him, except that his skeleton is displayed at a college in London, still dressed in one of his old suits.

"Exactly!" Mr. Herzog exclaimed. "That is one of the best explanations of the Panopticon I've ever heard, Carlton. I mean it. Very well done. Don't stop; don't stop. Speak. Enlighten your classmates. Can you tell us how the Panopticon worked? Can you tell us exactly *how* Bentham intended to convince prisoners that they were being watched all the time?"

I nodded, blushing. All those eyes were still on me. "Uh . . . yeah," I said. "See, a panopticon is a circular building, like a donut. All the prison cells are built in the donut part. There are no windows on the outside wall, so the prisoners can't see out. But there's a slim tower built right into the middle of the donut hole, where the guards are. So all the prisoners are isolated from one another in their cells. Plus, all they can see is this tower through their bars—which has all these darkened windows, pointing back at *them*." I hesitated, chewing my lip, wondering if I was making any sense.

Mr. Herzog held up a piece of chalk. "Maybe it would help if you drew it?" he suggested. "I don't know if you can draw, but sometimes a person with a gift for prose can apply that gift to a two-dimensional image." He raised his eyebrows. "You dig?"

I smiled back at him like a fool.

"Yeah, I dig," I said—and at that moment, as corny as it sounds, Mr. Herzog and I might as well have been the only two people in the classroom. "I'll give it a shot."

62

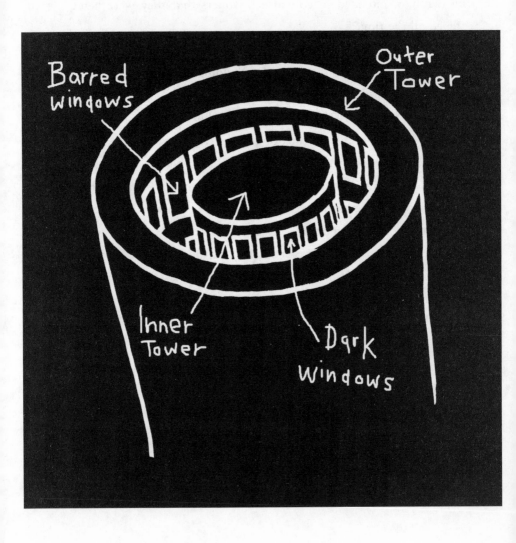

20

THE FORTRESS OF ETERNAL LIFE

"So here's how it works," I said. "Right before the prisoners get locked up in the donut part, they're warned that armed guards will be in the tower at all times, watching them. And because of the design, the prisoners *believe* it. But the guards don't even have to be in the tower. The prisoners can't see them, anyway, because the windows are dark. So the prisoners just *believe* they're there. So they don't try to rebel. Get it?"

I turned back to the class. Those fifteen pairs of eyes were still on me.

Not that I even need to say it, but there's nothing I hate more than being the center of attention. I get clammy and have trouble breathing and all the rest of that crap.

"Heavy," Mr. Herzog finally murmured. "Carlton, that was extraordinary. If you don't mind my asking, how do you know so much about Jeremy Bentham?"

I bit my lip.

"It's okay," Mr. Herzog encouraged softly. "Go on. You're doing great."

"Well, my dad is using the Panopticon as inspiration for this . . . project. He's, um, an architect."

"Really! Interesting. Is he designing a prison?"

I shook my head queasily. *Why did I open my big mouth?* "Uh, no. He's designing this—thing. It's sort of a giant freezer for rich people who are scared of dying."

"Say what?"

"It's true," I admitted. "See, the people who hired him, his clients, after they officially 'die,' they want a bunch of doctors and technicians to cryogenically freeze them. The theory is that they'll be stuck in suspended animation all the way into the future when people finally figure out how to raise the dead and cure all illness. Then the doctors of the future will thaw them out. You know . . . so they can, like, live forever."

Mr. Herzog cocked his head. "Are you jiving me?"

"No," I mumbled. "I wish I was. My dad is designing a giant freezer based on the Panopticon. He calls it . . . he calls it . . ." I couldn't even bring myself to say the words.

"*What?*" somebody hollered, mocking me with glee. "What does he call it?"

"The Fortress of Eternal Life™," I confessed.

"HA!" Bryce Perry laughed.

Everybody else laughed, too. This time, I admit, I had to laugh along with them. The Fortress of Eternal Life™ wasn't just a silly name: It was the dumbest, most overblown, most pretentious name of all time—which meant that it fit my stupid father and his stupid freezer for crazy millionaires who wanted to live forever perfectly.[21]

---

[21] It would take a whole other book to explain why my dad actually *agreed* to design the Fortress of Eternal Life™, and how absolutely ludicrous it was on every level. Suffice it to say that Dad has met and befriended a lot of rich nuts during his career. (Water seeks its own level, as the saying goes.) To give you an example: The floor plans have been finished for ages; the materials are ready to go—yet to this day, he still doesn't even know where he's going to build the damn thing. He can't build it anyplace where there might be a hurricane, flood, earthquake, drought, or catastrophic war in the next thousand years, because the foundation might get damaged. As you can imagine, this rules out every possible location on the planet. Also, several of his clients want it built near "holy sites"—the Vatican, the pyramids, the Taj Mahal, whatever—in case there's actually a God (or gods). I am not making this up. I really wish I were.

21

A BIG LOAD OF BS

"Carlton, I apologize for putting you on the spot for so long, but I just want to ask you one more question." Mr. Herzog said.

I handed the chalk back to him, avoiding everyone's gaze. "Sure," I mumbled.

"Since today's topic is inspiration, why the Panopticon?" he asked me. "What is it about the Panopticon, specifically, that inspired your father? Because it seems to me—and I'm speculating here—but it seems to me that the people who hired your dad might not like the idea of being frozen in a place whose design was inspired by a prison."

I lifted my shoulders. That was a good point. Then again, my dad's clients were crackpots.

"Do they know about the inspiration?" Mr. Herzog asked.

"Yeah, they know," I said. "But in a weird way, it makes all these rich weirdos feel safe. I mean, you can ask my dad. They *want* to make sure that they're being watched all the time, so if anything goes wrong—like if the freezer breaks down or whatever—they know that somebody will be right there to fix the problem. Of course, they'll be dead . . . so they won't really know . . . so by using the Panopticon, my dad is sort of *convincing* them that they'll be watched all the time."

Mr. Herzog nodded thoughtfully. "I guess that's my real question, Carlton," he said. "*Will* they be watched all the time?"

I sighed. "Like I said, that was the genius of Bentham's design. As long as people *believe* they're being watched all the time, then they'll feel safe."

"That is such a big load of BS," Bryce muttered under his breath.

"Bryce!" Mr. Herzog snapped. "You'd like to add something?"

Bryce sneered. "Yeah, I would, in fact." He glanced around the classroom, drawing in everyone's attention, and then turned his genetically perfect blue eyes on me. "You think that being watched all the time makes a person feel safe, Carlton? You're such a dope, dude! I mean—wasn't that the whole point of the summer reading, to prove the opposite? Like . . . why else would they assign us *1984* and *Brave New World*? Duh! To teach us that we *are* being watched all the time! To *show* us what it's like to live in a totalitarian regime! Because that's what CM is!" He waved his hands, suddenly animated. "I mean, look at what goes on at this school! The faculty never stops spying on us! We're all a bunch of neurotic, paranoid jackasses! They force us to lie and to cover for those lies! I say, rise up, people!" He smirked at Mr. Herzog, and then slouched back into his chair and stared at me. "Dig?"

A bunch of kids laughed.

Mr. Herzog laughed, too. "'My motto as I live and learn,'" he quoted, "'Dig, and be dug, in return.'"

"What's that supposed to mean?" Bryce grumbled.

"Whatever you want it to mean, Bryce," Mr. Herzog said gently. "It's a line from a Langston Hughes[22] poem. He was a true revolutionary, just like you and my man Carlton here." He turned to me. "Carlton, would you like to retort?"

I stared back at Bryce.

He blinked a few times. His lips twitched. His expression never changed, but his gaze flitted away from me. And I felt sad staring at him, sad for the *both* of us—even though I wanted to smash *his* head with an ancient Nordic weapon, as well.

"You know, you're right, Bryce," I said finally. "I think some of us do believe that we're being watched all the time here. The question, though, is: Are we *really*? Maybe. But in the end, you know . . . it doesn't even really matter, because we believe it. So even though the faculty seems repressive and totalitarian, on some level, they've convinced us that they care about us. Otherwise, they wouldn't waste all that energy watching us all the time, right? And that's sort of comforting. *That's* what makes us feel safe, whether it's true or not. Just like with my dad's big stupid freezer."

---

[22] Langston Hughes lived from 1902 to 1967. He was a poet and writer, and one of the key players in the Harlem Renaissance. He defines "cat" in the Herzogian sense of the word.

22

KNOCK, KNOCK

I didn't see Bryce Perry for the rest of the day, Thank God.

I decided to take the rest of the day off, in fact—to hide in my room and doodle, seeing as being the center of attention during first period came close to inducing an ulcer. Besides, the dirty look Bryce shot me as he sauntered out of creative writing had sent a very clear message: *Time for another swirlie, butt munch!*

So I didn't have a choice. I *had* to hide.

Sure enough, that night, I was awakened by a clumsy and all-too-familiar knock on my door. I groaned, rolling over and squinting at my clock.

"Psst!" Bryce whispered. "Carlton! Open up, okay, bro?"

It was just before midnight. Since it was a Friday, it really wasn't all that late. Check-in isn't until 11:30 P.M. on Fridays. Most kids in the dorm were still up. Most kids in the dorm had other kids to be up *with*. Not that I felt sorry for myself or anything.

"What is it, Bryce?" I answered hoarsely.

"Just open up, dude."

I yawned. "Look, can't we do the swirlie tomorrow? I'm tired."

"Who said anything about a swirlie?"

"What do you want?"

"We need to borrow your room," Bryce said.

I sat up. "Excuse me?"

"Just let us in, okay, bro? My stereo's busted, and I'm default host for this year's first Who-Would-You-Bang Forum. Kyle said he'd host it, but his stereo still hasn't been shipped yet.[23] He's getting the sub-woofers custom made in one of his dad's factories, but there's a strike or something."

My head drooped.

I had actually been hoping that Bryce and Kyle and their friends would be bagging the whole Who-Would-You-Bang Forum this year. But that would have meant that they'd actually grown up a little over the summer. *I* certainly hadn't grown up.

The Who-Would-You-Bang Forum was a stupid tradition Bryce and Kyle and their stupid friends invented last fall, wherein whatever stupid sexist pigs were available would gather in some idiot's room after lights-out and listen to Led Zeppelin and discuss the "progress" of certain CM chicks: who looked good, who looked bad; who had gotten fat or undergone plastic surgery; who they'd already banged and, most important, who they *wanted* to bang. Needless to say, I'd never been invited. I'd never wanted to be invited. Not in the least. Although maybe I was a tiny bit curious . . .

"Come on, Carlton," Bryce pleaded. "Let us in. My stereo's busted."

"If you took better care of your stereo, it wouldn't—"

"Okay, *Mom*," Bryce interrupted flatly. "Look. Maybe you

---

[23] Kyle Moffat is the son of Dale Moffat, CEO of Moffat Stereophonics, one of the country's largest suppliers of turntables for DJs. You've probably seen their logo on MTV: **MOFFAT IS MO' FAT**. I mention this because it's funny, seeing as Dale Moffat is a right-wing gun nut who spends untold millions a year on conservative causes, seeking to oppress the very people who have made him rich. Also, his son is the biggest wiener I've ever met. Fortunately for Kyle, his wiener-ness is offset by the same evil-troll-scientist good looks as his best buddy, Bryce Perry.

don't understand the situation. Let me rephrase as multiple choice: I can A) torture you worse than any swirlie imaginable; B) use your room; C) tell Mr. Watts you snuck out last Thursday night; D) all of the above."

"Uh . . . what was C again?"

Bryce laughed. "C is exactly what you said in class today," he replied smugly. "This place is like your dad's Panopt-o-thing. People are watching all the time. You of all people should know that, dude."

Oh, brother. I buried my face in my hands.

"Look, you can be in on the forum if you want, all right?" Bryce offered.

"Really?" I said in the driest voice I could muster. "I can stay in my own room? That's kind of you, Bryce. I appreciate polite blackmail." I threw the covers aside. "This means a lot to me. I get to hang out in my own room to attend the special secret gathering of a bunch of horny, misogynist schmucks. I can't think of any way I'd rather spend my Friday night!"

Bryce laughed. "Misogynist?[24] Is that an SAT word? What's it mean?"

"Look in the mirror," I mumbled.

---

[24] mi-sog-y-nist \misojinist\ *n.* A person who hates or denigrates women.

23

THE WHO-WOULD-YOU-BANG FORUM

Minutes later, I found myself shoving an ancient cassette of *Led Zeppelin II* into the tape player. We couldn't use the CD player for tonight's all-important meeting, obviously; it was still stuck on eject. The little tray stuck out from my stereo like a raised middle finger, saluting all of us. Not that Bryce acknowledged or apologized for the damage he'd done. He didn't even notice it. Or he pretended not to. He simply tossed me the cassette and flopped down on my bed, then instructed me to fast-forward to "The Lemon Song."[25] He didn't say please, either.

Kyle Moffat flopped down right beside him. Apparently, the forum's attendance had dropped considerably. Bryce and Kyle were the only stalwarts. Nobody else came.

A couple of grand philosophical questions ran through my brain while I cued up the track. Mind you, I was tired and grumpy. But in

---

[25] I'm not sure why the Who-Would-You-Bang Forum members insisted on listening to Led Zeppelin, although "The Lemon Song" is a particularly horny and misogynistic track. I have to say, though, it kicks ass—especially the bass solo in the middle. Maybe Bryce and Kyle listen to Led Zeppelin because Zeppelin's music is so old and pat that it has somehow become cool again? Who knows? For my part, I have to admit, Led Zeppelin is one of my favorite bands. They're one of Dad's favorites, as well. Neither of us listens to much music that wasn't made by occult-obsessed English rock groups between 1966 and 1978 (Black Sabbath, Yes, etcetera). It's sort of weird, especially since neither of us is really into the occult. Weirder still, it's pretty much the only thing we have in common. Well, except for misanthropy and a love of drawing. And our tartan, I guess.

order, they went: *Why IS Bryce such a jerk, anyway? Does he have his own Enemy Within? Is he just a sad, lost, spoiled child, like me? Has fate locked us into this perpetual battle: two of the same breed—one the victim, the other the victimizer? And what about Kyle? Is he part of all these grand philosophical issues, too? Does he have Enemy-Within type stuff going on? And is their constant torture, along with my wussy acquiescence, simply a classic case of an age-old, boarding school dynamic? Are we just acting out roles? And—*

"What's taking you so goddamn long?" Bryce demanded.

"Sorry," I mumbled. I pressed Play.

"The Lemon Song"'s heavy, bluesy opening guitar riff filled the room. Once the drums kicked in, I couldn't help but nod my head along in time.

"You a Zeppelin fan, Carlton?" Kyle asked.

"Big time. I love Zeppelin."

"They suck," he said.

"Oh." I sat down at my desk, exhausted. I should have known that any answer I gave would be the wrong one, no matter what. "Well, why do you listen to them?"

"I don't. Not unless I'm at the Who-Would-You-Bang Forum. It's the ritual." He affected a mystical tone. "It's a secret. We can't tell you."

"Poor me," I replied dully. "I'm dying to know what that secret is, Kyle. I'd sell my soul to Satan[26] himself to hear you tell it."

"How about you tell *us* a secret?" he suggested. "Then I'll think about it."

"I don't have any," I said. "No good ones, anyway."

"Hey, ladies?" Bryce said. "Can we get started here?"

Kyle sat up straight. "Yes! I say we start with the forum's newest stud. Mr. Carlton Dunne, the— What is it? The sixth?"

---

[26] Legend has it that Jimmy Page, the guitarist of Led Zeppelin, sold his soul to Satan in exchange for success and fame. The jury's still out on whether this legend is true. The jury's also still out on whether this legend is spooky or just plain goofy. I guess it depends on your mood. Jimmy Page was born in 1944.

"The fourth, Kyle. The fourth."

"Mr. Carlton Dunne the fourth," he proclaimed. "Stud at large."

"Nah, he's better than a stud," Bryce said.

"Yeah, he's a *stallion*," Kyle said.

"Better than a stallion, even," Bryce said.

"Yeah. He's a . . . he's a . . ."

"He's a *mare*," Bryce said.

Kyle laughed. "A mare is a female horse, you dope."

Bryce smiled wickedly at me. "My point exactly, ladies."

I rolled my eyes. Maybe I'd given Bryce a little too much credit. Maybe he didn't have an Enemy Within. After all, having an Enemy Within requires a certain sort of intelligence, and judging from tonight's conversation, Bryce's IQ had fallen to something about on par with a squirrel or some other furry rodent.

"Aren't we supposed to get started?" I said.

"Right. So how about it, stallion?" Kyle asked. "Who would you bang? Or rather, who *have* you banged?" He drew in his breath and clamped a hand over his mouth, as if he'd made a terrible faux pas. "Whoops . . . my bad! You haven't banged anyone. You're a virgin."

"You're right, Kyle." I was too tired to put up a fight. "But so what? I'm only seventeen. Who cares if I'm a virgin? Besides, I'd rather lose my virginity to somebody I'm really into. Instead of, say, to Cindy Henderson, that promiscuous fourth-former with the buck-teeth. The one you thought was so tasty. You did lose your virginity to her, didn't you?" I glanced at Bryce. "Both of you?"

Kyle's lips tightened. He didn't look too happy. For a second I was worried he might pick up where Bryce had left off and destroy whatever belongings were left to destroy in my room.

"Okay, okay, guilty as charged," Bryce chimed in, clapping Kyle on the shoulder. (Whether this was out of solidarity or to ease the tension, I wasn't sure.) "But don't you want to prove yourself, Carlton? I mean, since you're such an idealist? Tell us: Who would *you* lose your virginity to? Who would you bang?"

I slumped back in my chair. "Nobody at this school," I said.

"Point well taken. But we can't leave it at that. This is the Who-Would-You-Bang Forum. You must divulge. You must prove yourself."

My eyes darted between the two of them. I knew they weren't going to let me off the hook. I also knew that any answer I gave would again be the wrong one. It would provoke raucous laughter at best and another swirlie at worst.

So there wasn't much point in trying to make up something to save myself.

I might as well tell the truth, I realized.

And as "The Lemon Song" blared in the background, I began to think—seriously, for the first time ever, in any sort of non-comic-book-oriented way—about whom I'd want to lose my virginity to.

"Well, it would be a girl I haven't met yet," I began. I stared into space. I thought about girls I knew. There weren't many. I could only think of Night Mare, Jessica James, and Bee A. Vixen—and I didn't even really *know* any of them, not even Night Mare. "She wouldn't be rude or pretentious or sex obsessed or much older than me, either. She'd be superintelligent and strong . . . but not so strong that she'd be all flexed up or anything. She'd be tall. And blond. She'd have a sense of humor. She wouldn't wear much makeup. She'd teach me how not to be scared of other people—"

"Carlton?" Bryce interrupted in a deadpan voice.

"Yeah?"

"I really think you need to sneak out of your room more often," he said.

Then both he and Kyle burst out laughing, as if that were the funniest joke anybody had ever told.

24

NOT-SO-DIVINE INTERVENTION

My face turned bright red. Given my propensity for blushing, my skull would melt by Columbus Day in a puddle of goop. On the plus side: A quality head melting would at least put me out of my misery. I resigned myself to a long night of humiliation at the hands of two jackasses—when, out of nowhere, my cell phone rang.

Both Bryce and Kyle stopped laughing. They looked as confused as I felt. I dug the phone out of my pants pocket. It was Dad. I sat on the edge of the chair, staring at the caller ID. What in God's name was Dad doing calling me after midnight on a Friday? Maybe he thought he would wake *me* up with a random call at a late hour, just to prove how annoying it was. I couldn't think of any other reasonable explanation.

"Who is it, stallion?" Kyle teased. "Your secret honey? A super-intelligent blond chick who isn't all flexed up? The one who's been sneaking into your room so much lately?" He stood up and grabbed Bryce's arm. "Come on. Let's hold the forum somewhere else. We should leave him alone so he can talk dirty."

"But your mother doesn't *like* it when I talk dirty, Kyle," I joked. "Besides, she hasn't been sneaking into my room that much lately."

Bryce laughed.

Kyle scowled at him. Then he made a dismissive *pffft* sound and pulled Bryce out of the room.

"What about my tape?" Bryce started to ask, but Kyle slammed the door.

Well. That was easy. Who knew what a hackneyed comeback could accomplish? It could actually get rid of two misogynist jerks. Had I offended Kyle? (*Did* he have an Enemy Within? If so, I felt sort of bad. But not too bad.) I clicked the answer button.

"Hello? Dad?"

"Hello, Carlton!" he said. His voice sounded strange and high-pitched.

"What's up?" I asked. "Is everything okay?"

"I don't how to tell you this. We have a situation."

I felt a shudder. The last time he'd used the word "situation" was spring semester last year, when Miss Krebs had called to tell him that I'd failed to show up for my trig exam. And even though *this* semester was only two weeks old, I'd skipped about half my classes so far. CM must have notified him. So they really were watching me. It was actually sort of encouraging. "Mr. Watts didn't call you to tell that I've been skipping a bunch of classes, did he?" I said quickly. "Because, listen—"

"Of course not. Nobody called."

"Oh." I blinked, my mood sinking. "So . . . what's wrong?"

"Carlton, how would you like to go away on a vacation with me?" he asked.

25

THE LAST VACATION WE EVER TOOK AS A FAMILY

I wasn't expecting that.

Obviously, for one, I couldn't go on vacation with him. I may not have been attending classes, but I was still at school. I'd just returned, to be more exact—meaning I'd come off four whole months of vacation with Dad, most of which had been spent avoiding each other in our two homes.

I wondered if he was drunk. But he wasn't a drinker. Maybe he was on some kind of designer prescription drug one of his kooky clients had given him? He did sound slightly altered, as if he'd ingested a balloonful of helium. He definitely wasn't in his right mind (whatever that was), because he should have remembered as well as I did what had happened on our last official family outing.

We'd gone to the Bahamas over Christmas with Martha and Olivia. Upon our return, Martha had filed for divorce.

26

CONRAD MACSCHTOON

I knew the exact moment when I knew their marriage wouldn't survive the trip. It was when Dad insisted that we "exercise our mental organs."

In addition to being negligent and delusional, Dad is also fiercely competitive. He loves to show off his rapid-fire intellect whenever he can. Hence, vacations are never really *vacations*, per se; they're more like intensive seminars held at some gorgeous, scenic retreat. In this case, it was a pristine Caribbean beach, attached to a swank hotel called Junkanoo. Instead of relaxing on the sand and splashing in the surf, Dad suggested we play Twenty Questions, for the reason mentioned above.

"It'll be great fun," he said.

"Can I play, too?" Olivia piped up.

Dad hesitated for a second.

At first I thought he was going to say no. I really did. It certainly would be in keeping with his character to deny a sweet little four-year-old girl the chance to join in a family activity, when ostensibly, this was the sole purpose of our vacation. The way Dad saw it, however, playing Twenty Questions was serious business. It was mental-organ exercise. It was not for children.

He truly believed this.

One other little detail: Up until that point, Martha, Dad, and I had been sitting in complete silence. Dad had actually brought his laptop along to the beach to do some work, an act of misanthropy so offensive it even bothered *me*. In passive-aggressive response, Martha had brought a large vodka tonic and a paperback. I'd brought the latest Marvel comic. Olivia, however, had brought her cell phone. She'd spent the entire time engaged in a loud and spirited debate with her imaginary friend, Conrad MacSchtoon.[27]

"Can I play Twenty Questions, Dad?" she repeated, cupping her hand over the phone's mouthpiece.

"Well, okay," Dad told her. "You can go first. But if you want to play, you have to think very hard, sweetie."

"Okay, Dad."

"You have to think of somebody we all *know* but would have a hard time guessing," he instructed her. "Do you understand?"

"Yes, Dad," she said patiently. "I think so. I've seen you play."

"You have to think of somebody famous. But not so famous that—"

"I think you've explained it, dear," Martha interrupted, forcing a smile. She rattled the ice cubes in her vodka tonic. "You understand, don't you, Olivia?"

---

[27] A while back, Dad gave one of his old cell phones to Olivia to play with. I suppose this was in keeping with his tradition of giving weird and inappropriate gifts to his children. Yet somehow Olivia took to this discarded appliance with the same all-consuming fervor I took to the coffee-table book. The keypad didn't function; the battery was long dead, but it didn't matter. Within hours, she'd invented an imaginary phone friend: Conrad MacSchtoon. She began calling him incessantly. After a few months, everything else fell by the wayside, *everything*—cleaning her room, saying please or thank you, changing her socks . . . The few times Dad hung around with her long enough to pay any real attention to her (usually to scold her about her new rebellious behavior) she would always tell him that she was too busy to worry about silly things like "cleanliness." How *could* she worry? She was on the phone, taking care of EXTREMELY important business with her good friend Conrad MacSchtoon. Dad would just have to deal with it. Often, she would turn to Martha or me for support. We always backed her up wholeheartedly.

Olivia nodded. "Good-bye, Conrad!" she cried cheerily into the phone. "I have to go!" She closed it and stuck it in the sand. Then she scrunched her little eyebrows together, thinking very hard for a very long time. Finally, she nodded again.

"Okay," she said. "I've got someone."

I glanced at Martha. She winked at me. We both smiled.

"Is it a . . . *ma-a-an?*" Martha asked, drawing out the word.

Olivia giggled.

"Is it a man named . . . Conrad Mac-*Schtoo-oon?*" I asked in the same goofy voice.

Olivia giggled again, looking sheepish. "Yeah! But how did you know? That's only two questions!"

Then we all giggled.

All of us except Dad, that is.

Dad shook his head. "Conrad MacSchtoon doesn't count, sweetie," he informed her. "Conrad MacSchtoon isn't real."

Martha and I exchanged another glance.

"Um . . . Carlton, dear?" Martha stated tersely. "I think we can let this one count. Olivia just wants to play."

"I know, but she's already four," Dad replied. "She should know the difference between what's real and what's not."

"Please," Martha scoffed.

Dad's lips turned downward. "What?"

"How can she tell what's real and what's not!" she yelled. "Look at you! You're obsessed with a feud that doesn't even exist—and you refuse to seek therapy! You say therapy is for whiners! You pay more attention to a letter opener than you do to your own daughter! Let me ask *you* something, Carlton. Is the Forba Clan real? Answer me that!"

Dad didn't answer. His jaw tightened. His eyes simmered with rage.

Good grief. I closed my eyes, wishing I were anywhere but on this beautiful beach. Then I snuck a quick peek at Olivia.

Fortunately, Olivia didn't seem to notice that anything was wrong. She was already back on the phone, happily chatting away with Conrad MacSchtoon.

27

TRILLING R'S

"Carlton?" Dad asked, his strained voice whisking me back from the Bahamas to my lonely little room at Carnegie Mansion. "Are you still there?"

Led Zeppelin's "Thank You" was now playing on the stereo, its lines about inspiration softly and abysmally apropos.

"Yeah, I'm still here, Dad," I mumbled. I stood and began pacing. "But I don't really think I can go on vacation with you. For one thing, school is in session right now." I held my breath, frightened of what I was about to ask. "Look, Dad—are you all right? What's going on? Why are you calling me?"

There was a brief silence.

"Carlton, I've been kidnapped!" he shrieked. "He finally did it! The head of Clan Forba! He really has lost all his money! They thought I had the proof, but I don't! I swear to God." He ran out of breath. "Listen, I'm in Orkney—" *CRACK!*

I flinched, shoving the phone away. *Yikes.* Somebody on the other end had swatted his phone from him. Either that or batted it with a tire iron. I tentatively drew my own phone back to my ear.

"Dad?" I whispered.

"Bring the pr-r-rue-ef to Edinbur-r-r-gh," a Scottish voice said, trilling the R's in a singsong lilt. "Aweet instrookshin. You 'ave forty-eight hours. Oor ya dad is 'aggis."

Click.

"Dad?" I whispered again.

There was no response.

I stood still for a moment.

Then I laughed. Ha! This had to be a sick joke. Of course it did. Dad's sense of humor was . . . Well, actually, he had no sense of humor.

I stopped laughing.

I felt a needling in my gut, as if somebody were poking around in there with a large and very sharp safety pin.

There had been real fear in Dad's voice.

I'd never heard him sound that weird or distraught. And what about the guy who'd cut in? He'd sounded even *weirder*—and definitely not like someone who was joking around. He sounded like a soccer thug. (Not that I'd ever spoken with a soccer thug, or any thug, but the analogy seemed reasonable at the time.) Also, what did "aweet instrookshin" mean? Maybe "await instruction"? And what did *that* mean? That Dad's insane rants about Clan Forba *weren't* insane? That the demented nut job had *justification* for his dementia? And what in God's name was the "proof"?

Okay, I said to myself. I shoved the phone back into my pocket and started pacing again. The little needle in my gut was now pricking at my spine. *Okay. Calm down. Think for a second.*

But I couldn't.

This was bad. This was very, very bad. Either Dad had at long last gone completely crazy, or he had truly been kidnapped by his archenemy.

That wasn't even the worst of it, though. The worst of it was that I had to deal with this situation, whatever it was. If what Dad was saying were true, I had to sneak out and fly to Scotland in the next forty-eight hours by myself.

I couldn't do that.

I couldn't because . . . well, for one thing, I didn't even know what the "proof" was. So how the hell could I possibly bring it to Orkney or Edinburgh or wherever? Besides, if I snuck out of school again, I knew I would wind up surrounded by psychopaths. Bee A. Vixen, Roger Lovejoy . . . these were the kinds of people you met when you splashed around in the ocean of mankind. I'd learned my lesson. The real world was cold and ugly. It was not a place for misanthropes, for guileless poster boys for scams. Dad had gotten himself into this mess, and Dad could get himself out of it. He was a resourceful, intelligent grown-up. He'd had lots of experience with the real world. He lived in it.

I lived at boarding school.

This was *his* responsibility.

Right. And seeing as this was *his* responsibility and *his* reality—I decided to do what I always did when I wanted to escape *my* responsibility and *my* reality.

I retreated into my mental prison and busted out the sketch pad.

PART II

28

CRACKED, COWARDLY WIMP

At 6 A.M. Saturday, I finally stopped drawing. I wore out an entire eraser and sharpened my pencil down to a two-inch stump. I felt as if I were on drugs.

The finished strip was not my finest. I doubted it was *New England Sentinel* material. Not a whole lot of concentration had gone into it. Dad's kidnapping had little to do with the quality of my work . . . at least not directly. No—and sad to say, this illustrates just how much of a cracked, cowardly wimp I was—it had mostly to do with how I'd been thinking about *MAD* magazine the whole time. In particular, I'd been thinking about Alfred E. Neuman's[28] famous signature line.

The line goes: "What—me worry?"

---

[28] If you're unfamiliar with Alfred E. Neuman (God help you if you are) and want to form a mental image, he has been described by various critics over the past fifty years as "a grinning nebbish [with a] s***-eating smile" who is "more a mental defective than a lunatic" . . . "unkempt and unattractive" . . . "everything that parents prayed deep down their kids wouldn't turn into—and feared they would."

29

A CURIOUS AILMENT

When I first started sneaking away from Dad in bookstores to feed my growing comic-book addiction (the only times I ever felt safe out in the real world by myself), one of the first big collections I discovered was *Sandlot Peanuts*: a *Peanuts* anthology dedicated entirely to strips about baseball.

I was seven at the time, and not a huge baseball fan, but some of the strips were pretty funny.

Anyway, there was one that always stuck with me. In it, Charlie Brown develops a curious ailment. His head turns into a giant baseball, with the stitching and everything. Suddenly, he sees baseballs everywhere. Anything round becomes one: an ice cream cone, the sun, whatever. Naturally, Charlie Brown starts to get anxious, and he's an anxious guy to begin with. Nothing will stop the hallucinations or cure the rash on his head. But after consulting with Lucy (the *Peanuts* in-house shrink) and various other characters, he realizes the problem. He's obsessed with baseball, unhealthily so, and he needs to take some time off. So that's what he does. He tries his hardest not to think about baseball for a whole entire week. And at the end of this probationary period, he sits on a hilltop at dawn, anxiously awaiting the sun as it begins to rise . . .

If he sees a giant baseball, he knows he's doomed . . .

And it's not a giant baseball.

Of course, it isn't the sun, either. How could it be? This is Charlie Brown. Nothing ever works out for him. Failure is the defining feature of his existence. Instead, it's the face of Alfred E. Neuman, smiling back at Charlie Brown with that s***-eating smile and asking the question he'll be asking for all eternity.

"What—me worry?"

30

THE POINT OF THAT DIGRESSION

The point of that digression—

Well, there are a lot of points.

When I first stumbled upon this strip, I was a comic-book novice. I was *more* than a novice; I still hadn't discovered *MAD* yet. So I asked one of the store clerks: Who was this mysterious big-eared, gap-toothed figure, and why was he appearing in a *Peanuts* anthology? It was obvious even to me that Charles M. Schulz hadn't drawn him.

"That," the store clerk replied, "is my god."

It bears mentioning that the store clerk turned up his nose disdainfully as he spoke—and that he was stick thin, pockmarked, and had the worst breath of any human being I've ever encountered in my seventeen years. Also, he wore his name tag upside down. Back then, I didn't understand why. But having returned to this same store several times since (he still works there) and having grown a little older, I've come to realize that his inverted name tag is supposed to announce to the customers: *I am a rebel. I do not play by the rules. I am the smartest rebel you will ever meet. I know all there is to know, and I will go out of my way to make you feel bad about it. That is why my name tag is upside down. You meet a lot of people like me at places like COMIC EXPO.*

"But who is he?" I asked him.

"He is Alfred E. Neuman. He is the mascot of the greatest satirical organization in the free world. You don't know it, but you've stumbled upon an historical document of extraordinary magnitude. This marks the only comic book crossover ever between *Peanuts* and *MAD*.[29] It is the only place you'll ever find Alfred E. Neuman and Charlie Brown in the same strip."

"Oh," I said. I felt very dumb. "What's *MAD*?"

He snorted. "*MAD* is quality, my friend," he said. "*Peanuts* is crap."

"So . . ." I hesitated. "I'm sorry. If one is quality and the other is crap, then why are these two guys in the same strip?"

"That's a very good question. Probably because some rich fat-cat executive somewhere said, 'You know how we can make a lot of money? Let's do a *MAD-Peanuts* crossover. Let's impose the brilliant reality of *MAD* upon the specious reality of *Peanuts*, even though such an imposition makes no sense.'" His voice rose. "'Let's dumb down *MAD* for the sake of a few dollars, because we don't give our readers any credit!' Do you understand, my friend?"

Needless to say, I did not understand.

It was only after I found out my father was kidnapped that I began to get it. Because the *real* point of the digression is this: When I finally quit drawing that fateful morning, the sun was just starting to come up. And I stood at my dorm room window, staring east over campus. And everything was still and quiet. And I felt very much like Charlie Brown, only in reverse. I was *praying* for a big hallucination.

---

[29] I'm not sure if this particular strip is the only crossover between the two comics. Judging from the guy's officious tone, though, *he* certainly believed it was.

I was *praying* for the face of Alfred E. Neuman. I was praying for any reality—however brilliant or specious—to cross over to *my* reality, to blot out my father's kidnapping.

But it was not meant to be. No, I just saw the same old fiery ball rise over CM, a spotlight shining down from the heavens, announcing: *Ladies and gentlemen, I present to you Carlton Dunne IV, the cracked, cowardly wimp who refuses to deal!*

31

A SLIGHTLY SURREAL ENCOUNTER

So I dealt. Or I tried.

My hands shaking, I gathered up the dirty laundry strewn across my floor and shoved it in a knapsack—along with a toothbrush, a stick of deodorant, my sketch pad, and my pencils. Then I hopped out my window and scurried across the quad. I didn't have much of a plan, other than catching a cab to the Brookfield Metro-North station so I could grab the first train to Manhattan. My brain squirmed with paranoia, just as it had the night of COMIC EXPO.

You know this is a mistake! my brain told me. *You know it!*

When I reached the cabstand a few minutes later, I was about to barf again.

Until I saw who was waiting there.

It was the same cabdriver who had driven me to the Meriden Ramada.

Aside from chirping birds, the entire town was silent and deserted.

Everyone was asleep except this one pleasant old man, sitting alone on a bench near his taxi, reading the *New England Sentinel*. In retrospect, it probably wasn't that strange a coincidence. Brookfield is pretty small, so there probably aren't that many cabdrivers to begin with . . . but still, it was sort of odd.

"Hi," I said. "Remember me?"

He looked up from his paper and smiled. "Running away again, are you?" he asked nonchalantly.

"In a way," I admitted.

"Well, good for you." He folded his paper and stood, then opened the back door of his cab for me. "If somebody sent me to Carnegie Mansion, I'd run away, too. From what I've seen, the kids who go to that school are real douche bags."

52

FOCUS

The cab screeched up to the station just as the 6:45 express was pulling in. Perfect timing—since it didn't allow me to consider too deeply what I was, in reality, *doing*. I simply shoved the fare into the driver's hand, thanked him, and dashed on board.

The doors closed. I collapsed into the seat. My lungs heaved. My body was drenched in sweat. The back of my T-shirt clung to the vinyl upholstery.

The car was empty, a big relief. The train lurched forward.

Whew. I tried to breathe evenly, to focus. If there were ever a time for bullet-point thinking, now was it. But the bullets had scattered to the four winds. *I have forty hours! The clock is ticking! I have to find the proof. What is— Wait, what is . . . no, what was I thinking just two seconds ago? Hold on. Maybe I should . . . What should I do? Call Martha. Right. Call Martha and find out what she knows and what she's heard—*

I fumbled for my cell phone and looked up Martha's number in the little directory. Thank God it was still there. I'm not sure why I held on to it. Actually, that's not true; I knew exactly why. I still clung to the secret hope she would forgive Dad for being such a jerk and that she would come back to our family.

"Carlton?" she answered in the middle of the first ring.

"Hi, Martha? Are you okay?"

"Yes, yes," she said quickly. "Where are you?"

"I'm on a train to Grand Central. I should be—"

"Are you safe?" she interrupted.

"Am I—" The question took me by surprise. "Yeah. I guess so."

"Oh, thank goodness." She let out a long shaky sigh of relief. "Thank goodness you're safe. It's so good to hear your voice."

I opened my mouth to say thanks. The word got stuck. A tear fell from my eye. It splattered on the leg of my jeans. *Jesus.* I was crying. No, no, no. This was all wrong. I hadn't cried in a long time, maybe not since Mom died, and never over the phone. But the moment she asked me that one little question—"Are you safe?"—the freaking dam burst.

"Carlton?" she said.

I sniffled. "Yeah?"

"I lost your cell phone number when I moved out, and nobody at Carnegie Mansion is answering the phones. I guess everyone's still asleep. I couldn't track down your dorm adviser. I've been going crazy."

"Has anyone—" I gulped, drying my cheek with my knuckles. "Sorry. Has anyone called you? You know, anyone Scottish?"

"Yes," she said. "The head of Clan Forba called me. He has your father. He's real, Carlton. The feud is *real.*"

33

SAUL WHO BECAME PAUL (NOT THAT I'M A CLOSET JESUS FREAK)

Martha gave me a bit of time to process the information. She's a sharp lady, so she knew it might take me a while. I could hear her breathing softly on the other end, allowing the words to sink in. I felt a little like that guy in the Bible who got blinded on the road to Damascus: Saul who became Paul. He grew up believing one thing zealously—so much so that he persecuted people for *not* believing it. Then suddenly the truth struck him, and in an instant his perspective flipped—so much so that he changed his name and whole entire identity.[30]

Likewise, I'd grown up believing that the feud was a bunch of hooey. I'd persecuted Dad for believing in it. Maybe not to his face, but I'd persecuted him plenty in my head. And now, struck by the truth on the railroad to Manhattan . . . well, a new name and new identity might not be a bad idea. (If only for safety's sake.) My family truly *had* an enemy. Dad truly *had* been kidnapped. Until this very moment, a big part of me still hoped that the last seven hours had been make-believe.

[30] When I say "the truth," I'm not saying that I necessarily believe in the Bible. I'm just saying that this is what Saul who became Paul believed. To be honest, I've never even read the Bible, other than parts of the Old Testament for third form English. I did read *The Comic Book Bible* by Rob Suggs, however, cover to cover. Not because I'm a closet Jesus freak or anything. I was just kind of curious.

"Man," I finally breathed. My voice was hoarse.

"I know, sweetheart," Martha said. "I know. It's hard to take."

I nodded. I heard a strange mewling sound in the background. "What's that?" I asked. I thought it might be her cat.

"I'm sorry," she muttered distractedly. "This whole situation has taken a huge toll on Olivia."

"That's Olivia?" I cried, aghast.

"Yes, but, Carlton, I need you to hold it together, all right?"

No problem, I wanted to say. But a few more teardrops fell on my jeans. It wasn't a downpour, more of a drizzle—but still the kind of rain that is a big fat nuisance when all you want to do is plow forward and hug your half sister and all the rest of that junk that sucks talking about.

"Would you like to talk to her?" Martha asked. "I bet it would do you both some good. I know that Olivia would love to talk to her big brother." She fiddled with the phone, covering it with her hand. "Right, sweetie?"

"Just tell Carlton I want him to bring Dad back," Olivia's tiny voice said from somewhere faraway. "If he brings Dad back, I'll let them both talk to Conrad MacSchtoon, okay? Conrad doesn't like to talk to anyone but me. Tell them both."

Hmm. I should probably hang up soon. Yes. This was slightly too much to handle. I could hang up and draw. Or I could enjoy the view out the window, which was really quite beautiful. Smokestacks, factories, garbage dumps, landfills . . . The ride from Winchester to Manhattan is on one of the more scenic Metro-North routes. Until you reach the Bronx, that is.

"Carlton?" Martha said.

"Yes?"

"Where are you going?"

"I'm going to our place on Madison Avenue," I said. I tried my best to be calm. "Hey, that reminds me, do you know what the 'proof' is?"

"No, but I'm sure it's got to be some sort of document that your father keeps in his private study there," Martha said. "You know, he had a whole file on the Forbas. I never paid any attention to it, because . . . well, with your father's obsession . . . and he didn't like me getting near his letter opener . . . " She didn't finish. She didn't have to.

"Can you meet me at the apartment in a little while?" I asked.

There was no reply. I heard Olivia sobbing quietly.

"Martha?" I pressed.

"I can't, Carlton."

"Why not?"

"I can't go to the apartment because it's part of the terms of the divorce," she said. "Your father filed a restraining order against me. I can't come within five hundred feet of the entrance. Not unless I'm there to pick up or drop off Olivia. Even then, I'm only allowed in the lobby and only if he's waiting there, too."

For a blissful, appalled moment I forgot everything except how much of a jerk Dad was. "Are you serious?" I yelled.

"Yes, but now it makes sense. He was trying to protect me, and he couldn't tell me why. The head of Clan Forba knew where he lived. Now I know he insisted on these terms because he didn't want to endanger Olivia or me. He didn't want us near him."

"Oh," I said. I needed to keep running my mouth; otherwise I'd start bawling again. "He never mentioned the terms of the divorce to me. But listen, since I'm technically a resident there, too, can't I meet you in the lobby? I—"

34

BEEP!

Somebody was calling on the other line.

"Hey, Martha, can you hold on a second?" I didn't wait for her to answer. My hand shook violently as I clicked on the Accept button. "Hello?"

"Car-r-r-l-ton Doon?" It was that same Scottish voice.

"Yes?" I whispered, glancing around the empty train car.

"Where're yoo?"

"I'm on my way to New York right now," I heard myself reply. It was as if another person were speaking. The words just popped out of my mouth. "Listen, I need to know what the proof is and where it is, okay?" I added shakily. "If you really want to end this thing—"

"Auld maid's bairns are aye best brocht up![31]" the man snapped. "You're doin' the listenin'! Ya know where und what the pr-r-r-uef is. Ya git it, und ya take British Airways tonight, the seven oh-cluck Edinburgh dee-rict frum jay-uff-key. Look for the crest of the serpent . . ."

I clutched the phone, trembling. I understood only a fraction of

---

[31] This is an old Scottish aphorism that means: "Don't offer advice about that which you do not know." I didn't learn what it meant until much later, of course. At the time, it sounded like complete gibberish, which made it all the more frightening.

what he was saying. His brogue was like Muzak: awful and unintelligible, yet insidiously hypnotic.

"Ya hear me? The dugger! The dugger!"

"The what?" I asked.

"YA KNOW! TILL THE CUPS UND YOOR FAH-VER IS 'AGGIS!!!"

"I till the what, now?"

"The police, ya ponce! Doon't tell tha police. Weet for me cull—"

Oink.

I blinked. Was there a pig or hog in the background? What the hell was going on?

"See ya in Edinbu-r-r-rgh, Carlton Doon tha Furth," the man finished.

With that, he hung up.

35

PROBLEM SOLVED—MISSION COMPLETE—AFFIRMATIVE

Until he'd mentioned the cops, I hadn't even considered notifying them. I didn't know why. (Possibly because I'd led the most grotesquely sheltered life imaginable?) I clicked back to Martha's line—and then, with the unconscious speed associated with a bodily reflex, such as gagging, I turned off the phone.

I sat there for a second.

Why did I just hang up on Martha?

Oh, right: because I couldn't handle hearing Olivia cry again. If I heard her cry, then *I'd* start to cry. Then an ugly domino effect would ensue where I'd lose all control and I'd notify the cops and Dad would be killed and all would be lost in an apocalypse of my cowardice and panic and inability to deal.

Yes. So . . .

I didn't even need to call Martha back. She knew I was safe. Besides, she couldn't help me. She didn't know what the "proof" was. And even if she did, she still couldn't get within five hundred feet of the apartment. If she did show up there to meet me, whatever doorman on duty would ask what was going on, seeing as she was banned from the premises . . . No, best not to get anyone else involved. I had to protect Martha. I had to protect Olivia. The only way to accomplish this would be to leave them out of it from now on. Above all, control was of the essence.

I needed to stop being so goddamn emotional.

That's when it hit me: There was only one entity in this world that was totally unemotional and completely in control. (AND virtually indestructible, to boot.) It was a certain kind of comic-book robot—found only in the rare *Magnus, Robot Fighter, 4000 A.D.* series. Which meant I needed to transform myself into one. I knew just how, too: Suspend the rules of grammar by dropping all definite and indefinite articles.[32]

Think in flat monotone. Focus on mission. Find "proof" at apartment. Withdraw $$$ from checking account. Report to JFK. Fly to Edinburgh on Dad's credit card. Locate "crest of serpent." Meet Forbas. Make peace. Bury feud. Learn definition of "dugger" (sp?) and "ponce" (sp?). If peace fails, destroy Forba clan in vengeful bloodbath. Reunite Dad and Olivia. Restore family. Ensure reconciliation of Dad and Martha. Drop out of CM. Get syndication for comic strip. Lose virginity to adoring groupie. Live happily ever after. Problem solved—Mission complete—Affirmative.

Well, that was easy. That was some nice bullet-point, *Magnus, Robot Fighter*, thinking, if I do say so myself. The downside was that it left me with nothing to do until I reached Grand Central. Fortunately since I was a robot, I was in no danger of bawling again. I could just sit and feel absolutely nothing.

---

[32] I'm not sure why the robots in the *Magnus, Robot Fighter, 4,000 A.D.* comics speak without using "the" or "a" or "an"—or why other rules of grammar managed to fall by the wayside. Then again, it was created by a bunch of weirdos in the early 1960s (under the pseudonym of "Robert Fighter") who seemed to take great pleasure in truncating not only the human language but also the human body. Every single human being in that series is drawn top-heavy with massive torsos and stumpy legs, like a gorilla. Even women.

36

A KEY TO UNDERSTANDING SCOTTISH BROGUES

No, I didn't really *believe* that I'd transformed myself into a robot. It was only pretend. (Sort of.) I hadn't quite lost my mind. (Yet.)

The train arrived about an hour later. I caught a cab outside the station on Park Avenue. Since it was a Saturday morning, there wasn't much traffic. I zipped right uptown to our apartment on Madison Avenue and 82nd Street.

I mention these boring details to illustrate how sane and in control I was.

In fact, I even managed to accomplish something productive during that time. I created a Scottish pronunciation key for myself, so I'd have a tool to help me figure out what the hell the Forbas were saying in case they called again. I memorized it, too.

Our building's chattiest doorman, Walter, was sitting on a stool under the awning. He looked just as I'd seen him last when I'd left for school. His bulbous face was red. The color contrasted pleasantly

PRONUNCIATION KEY

You = "YA/Yoo" (hard U becomes soft A or exaggerated U)

Tell = "TiLL" (soft E becomes soft I)

Cops = "Cups" (soft O becomes soft U)

And = "Und" (soft A becomes soft U)

Father = "FA-VIR" (hard TH becomes soft V;

soft E becomes hard I followed by TH)

F = "UFF" (soft E occasionally becomes soft U)

K = "KEY" (hard A becomes hard E)

with his bright green uniform. Finding him there was oddly reassuring. I could almost imagine that nothing had changed.

He hopped up and opened the cab door for me with a big smile.

"How ya doin', Carlton?" he asked. "Home for the weekend, are ya?"

"Yup," I lied.

He escorted me into the lobby.[33] "Dad's throwing a big brunch, eh?" he asked.

"Uh . . . not that I know of," I mumbled distractedly, hurrying into the elevator. *No, sorry, Walter. Dad's been kidnapped. No big brunches for a while.* I poked at the seventh floor button. "Why do you ask?"

---

[33] The lobby of our building is furnished like a 1920s gentleman's smoking club: lots of low lamps and Oriental rugs and big leather chairs. When I was younger, I liked to imagine that the doormen got together there when nobody was looking and smoked cigars and sipped brandy and talked about what stuck-up losers the tenants were—especially my dad.

"I let the caterer up about an hour ago," he said. "She had the key to your apartment, so I knew your dad had arranged it. Not the warmest gal. Spoke with a funny accent, too. I said, 'Early to be working on a weekend, eh?' And she said . . ."

I couldn't hear him anymore. My heart had started pounding like artillery. His lips were still moving as the door slid shut—uttering what, I don't know.

37

THE SHATTERED BUST OF FRANK LLOYD WRIGHT, AMONG OTHER THINGS

The smart thing would have been to press the DOOR OPEN button and run like hell. Unfortunately, such decisive action requires limbs that function. I stood there, a gelatinous fool, as the elevator whisked me up to certain death.

In our building, apartments take up entire floors. There's just a tiny little hall that separates the elevator door from the front door. To put it another way: About three seconds later, the elevator would basically open up right into my home, where the "caterer" would be waiting.

This is what happens when your rich dad owns an apartment in New York. You live part-time in a so-called high-security building that affords no security at all. You live in an apartment that allows an enemy clan member to fool a chatty doorman into gaining access with nothing more than a stolen key.

I am walking into an ambush. I am going to die.

The elevator opened. Our front door was open, too. The key was in the lock. This was it. The moment of my death! Morning sunshine streamed in from the living room, casting a bright glare over the marble floor. I cringed, waiting for the gunshots . . .

A horn honked on the street far below.

Interesting. If I'd heard that, I should have been able to hear Scottish battle cries or pistols blasting. But the apartment was deathly silent.

I squinted into the foyer, fingers poised over the DOOR CLOSE button.

"Hello?" I called. My voice cracked.

No answer. I summoned some courage and crept out. The elevator shut behind me. *Oops.* I probably should have held it.

"Hello?" I called again, a little louder.

Still nothing. I rounded the corner to the hall that led to Dad's study—

"Yikes!" I screamed.

Nobody responded. But the mysterious visitor had been here. And she'd been busy, too. Crumpled letters and architectural plans lay strewn across the hall floor, and the mess spilled out from Dad's study—as if a recycling truck had dumped a white-paper-only load through the door. I backpedaled a few feet. Yet even in the midst of panic, I noticed that the door at the end of the hall was open . . . the door that led to the building's stairwell. We never opened that door. So maybe the "caterer" had already left. Maybe she'd found what she was looking for. Maybe she'd found the "proof" and would now let Dad go, and we could all just forget about the whole damn feud and call it quits.

I decided to pretend that this was true. It made things easier.

Holding my breath, I tiptoed through the debris.

My knees wobbled. I had to clutch the doorframe to keep from keeling over when I peered into Dad's study.

What a freaking disaster.

She'd completely ransacked the room. She'd *destroyed* it. The drafting table was overturned; cabinet drawers hung open; every painting had been torn from the walls, every book had been yanked from the shelves . . . and any object large enough to conceal something inside it—be it a coffee mug, goldfish bowl, or the ceramic bust of Frank Lloyd Wright[34]—had been shattered.

I stepped toward the upside-down drafting table.

Amazingly, its lone drawer was still closed. Then I remembered why: It was *always* locked, because this was where Dad kept his precious Dunne family heirloom, the antique letter opener. I crouched beside the keyhole. The fake caterer had clearly tried to break it open. The paint was chipped. *Sucker!* I thought. She hadn't been able to find the key, of course. Dad didn't keep the key in the study. He didn't want *anyone* getting inside that drawer. He'd even hidden the key from me. Or so he thought.

What he didn't know is that I'd spied on him many years ago, the night he slipped it under his bedroom rug.

I'd spied on him because I couldn't believe that he was hiding his stupid drawer key from his own son, seeing as his own son didn't want to touch his stupid letter opener in the first place.

[34] Frank Lloyd Wright lived from 1867 to 1959, and is probably the most famous architect in the world. He designed, among other things, the Guggenheim Museum—which if you think about it, looks a whole lot like Bentham's Panopticon. Maybe that's why Dad displayed his bust. Either that or Dad is just a big geek.

38

TWO EPIPHANIES

There's a certain feeling you get when you realize that you've been an idiot. Rather, it's the feeling you get when you realize that the obvious has stared you in the face and you've been too scared or blind to see *anything*. It's sort of akin to what Bruce Wayne must have felt when that bat came crashing through his study window,[35] or what it feels like to be slapped in the face by a beautiful girl. (Or so I imagined, in the case of the latter.) You can't help but smile. In a flash, I was stumbling through the wreckage and out the door.

Carlton, you dope, I groaned to myself. I hurtled down the hall to Dad's bedroom, nearly falling on my butt as I skidded to a halt. *The "proof" has to be the letter opener. Why else would Dad have made such a big deal about it for all these years?*

Crouching on all fours, I dug the drawer key out from under the rug—a psychedelic Persian monstrosity that weighed probably four times as much as I did—then bolted back to the overturned drafting

[35] This is a reference to *Batman* #404—the all-important, historic comic when Bruce Wayne adopts the alter ego of a bat to wage war against the seedy criminal elements of Gotham City, those responsible for his parents' murder back when he was a child. This comic appeared in 1940, written by Bill Finger and illustrated by Bob Kane. Bill Finger lived from 1914 to 1974; Bob Kane lived from 1915 to 1998.

table. My hands were almost shaking too much for me to open the damn thing; I must have jabbed at it a dozen times before the key finally slid into the lock and turned. The drawer popped open. Since the table was upside down, it took some doing to dig the letter opener out. I had to lift the tabletop; the letter opener was buried beneath what felt like a large manila envelope . . . *there*. My fingers wrapped around the cold metal hilt. I whipped it out and held it aloft, prepared to shout in lunatic triumph: "The proof, you bastards!"

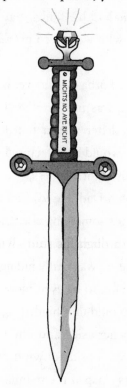

I didn't shout anything, though.

I didn't because . . . The letter opener was a piece of junk.

I'd never really gotten a close look at it before. Dad hadn't let me within ten feet of it. But now that I was actually *holding* it . . . I sat there on my knees, frowning at the cheap brass blade. Its metal was the color of pee. It was nicked and scratched. The hilt was inlaid with cheesy fake gems. Most of them were pink. The inscription was so filthy and poorly carved as to be barely legible: MICHTS NO AYE RICHT.

It looked like something that would go for two bucks at a yard sale.

I was a little confused.

Obviously, I'd *seen* the letter opener before, long ago. Somehow, though, it had grown fabulous and magical in my memory over time. It had become the Excalibur of letter openers. This didn't make sense. Dad was a smart guy. He had his faults, but he appreciated the finer things. He had taste. So why was he so protective of *this*? How—

This isn't the proof.

No. It couldn't be. Mr. Forba or whoever he was wanted me to bring the proof overseas. There was no way that I could get on a plane to Scotland with a big huge letter opener that looked like a knife—even with a blade *this* dull. He would have factored airport guards and X-ray machines into his demands, right? (Unless, of course, he was a dope, too. But he'd managed to snatch Dad. He *was* crafty.) No, the way I saw it, the Forbas were looking for something else. Dad must have deliberately used this letter opener as a distraction for all these years—to draw our attention away from what he was *really* hiding. It would certainly be in keeping with Dad's behavior, to be even more secretive and duplicitous than necessary. But what could that hidden something be?

I tossed the letter opener aside and lifted the drafting table again, digging blindly through the upside-down drawer.

This time, my fingers clasped the manila envelope.

39

POP-SICLE

Aha. I yanked the envelope out. It was covered with dust and unlabeled. Like me, Dad anally labeled everything. THIS was the proof. What else could it be, really? Nothing left in the study was even remotely salvageable. Everything else had been mangled or ripped to shreds or smashed to bits. Plus, Martha had told me that Dad kept an entire file on the Forba clan. He must have been trying to hide it in this envelope with the whole letter-opener-as-distraction ruse.

I tore the envelope open.

There were several sheets of paper inside, thick like vellum.

And I swear—by everything that is holy and everything that *isn't*—this is what I found printed on them:

THE FINAL TESTAMENT OF CARLTON DUNNE III

TO BE OPENED BY BRIAN SAMPSON,

ESQUIRE, UPON MY PASSING
AND PRESENTED TO MY BELOVED ONLY SON,
CARLTON DUNNE IV

Dear Carlton:

As you know, I'm clinically dead. I say clinically because I have instructed my attorney, the man who gave you this envelope, Mr. Brian Sampson, to ensure that cryogenic technicians will freeze me to –103 degrees Fahrenheit and install me in cell 5M of the Fortress of Eternal Life.™

That's right. I'm going in. I reserved my own cell, the very last one. I never told you because I know how you feel about my work, and about this project in particular. You think it is bulls***. I don't blame you. As much as I appreciate my clients' generosity, those who financed the building of the Fortress are, without exception, wackos. But I do have my reasons for joining them in suspended animation, which I will address shortly.

By the way, have you ever seen the television commercial for the Hair Club for Men? The president tells the audience: "I'm not just the president, I'm also a client." That goes for me now, too. "I'm not just the architect, I'm also frozen inside the building." Don't be sad or angry though. Look at it this way: I'm no longer your pop. I'm a Pop-Sicle.

That was an attempt to be funny.

I know you comic-book types appreciate a good

joke. I do, too. I never told you this, either, but I was so opposed to all your comics only because I was worried you would become an unhappy shut-in, like me. Don't let that happen, Carlton. You have so much love, talent, and warmth to share. Don't f*** it up.

There are some other things you deserve to know, some things I've kept from you your whole life, so I'll get right to them.

I've lied to you, Carlton. I've been lying to you ever since I told you about the feud and swore you to secrecy. Angus Forba didn't burn down Birsay because Malcolm Dunne took back what was rightfully ours. He burned it down because Malcolm Dunne was a crook. Malcolm robbed and abused the townsfolk until they finally rose up against him. The only reason history wrote the Burning of Birsay in our favor is because Malcolm Dunne inspired so much fear.

I can't tell you any more than that. Some secrets I have to take with me to the Fortress of Eternal Life™ or, if fate decides otherwise, to the grave. I've always been too ashamed to tell you the truth. Maybe someday I won't be. What I can tell you is that the Forbas want what's theirs. And on some level, they deserve what's theirs. But know this: They are just as rotten and hypocritical and crooked as our clan. They've threatened me with violence. I've never crossed that line, nor did my father, nor did my father's father. The Forbas started threatening me right after your mother died, if you can believe it. They didn't even have the decency to let me mourn, because their fortune was slipping away.

Until that point, the feud had been conducted in a gentlemanly fashion.

One last confession: Your mother's death changed me in the worst way possible. It made me scared of pain. I didn't want to hurt like that ever again, so I kept everyone at a distance. When I met Martha, and I began to fall in love with her, I pushed her away. I pushed her right out of my life. It's one of my biggest regrets. The only bigger regret is pushing you and Olivia out of my life. I let a struggle inside me become a struggle with the people who matter most.

I'm so very, very sorry, Carlton. I'm sorry for cursing so much, and for sending you away to boarding school, and for being so competitive, and for being such a lousy dad. But it was always my destiny, I suppose.

The Forbas can threaten me all they want, but if they try to kill me, the joke will be on them, because I will live forever in the Fortress of Eternal Life™. And when I'm healed and thawed—be it a hundred or a thousand or a million years from now—I will put an end to the feud. I won't harm the Forbas' descendants, either, because that would mean stooping to their level. I will simply tell the truth.

With all my love and apologies,
Dad

P.S. Please remind my attorney that I insist on being stored in cell 5M with the following items, also frozen instantaneously and intact to −103 degrees Fahrenheit, upon my clinical death:

- My letter opener
- One (1) iPod loaded with the complete collections of Yes, Led Zeppelin, Black Sabbath, and the original cast recording of Jesus Christ, Superstar
- One (1) 11 x 14 sketch pad
- Four (4) presharpened graphite drafting pencils, black
- Four (4) erasers
- Two (2) foot-long chicken salad hoagies, extra mayonnaise and bacon
- Four (4) bags Sour Cream and Onion potato chips (Utz)
- One (1) case Diet 7UP
- The framed photograph of Martha, Olivia, and you taken during our vacation in the Bahamas.
- One (1) folding chair
- One (1) folding table

40

PIRATES

For a long time, I sat perfectly still on the floor. I sat in the middle of that destroyed study, clutching those papers in my hands. And a memory floated out of the dark recesses of my brain—a memory long buried by tragedy, I guess, and conjured by my thoughts of Batman—the memory of the drive to my mom's funeral in a long black limo, back when I was five.

I think it bears mentioning that this is also my very *first* memory, which is kind of funny. I mean . . . My memories begin with a funeral. You usually don't think of anything beginning with a funeral. Funerals are supposed to mark endings—THE ending, really—although my dad might argue otherwise if you freeze yourself when it's all over.

Besides, some cultures believe that death is just the first step on a long, mystical journey. The ancient Egyptians even loaded their tombs with snacks and gold coins and extra clothes, so that the dead wouldn't leave empty-handed. And sitting there on that floor, I remembered thinking about *that*, too . . . how I'd thought of loading Mom's coffin with a few basic items: her asthma inhaler, one of Dad's drawings, and maybe some money, just a few bucks, in case her mystical journey also involved taking a cab or limo.

I even remembered telling this to Dad on the drive to the cemetery.

"Don't talk that way, Carlton," he'd snapped. "When you're dead, you're dead. And who in their right [#%$*] mind would bury money?"

Before I could reply, his cell phone rang. He took the call and immediately began barking at someone. I wondered why he was so grumpy, aside from Mom's death. Using my five-year-old logic, I figured it was because he was wearing a suit, and he hates wearing suits. *I don't like you in your suit, Dad,* I'd thought angrily, and immediately felt ashamed. Even then, I'd known he was all I had left. But I also knew now that I must have grown up a bit, or at least changed since then, because I didn't feel so ashamed anymore. I'd never liked him in a suit. I still didn't. Not even in his ruined study—not even knowing he was kidnapped, not even knowing all he'd confessed in this letter.

But "like" has nothing to do with "love," right? I asked myself.

I couldn't answer.

Pirates, though, I wanted to tell him. Pirates would bury money.

47

DREAMLESS SLEEP

After that, my breath came slow and evenly.

My heart beat at a steady pace.

Incredible. The letter, the memory of my mother's funeral, the destruction around me—all of it did the trick. It did what fear alone couldn't do. It turned me into a robot from the *Magnus, Robot Fighter, 4000 A.D.* series. It fixed me.

I know I should have felt something, but I didn't. And this sudden icy numbness should have made me very scared about my already precarious psychological state, but it didn't do that, either. It had unleashed something inside me, and that something was a big black void. It was pure emptiness.

Calmly, mechanically, I folded Dad's final testament and shoved it into my knapsack. I wasn't sure if this was the "proof." I sort of doubted it was, seeing as its contents didn't technically *prove* much. Not in the traditional sense. But I figured it was something worth holding onto. At the very least, it wasn't safe here.

Neither was I, probably.

Dad's kidnappers were waiting for me in Edinburgh. For all I knew, their mysterious female cohort might return to the apartment.

It was time to leave.

So I strolled down the hall to my room. I grabbed my passport and exited through the back entrance. I hurried down the seven flights of stairs into the alley—so I wouldn't have to see Walter again. I didn't bother closing any doors behind me.

The big black void began to fill with a thick white fog.

The fog grew thicker as time went on, keeping me at a safe distance from every mission I accomplished. It shrouded me as I hopped in a cab to JFK . . . shrouded me as I withdrew $1000 in cash from my checking account at an ATM . . . shrouded me as I charged a one-way first-class ticket to Edinburgh on Dad's forbidden credit card: seat 2A on Flight 19, British Airways, seven o'clock direct.

Go, Magnus, Robot Fighter, 4000 A.D.

It was 11 A.M. The flight didn't depart for another eight hours.

But those hours could have been millennia, or they could have been microseconds. To a robot, the passage of time has no impact. A robot doesn't experience *any* emotion, and that includes boredom. I ate a chicken salad hoagie in the terminal; I drank a Diet 7UP; I went to the bathroom a few times. Other than that, I sat and stared. Only two thoughts occurred to me, back to back, as if endlessly played on a programmed loop: *You are doing this for Olivia. You are doing this so Olivia doesn't have to suffer the loss of a parent. You are doing this for Olivia. You are doing this . . .*

I was so detached that I didn't even think to doodle in my sketch pad.

And when it came time to board the plane and sink into that plush first-class seat, the fog turned to a drowsy stupor. A stewardess passed by with a tray full of plastic champagne flutes.[36] She smiled at me in a way that reminded me of Martha.

It was only then that I started to cry. Bad form for a Magnus, Robot Fighter.

So I took one of the flutes and slurped down in three gulps, then handed it back, nearly gagging. The drowsy stupor segued seamlessly into a dreamless sleep.

---

[36] Flight attendants never card teenagers on international flights. I don't know if drinking laws are different on planes, but it's true: You can be thirteen years old, and they'll still serve you free champagne.

42

AN EVEN THICKER FOG

"Excuse me. Excuse me, young man?"

Somebody was shaking my arm. Somebody with an English accent.

My eyelids fluttered open. It was the stewardess. She looked blurry. For some reason, the plane was now suffused with a horrible white light.

"I filled out your customs card," she whispered. She handed a large ticket to me. "I didn't want to disturb you. You looked so sweet and cute."

I gaped at her as she scurried off down the aisle. Drool hung from my chin. This was odd, as my mouth was bone dry.

I wiped the drool away. I had no idea what was going on. It took me several more minutes to realize that the plane was about to land.

A few seconds after that, the wheels struck the runway.

My head bounced. I glanced at the customs card. The stewardess had indicated that I was a student and that I was traveling abroad for a study program. Why she had done this, I couldn't say. But why question it? Whatever this ticket said, it was better than the truth. I groggily signed at the bottom, swearing to its authenticity.

I stuck to this convenient lie as I filed out and cleared customs, and exchanged my dollars for pounds: big white bills that looked and felt fake.

I splashed my face in a water fountain.

Wake up, I ordered myself. *A grown woman called you sweet and cute, for God's sake! Someone other than Martha! Wake up! Start feeling emotions again!*

I couldn't seem to obey my own command. I trudged forward. My sneakers clomped on the tile floor of Edinburgh International Airport. I patted various pockets, checking to see that I still had wallet and passport and cell phone. All there. I gripped the straps of my knapsack, knowing that my father's letter was inside—wondering if *this* would trigger an emotional response. No dice.

A pair of sliding doors parted.

Happy Scots chattered all around me in incomprehensible brogues. Most were crawling into tiny black taxis the size of go-carts.[37] The steering wheels were all on the wrong side. I shivered, searching for something resembling "the crest of a serpent." A flag? A tartan? Nope. A small problem: Aside from the cabs and the Scots in my immediate vicinity, I couldn't see a goddamn thing. It was as if the thick white fog had blown out my ears and settled over the entire city. I'd never seen or felt a fog quite like it. It was like refrigerated cotton. How the hell had the plane even landed?

I needed to go someplace quiet. Somewhere to get my head together. The kidnappers were due to call again with further instruction—so preferably someplace far from any other people, as

---

[37] One particular brand of Mini, popular with Scottish drivers, is the French *Deux Chevaux*. Literally, this means "two horses." Translation: the engine is so small that it's only two horsepower. Maybe that's an exaggeration, some sort of self-deprecating joke created by the manufacturers. Maybe the name is supposed to be funny.

well. I spotted an empty bench on the other side of the street, across from the pickup and drop-off area. It would have to do.

I shambled across the street. I didn't see the black van screeching toward me.

43

THE DAM BURSTS AGAIN

"LOOK OUT!!!"

What the—

Tires squealed.

From out of the fog, a pair of headlights bore down upon me. I froze. What happened next was all so swift and confusing that it was more a bullet-point montage of disparate images than an actual *event*:

- SOMEBODY TACKLED ME OUT OF THE WAY . . .
- MY HANDS SMACKED THE PAVEMENT . . .
- I ROLLED END OVER END . . .
- I CAUGHT A GLIMPSE OF A BLACK VAN, SPEEDING AWAY . . .
- IT DISAPPEARED IN A CLOUD OF EXHAUST . . .

And all at once, I was lying flat on my back, staring up into a girl's face.

She crouched over me on all fours, gazing down worriedly. Her eyes were bright green. She had long curly blond hair, so long that it brushed over my cheeks. Aside from a few freckles, her skin was blemish free, as pristine and pale as the fog above us. Her lips were red and curvy, like the lips of a child. But she definitely wasn't a child. She looked to be about my age, but she was bigger and stronger than me.

She was gorgeous. She might as well have been the girl I'd described to Bryce and Kyle, back at the Who-Would-You-Bang Forum.

And she had just saved my life.

"Are you all right, mate?" she asked in a brogue even thicker than my dad's kidnapper's. It sounded more like: *"Err-ya-reet, meet?"*

I swallowed. "Yeah."

"Are ya sure?"

I bit my lip. I didn't want to say much more. But I could feel it all welling up inside me—everything I'd been through . . . everything I'd suffered in the past day, the past two weeks, the past seventeen years—and then out it came. I was no longer a Magnus, Robot Fighter. I was a babbling idiot.

"I don't know—I mean, oh my God, thank you so much. You don't understand . . . My name is Carlton Dunne the fourth, and I'm an American, and I'm here because my dad has this enemy, and his enemy kidnapped him . . . See, even though we're American, we're originally from Scotland, and this clan hates us . . . and I probably should have gotten the license plate of that van but I'm so freaked out . . . because, look, this is only the second time I've ever snuck out in my life. I mean, I go to boarding school . . . but I'm really bad with people and I'm a misanthrope but I also trust whoever I meet absolutely no matter what and I never listen—"

THWACK.

The girl slapped me in the face.

"Get hold of yourself, lad!" she cried, laughing.

I blinked.

Funny. Less than twenty-four hours ago, I'd hypothesized about what it would feel like to be slapped in the face by a beautiful girl.[38]

Now I knew.

As it turned out, I'd been half right. I *was* angry. But as far as the grinning went . . . Nah. That wasn't part of the equation.

[38] See Chapter 38

44

BLUNTNESS IS A QUALITY I ADMIRE

"How long are you going to sit there drawing?"

I didn't answer.

"Look, for the last time, I'm sorry I slapped you," the girl said.

My cheek was still smarting. I kept my eyes glued to the sketch pad. I kept my mouth shut. For all I knew, if I opened it again, she might hit me again. Mostly I was hoping that if I ignored her, she'd leave. What the hell was her problem, anyway? She'd followed me to the empty bench. She'd been sitting here pestering me for the past half hour, even though I hadn't said a word. I might as well have been wearing a bright neon sign that flashed GO AWAY. Were Scottish girls extra clueless?

Finally she snatched the sketch pad out of my hands. "Mind if I look at what you've got here?" she asked dryly. "I've heard Americans have trouble sharing—"

Bee-bee-beep. Bee-bee-beep.

My cell phone was ringing. *Jesus.* I could feel it squirming around in my pocket. My stomach twisted in a painful knot. I held up a finger, shushing her, and dug the phone out of my jeans. "Hello?"

"Hallo, Carlton Doon," the kidnapper rasped.

I turned my back on the strange girl.

"What do you want?" I whispered furiously, hunching over the mouthpiece.

"I want to grind ya to 'aggis. But that hasn't quite panned out for me, has it?"

I tried to think of a witty rejoinder. I was sure he was joking. In every comic book I'd ever read—or drawn, for that matter—the hero and the villain always shared a certain kind of semihumorous rapport. He was trying to scare me, the way a classic comic book villain would. He didn't *really* want me to die. Otherwise, he wouldn't have instructed me to come to here.

"Bluntness is a quality I admire," I heard myself tell him.

"What?" he spat.

"Bluntness—" I realized I sounded like a jackass.

"Bollocks," he hissed.

Right: This wasn't a comic book. This was my life, and a van had just tried to run me down. I'd been played for a sucker. My entire body felt as if it were liquefying, oozing through the slats in the bench. "Sorry," I mumbled.

"We need the proof! Your dad's in Stromness, and he'll die there in tha next three days if we don't get it. Join 'im if ya like, or don't join 'im. It's oop to yoo. Ye can cuil in the skin ye het in."

"I can what?"

"Yoo can do whatever yoo like, ya ponce!"

Click.

45

DRAWER'S FORGETFULNESS

The girl tapped my shoulder. "Who was that?" she asked.

"It was that kidnapper I was talking about. He, um . . ." My shoulders caved in over my scrawny chest. I couldn't bring myself to look at her. "You know, forget it. You wouldn't believe me if I told you, anyway."

I reached for my sketch pad.

She pulled it away from me. "Not so fast, mate. Of course I'll believe you!"

"You will?"

"A van just tried to run you down!"

I sighed, rubbing my eyes. "Oh, yeah. That."

"So what'd he say?"

"He said that he wanted to grind me to haggis."

She snorted. "A true Scot would never mention haggis. That's like an American saying 'I'll grind you into hot dog.' This man's a ponce."

I turned to her to ask her what the hell she was talking about.

I completely forgot about the question.

I forgot about how bewildered and upset I was. I forgot about the scratches and bruises I'd sustained from her tackle. I even forgot about my dad, and about Olivia and Martha, too. I forgot *everything* . . . and I know it sounds corny, but this weird blond stranger gazing back toward the airport with those distant green eyes (or maybe it doesn't sound corny as much as voyeuristic), all at once, her staggering beauty overwhelmed me. Not as a seventeen-year-old virgin but as a kid who liked to draw.[39] She wasn't sexy like Bee A. Vixen. She wasn't cute like Jessica James. She transcended any earthly comparison. She may have been a jerk, a certifiable madwoman, or worse—but in this fog, in this light, she almost reminded me of Signy.

"You know, it's weird," I started to jabber, against all better judgment. "For pretty much my whole life, or at least ever since I can remember, I've never really done anything on my own. I mean, I've always had somebody watching me—or at least I've always *believed* that somebody was watching me—and, now, I'm in this foreign country and people are trying to kill me and nobody's watching me. But *you* came out of nowhere, so I guess I want to say thanks again, because you saw me. I mean—"

"I ken your meanin' by your mumpin'," she interrupted.

"You what?"

"I UN-DER-STAND," she said, enunciating each syllable in an exaggerated Southern American accent. "YOU ARE WEL-COME."

I laughed in spite of myself.

"Buck up, mate," she chided. "You're still breathing."

"I guess that's a start."

"There's an old Scottish proverb: '*Greedy fowk heas lang airms.*' It means greed will make you do anything. Whoever took your dad is greedy and nothing more. So he'll be predictable. What else did he say?"

---

[39] Maybe a little as a seventeen-year-old virgin.

I shrugged and leaned back on the bench. "That he's holding my father in Stromness," I said. "He's gonna kill him in three days. And that—"

"You're lying!" she cried, slapping my arm.

I winced. "What?"

"Me dad is in Stromness!" she exclaimed, hopping to her feet. "I'm on me way to Stromness *right now*. That's why I'm here at the airport! Don't you get it?"

"Get what?"

"I can take you there! It's in Orkney. I can help you get to your dad and get these kidnappers! I can protect you!" She rubbed her hands together and smiled broadly. "This will be so great for me treening!"

I shook my head. "Your . . . what?"

"Me treening? This is me ticket! Protecting you will guarantee me place in Tulliallan history! I'm treening to be a cop!"

46

THE EXCEPTION TO THE OLD SCOTTISH RULE

I laughed. "I'm sorry. Did you say you were training to be a cop?"

She turned away sulkily, as if I'd just asked the most offensive question in the world. "Aye. Do you find it hard to believe that a girl can be a cop?"

"No, no. It's not that at all. It's just—"

"I've been accepted into the Scottish Police Services," she said proudly. "I shite you not. I'm one of the youngest ever. I'm only eighteen years eight months, and I got in. I'll show you." She dug a crumpled piece of paper out of her pocket and shoved it under my nose, flapping it open. "See?"

I blinked at it. It was an acceptance letter, all right. I supposed it looked official, too—stamped with a crest that featured a green-and-white tartan and two birds, pecking at each other. My eyes skimmed over the page, catching a few words here and there . . . *Scottish Police College . . . Tulliallan Castle, Kincardine . . . Dear Aileen . . . Congratulations! We look forward to providing you with effective training supporting the delivery of a high quality of police service to the public—*

She shoved the paper back into her pocket. "Listen, do you believe in fate?"

"I don't know. I've never thought about it much."

"I'm a little superstitious, meself." She grabbed my arm and yanked me off the bench, then threw a powerful arm around my shoulder, hugging me close as if we were old pals. "You're in great hands, mate. I'm going to be the exception to the old Scottish rule: 'Laws catch flies but let hornets go free.' Here's the thing: Saving you was a huge stroke of luck for me! When I tell the police I saved your life, when they know I've helped you find your father . . . Think about it! This is a *kidnapping* involving an American! If I solve it even before I *start* at Tulliallan, I swear to you, I could become Chief Inspector for all of Orkney in no time. And after that, it's on to the LAPD. Because that's what I *really* want to be: an American cop, you know? *Cops* is me favorite program. There's another old Scottish saying: 'Better a gude fame than a fine face . . .'"

Thankfully, my trusty listening problem kicked in again.

Once she mentioned that her favorite show was *Cops,* I was gone. But that didn't mean I didn't stop staring at her. I could be content just to watch her and let my mind wander elsewhere.

I knew her name now, too: Aileen.

Mostly, I knew that I had to accept her offer. What else was I going to do? Fly to Orkney by myself? I *owed* her for saving my life. That didn't even require any rationalization. Maybe Signy wouldn't consider protecting a helpless foreigner solely to advance her own career and star on *Cops*, but this girl wasn't Signy. This girl was a weirdo. Signy was a character I made up. It was important to remember the distinction, seeing that my life was in danger and I had three days to rescue my father.

"So we better be on our way," she concluded. "This is great! A real live case!"

She began dragging me back toward the airport.

"Wait a sec." I pulled away from her. "Don't you even want to know my name?"

She laughed gently. "You told me your name, remember? When you were lyin' in the street. The first thing you said was your name was Carlton Dunne the fourth. The *fourth*. Once I heard that, I knew you were a true Scot." She looped her arm around mine and winked at me. "You're a cocky bastard, aye?"

Cocky was not a word I'd ever considered using in describing myself, but I shrugged. And even though I wasn't superstitious, and even though I didn't believe in any sort of mumbo jumbo (not even the stuff I put into my own comics), I *was* starting to believe in fate. Or maybe not so much fate as self-fulfilling prophecy. Because from the moment Aileen had slapped me in the face, I had an awful premonition that my already horrible circumstances would most certainly get worse. It had happened at COMIC EXPO, and now it was happening in Edinburgh.

I'd accidentally splashed into the ocean of womankind, and without warning the riptide had come to drag me under.

47

HANG A LEFT AT THE SHACK

The flight from Edinburgh to Kirkwall, Orkney, was not luxurious. At least, not on the airline this Aileen girl chose. Maybe other airlines on this route are more comfy. I'm not sure. All I know is that we boarded a twin-propeller junk heap that looked as if it should have been condemned during World War II. I half expected a leather-faced mechanic in goggles to run out and manually start the engines.

The ride was a little bumpy. When you fly in a modern jet, you don't feel as if your insides are being stir-fried. Another benefit of flying in a modern jet: There are flight attendants. Also, pilots generally tend to stay above the mountaintops. Our pilot swerved and banked his way through lush green highlands and wispy tendrils of fog, as if taking us on a playful, low-altitude sightseeing tour. I honestly started to wonder if he even knew where he was going. I pictured him up in the cockpit, sticking his head out the window every so often, scratching his chin, and trying to spot a landmark. *Now I think I was supposed to hang a left at that shack down there . . . wasn't I?*

Aileen was as relaxed as a Zen Buddhist.

She kept up a one-sided conversation the whole time. She spoke of her father: He was a bit ill-tempered but very proud of her acceptance into Tulliallan. She spoke of her mother: Mum had died of cancer when Aileen was very young, like mine. She spoke of the house where she grew up: It was a little cottage on the Loch of Stenness. She spoke of her family's brand-new refrigerator. Dad didn't own it; he rented it. Was that common in the States? Did people rent their refrigerators? Rich people probably owned their own refrigerators. Can you imagine? Owning your own refrigerator!

I didn't respond. I clung to the armrests in white-knuckled terror.

"You should take a look," Aileen murmured. She pointed out the window. "There's Orkney. I'll drive us from Kirkwall to Stromness, where I live. You can see Kirkwall there. Lovely town. Famous for the ba.'[40] You've heard of the ba,' have you?"

No, I hadn't heard of the ba'. I didn't tell her so, though. To tell her so would mean barfing all over her.

She smiled and patted my arm. "First time on a propeller job, eh, Carlton? Ah, don't worry. This is the same model of airplane they use in the police force. Its safety record is nearly perfect. Mind you, they haven't updated the records since before I was born. But that's Orkney for you. Heh-heh!"

---

[40] As I later discovered, the ba' is an ancient ballgame played only in Kirkwall twice a year. On every Christmas and New Year's, the whole town divides into two teams, "Uppies" and "Doonies"—depending on where they were born: either "up" from the town's cathedral or "down" from it. At 1 P.M., a heavy leather ball (the ba' itself) is tossed into the square, across from the cathedral. The goal is for either team to smuggle the ball through Kirkwall's winding streets, back to their home territory. Many superstitions and feuds have grown up around this game. I mention this only because it seems to me that certain Orkney families seem to revel in making up any excuse for superstitions or feuds, no matter how silly.

48

MORDOR, LED ZEPPELIN, AND A WRONG PREMONITION

The drive from Kirkwall to Stromness wasn't much better than the flight.

Aileen owned a *Deux Chevaux*.

But what other car could she own? It was the least-safe car ever built. This girl was to safety what I was to normalcy: An invisible force field surrounded her at all times, repelling it. I'd actually felt hopeful as I stumbled after her through the parking lot at the tiny Kirkwall airport, past Mercedeses and Jaguars and Peugeots—until she climbed behind the wheel of one of those two-seat go-carts, with the steering wheel on the wrong side.

"You know, standard transmission in the UK is great for us lefties," she commented as I crawled in beside her.

"Neat," I said.

"You a lefty, Carlton?"

"Nope."

Then we were off. I held both my knapsack and her battered leather satchel in my lap. The trunk was too small for anything larger than a grapefruit. Aileen's bracelets jangled as she tugged at the gearshift and peeled out onto the highway.

Screeeeech!

My head slammed back in the seat. It was funny: Until now, I hadn't noticed her bracelets. Her beautiful face and my own horror demanded all the attention. But the bracelets were astonishing: silver and ornate and very old. The scaly double-helix design reminded me a lot of the sword hilts I'd copied from *The Illustrious Myths of Scandinavia* all those years ago . . .

But I couldn't look at them. I couldn't look at anything. I was too nauseated.

"So what do you think of Orkney?" Aileen asked after a few minutes, veering off the highway. The new road was barely wide enough for us, much less a car that met any civilized standards. "Pretty, aye?"

Pretty? I shot her a glare. Her face was earnest and serene. No, Orkney was not pretty. Orkney was a godforsaken wasteland. Orkney reminded me of Mordor, from *The Lord of the Rings* and the Led Zeppelin song "Ramble On."[41] There was a palpable aura of gloom and Evil. The sky was charcoal gray. In the mist, I couldn't see much more than weed-choked fields, dilapidated stone cottages, and a few desolate and jagged hills in the distance.

Of course, it probably didn't help that I'd allowed myself to be chauffeured by a stranger who—despite her beauty and law-enforcement aspirations—didn't quite strike me as stable. (*Rented refrigerators?*) But maybe I was overreacting.

"So look, Carlton," Aileen announced. "I'll check us in to an inn outside of town tonight so we can rest. It's perfect."

"We're not going to your house?"

---

[41] Subconsciously, it probably reminded me of Mordor because this is the hellish place in Middle Earth ("the darkest depths") where heroes and treasures are spirited away and held prisoner. "Ramble On" is a seminal acoustic Led Zeppelin ballad about Mordor. It was written in 1969.

She laughed. "Where'd you get that idea?"

I swallowed. "I don't know. I just thought, you know—since you said you lived in Stromness and all . . ."

"Come on, now! What do you think me dad would say if I showed up with some American bloke after being on holiday in Edinburgh? Oh, hallo, Dad. Here's a bloke whose life I saved. I'm trying to find out who kidnapped *his* dad. Heh! If me dad knew any of this, he would give me a good dressing-down. We have to lie low, Carlton. Out of sight. Anyhoo, where would you sleep? In me bedroom?"

I gazed dizzily out the window. I felt very small and embarrassed, and I wasn't sure why. I'd never said I wanted to sleep in her bedroom. Had I?

"I just need some time to do a little poking around the town," Aileen went on. She nodded to herself, thinking hard. "I need to stay someplace out of the way, a place that won't arouse suspicion. And this inn I'm thinking of . . . like I said, it's perfect. Give me a room for the night and one day—and I guarantee I'll find somebody who knows something about your dad. Orkney is an isle of gossips, you know. Scotland is the *land* of gossips." She glanced at me as she rounded a corner. The car nearly flipped over. "You know anything about Scotland?"

I shook my head.

"You *don't?*" she cried accusingly. "But you said your clan is from Scotland! You got to learn your history, mate."

"Well, I know a little history," I murmured. "I know about the battle of Culloden Moor.[42] I learned about that in third form European history. I also know that the guitarist from Led Zeppelin bought a castle here.[43] It's on Loch Ness. Right by the Loch Ness monster."

---

[42] The Battle of Culloden Moor was fought on April 16, 1746. It was the last battle ever to be fought on British soil—led by a hapless Scottish aristocrat named Bonnie Prince Charlie, who wanted to be king of England and Scotland. The British routed his army in less than an hour.

[43] Jimmy Page bought this castle because he knew that it was once owned by a famous black magician and occultist Aleister Crowley. Aleister Crowley lived from 1875 to 1947.

All of a sudden Aileen was cackling hysterically. "Brilliant!" she cried. She took her hand off the gearshift and swatted my knee. Her bracelets rattled. "You're funny. You a Zeppelin fan, Carlton?"

I turned to her. Wow. Talk about déjà vu. Less than forty hours ago (was it less than forty hours? The time difference was screwing with my head), Kyle Moffat had asked me that same exact question. Word for word. And I couldn't explain it, but I just had this *feeling*, another glimpse of the future: Whatever answer I gave would be the wrong answer this time, too. So why lie? I had nothing to lose.

"Big-time," I confessed once more. "I love Zeppelin."

I waited for her to laugh. I waited for her to slap me. She didn't. She just smiled back with that wondrous childlike smile.

"Me, too!" she exclaimed. "Me dad turned me on to Zeppelin when I was a girl. I like their earlier stuff the best." She sighed, turning back to the road. "It's a bit funny, you know. Me dad and I don't have much in common, other than the music we fancy."

49

DUNG

We didn't do much talking after that. I guess there wasn't a whole lot more to say. Besides, I was too out of sorts to make any more conversation. Anyway, it wasn't as if we could celebrate our new Led Zeppelin bond by popping in a CD. Neither of us had any CDs. The car didn't have a CD player, either. It didn't even have a radio.

Given the overall bare-bones vibe of Scotland so far, I don't know why I was surprised when Aileen swerved off the paved road onto an unmarked, muddy path.

The "inn" was a hog farm.

I was sure of this, because we were suddenly surrounded by hogs, some of which were about the size of Aileen's *Deux Chevaux*. There were no other cars on the premises. The engine sputtered into silence as Aileen parked. I hadn't even realized how deafeningly loud the engine was until this very moment—not until I could hear the snorting of the hogs, meandering around in the mud beside us.

"We'll have to do some chores in the morning," Aileen remarked.

"Chores?"

"Aye," she said, climbing out and slamming the door. Not surprisingly, the air was thick with the smell of hog dung. "We'll take a nap, then eat some supper, then go to bed. It's only fifteen quid a night, but you help around the house. We'll need the rest."

"Oh," I said, even though I had no idea what quid meant.[44] "Okay."

I decided not to ask any more questions after that. I was afraid of the answers. I tried to slip back into *Magnus, Robot Fighter*, mode. It was harder this time around.

Aileen led me through the mud to a crumbling three-story stone shack.

There, I met a grizzled Scottish couple who looked as if they'd spent the last ninety years bathing in fecal matter. I assumed they were the farm's owners, but their brogues were so thick that my internal pronunciation key couldn't begin to decipher what came out of their mouths. I didn't want to concentrate too hard on their mouths, anyway. They had maybe five teeth between the two of them, all rotted.

I wondered what a tourist brochure would have to say about Orkney.

Welcome to remote Scotland! The land of kidnappers and hogs and poop! The land that time and dentistry forgot! Only 15 quid a night!

The male half of the couple handed an old-fashioned kerosene lantern to Aileen and gestured toward a rickety stairwell.

"Oop ya go," he said with a gruesome smile.

"Thanks, love!" Aileen called over her shoulder.

I trudged after her. The steps were uneven and slanted. I tripped a

---

[44] As I later discovered, 100 quid = 100 British pounds = 124 Euros = 158 U.S. dollars (at the time).

few times, nearly tackling Aileen.

"Easy, mate," she said with a chuckle.

When we reached the second floor landing, Aileen jerked her head toward two doors down a narrow corridor.

"Only one of the rooms has a loo," she whispered. "You don't mind if I take the room with the loo, do you?"

"I don't . . . mind?"

She smiled. "Just knock if you need to piss."

Just knock if I need to piss?

"Thanks, mate!" Aileen said before I could answer.

She shoved a rusty key into my hand, then scampered down the hall and disappeared through the door on the left: *Smack!*

The floor shook.

Now—

I admit: I was exhausted and scared and lost. Even so, I've never really thought of myself as a demanding sort. I know that I'm rich and privileged, and I've grown up with more than most people and all the rest of it, but, honestly . . . amenities, possessions, they don't mean that much to me. Bryce Perry had destroyed most of my amenities and possessions, anyway. Still, when I stay at a hotel, I insist upon having my own bathroom. That's just how it goes. I'd spent the last two years sharing a bathroom *with* Bryce Perry at boarding school, so I knew what happened when you shared a bathroom with somebody. At best, you got no privacy. At worst, you got a swirlie.

But I didn't make trouble. I sauntered forward and stuck my key into the door on the right. It opened with a loud creak. I sniffed the air. Realistically, I wasn't expecting a Meriden Ramada luxury suite. This was a hog farm, after all. But in addition to there being no toilet or sink, my room was also without:

- **CLEAN SHEETS**
- **ELECTRICITY**
- **A PLEASANT ODOR**

It did have character, however. I'll give it that.

The bed was barely large enough for a cat, and ditch shaped, as was the floor. Both stank of mothballs. I could also see stains on the quilt—impressive on the stains' part, as the day was still overcast. Luckily, a gas lantern and box of matches sat on the nightstand. (By "nightstand" I mean whiskey barrel.) Next to the matches, there were two books: the King James Bible, and *Poems, Chiefly in the Scottish Dialect,* by Robert Burns.[45] I had to hand it to Aileen. This was definitely a great place to lie low. The Forbas would never think to look for us here. Why would they? No sane person would ever stay here—under any circumstances, *ever.*

In a panic, I yanked out my cell phone to call Martha.

I couldn't get a dial tone. I was out of range.

In that case, there wasn't much more to do than follow Aileen's advice.

So that's what I did. I lay down for a nap. I needed the rest, after all. I would have chores to do in the morning.

---

[45] Robert Burns lived from 1759 to 1796. He is probably the most famous Scottish poet. I can't say why, and I'm no critic, but his poems are funny and raunchy, and he was a farmer and the son of a farmer.

50

NEW MAGNUS, ROBOT FIGHTER, MISSION

When I awoke, it was pitch-black outside. I must have slept a long time. Maybe I'd missed supper. I probably had, which was a drag, because I was pretty hungry.

Somebody had lit the lantern and left an envelope beside it—

Oh, my God!

Somebody had lit the lantern. That meant somebody had been in this room. Somebody had *snuck* into this room. *While I was asleep!* They'd seen me! Snoring and God knows what else . . . I suddenly felt dirty, violated, in need of a shower. (Obviously, that wasn't going to happen, as there was no shower.) I fell out of bed and stumbled over to the whiskey barrel. The envelope lying there bore a sickening resemblance to the envelope I'd discovered in my dad's study, dusty and yellow:

> *TO CARLTON DUNNE IV*
> *FROM CLAN FORBA*

My heart seized. Not only had somebody snuck in, they'd followed me here.

In the darkness outside, a hog snorted. *Oink.*

And that's when the realization struck in a grisly groggy flash: *The innkeepers are in cahoots with the Forbas.*

Of course. When the kidnappers had first called, I'd heard oinking in the background. The kidnappers probably called from this very inn. The innkeepers might *be* the kidnappers. We'd walked right into a trap. They'd lured us here somehow.

"Aileen!" I heard myself shriek. "Aileen!"

"Carlton?" her muffled voice replied. There was a patter of feet; the door across the hall slammed. A second later, my own doorknob rattled.

"Carlton!" Aileen yelled. "Open up! Your door's locked!"

I fumbled with the doorknob. My fingers were moist. She burst inside, nearly knocking me over.

"What's wrong?" she asked breathlessly. She was wearing flannel pajamas.

"There's a . . ." I paused for a second. For some reason, she cupped her left hand over her mouth as she spoke. Maybe she felt as queasy as I did.

"Is everything all right?" she asked. She surveyed the room. Her green eyes were sharp and calm. "What's wrong?"

I jerked a shaky finger at the envelope. "Look. The kidnappers have been here."

Aileen bent over the whiskey barrel. She kept her hand at her mouth the whole time. Her silver bracelets glinted in the lamplight.

"Uh . . . why are you holding your hand over your mouth like that?" I asked.

"Me breath."

"What?"

"I haven't brushed me teeth yet, all right?" she muttered. Finally she let her hand drop just long enough for her to rip open the envelope. "I'm sorry. I know it's silly, but I'm very self-conscious about me breath after I nap."

"Uh . . ." I paused, suddenly wondering if I were still asleep, if this were all some odd dream. "You can go brush your teeth if you want," I mumbled.

"Great!" she whispered gratefully, covering her mouth again. "Back in a jiff!"

I stared at her as she pulled a single sheet of yellowed parchment from the envelope and placed it on the barrel. Then she darted out of the room. The parchment was burnt at the edges and inscribed with calligraphy. Of all the strange and scary things that had happened to me since my arrival in this freakish country, this mysterious delivery topped the list. Still, I couldn't help but think: *We're on the run from demented murderous kidnappers; the innkeepers might BE those demented murderous kidnappers; a weird parchment is sitting on my nightstand . . . yet Aileen seems more concerned about her breath than all of the above. New Magnus, Robot Fighter, mission: Redefine what "strange" and "scary" mean.*

51

SUPERSTITION IS MY RELIGION

Moments later, Aileen returned, minty fresh. She grabbed the parchment and sat on the bed, then slapped the mattress with her free hand, gesturing for me to sit beside her. "Sorry again about that, mate. Come sit."

I hesitated.

Aileen smiled. "I won't bite ya, Carlton. Not even now that I've brushed me teeth. Can I ask you something?"

"Sure."

"Are you religious? I mean, do you consider yourself a Christian or a Moslem or a Jew or a Hindu or anything like that?"

I shook my head. "I . . . no," I answered. "I mean I'm Christian, I guess, but not really. I don't go to church regularly or anything like that. Why do you ask?"

"Because I knew it!" she whispered, absently fiddling with one of her long blond curls. "I don't go to church, either. Because that's exactly how I feel! Especially after me mum died, ya know? And me dad *hates* that about me. He's a Christian man. And when he tries to get me to go to church, and I say no, he says: 'Because there's no toothpaste commercials, aye?' What he means is that the telly is my religion, and that I'd rather sit at home and watch *Cops*, because at least then all the tales of misery and redemption are broken up by happy, pretty people whose breath just got a whole lot better. Ya see?"

I tried to smile. I wasn't sure where she was going with this. "Oh," I said.

"What I'm tryin' to say, Carlton, is that you and I are the same, aye? You have your drawing pad; I have my toothbrush. I have my own rituals, just like you have yours. Because, you see, ever since me dad said that about toothpaste commercials and the Church, I've been obsessed with keeping me breath clean. Because he's right! I *do* need those breaks. Brushing me teeth makes me feel safe. Comforted. Us kids without mums, we need that, ya know? It allows us to escape the misery and drudgery, at least for as long as a commercial lasts." She laughed apologetically. "Sorry, mate. Listen to me ramble! I'm a bit daft, if you haven't noticed. So let's have a look at this, shall we?"

She began to pore over the parchment.

I eased myself down beside her. The bed's U shape mashed us together like two bits of cereal at the bottom of a bowl. Aileen didn't seem to notice. And I was relieved, because looking at this terrifying parchment kept me from telling her that she was right: I may not have been a compulsive tooth brusher, but I *did* have my own rituals . . . and burying myself in my drawings provided not only comfort and safety but also the vital commercial breaks that I, a kid without a mom, needed to take from misery and drudgery.

52

AGRICOLA'S DAGGER

To Carlton Dunne IV, heir to Clan Dunne:

I've made a discovery since last we spoke. You know not what the proof is. Your father told me so. I believe him. He is in no condition to lie. Now I tell you: The proof is twofold.

The first is a written confession. You must attest that the Clan Dunne stole Agricola's dagger from Clan Forba in 1214 and used its power to destroy us.

The second is the dagger itself.

Your father tells me you would not know Agricola's dagger were it right in front of you. I am not surprised. You are an American. All you know is MTV and Calvin Kline. You know not of our ancestors—the sorcerers and warriors from the dimmest mists of history, the builders of the Great and Terrible Circles, from Brodgar to Maes Howe.

In the thousand years before 1214, Clan Forba had wealth and power beyond that of any clan. We were the greatest red fish fishers in all of Scotland.

We owed our luck to Agricola's dagger.

When Julius Agricola invaded Scotland in the first century after Christ, he carried with him a silver dagger—blessed with magic and encrusted with jewels—given to him by the Oracle at Delphi. It imbued whoever possessed it with force and strength. As long as Julius Agricola carried the dagger, the Romans could not be defeated.

Yet in due time, a stealthy Pictish warrior—a Forba—stole the dagger from Julius Agricola. He turned the dagger's power against the Romans. He and his clansmen drove the Romans from Scotland within twenty years.

The Forbas then retired to Orkney. We settled the land. We lived in peace and prosperity for over a millennium, until a jealous neighbor stole Agricola's dagger from Angus Forba in 1214. That neighbor was Malcolm Dunne. He used the dagger's power to rewrite history in his favor, to build his own fortune, and to shame the Forba clan for eight hundred years. Red fish continued to bless us but in ever-diminishing numbers. As we Scots say, "Ane lie gar a hunder lee."

Now our coffers are empty. Our wealth is all but gone.

We want what belongs to us, Carlton Dunne IV. Find the proof and bring it to Castle Glanach. Do not contact the police.

It is Sunday night. You have until dawn Thursday.

CLAN FORBA

PS: You may continue to have cell phone problems, so we will contact you via parchment if necessary.

53

RED FISH, FUNNY FISH

I gulped, hanging over Aileen's shoulder. "What do you think?" I whispered.

She sniffed. "I think that whoever wrote this is a ponce. He misspelled Calvin Klein. It's bollocks, all of it. I told you, he was a ponce, didn't I?"

I shook my head. "But . . . I mean, what about the other stuff? Is it true?"

"Aye." She nodded and then handed the parchment to me. "Well, I don't know about your family business, but Julius Agricola did lose his dagger in Scotland. And many of us believe that's why he was defeated so fast and why the Romans fled."[46]

"What does '*Ane lie gar a hunder lee*' mean?"

"It means, 'A lie can be passed innocently, to a hundred different people, by people who don't even know they're lying.'"

I shrugged helplessly. I still didn't get it. I didn't get *any* of this. This whole thing, this whole feud . . . it all spun from a simple theft?

[46] A fact: The Romans did start abandoning their Scottish fortresses around A.D. 87, a mere twenty years after they invaded.

This was the terrible secret Dad planned to take with him into the Fortress of Eternal Life™? This is what he was so ashamed of? That some jerk ancestor of ours stole a stupid dagger from—

Dugger, I suddenly remembered.

When the kidnappers called me on the train, they hadn't been saying "dugger." They'd been saying "dagger."

Not that this revelation helped in any way. But at least I knew what the word meant now. I had a fairly good idea of what "ponce" meant, too.

"Do you know anything about the Forba clan?" I asked Aileen. "Have you heard of them before?"

She nodded and then stood. The mattress squeaked. For the first time, she seemed unsure of herself. She paced the warped wooden floor, avoiding my eyes, fiddling with her hair again. "They're well known in these parts," she muttered. "Carlton, I don't want to worry you, but . . ." She left the sentence hanging.

"But what? You already are worrying me."

"If your dad's kidnappers really are the Forbas, they aren't exactly poor and powerless, despite what they claim. Everybody here knows that the Forbas are really the MacCloughs."

Clearly the name was supposed to mean something to me. It didn't.

"Legend has it that many generations ago, the Forbas sired no sons," she went on. "They sired only daughters, and the eldest married a MacClough. Again, no one is certain, but the legend is, they used this to bury their past. They adopted the MacClough tartan and crest. And the MacCloughs *are* rich and powerful. They own a red fish fishery near the sea, near where their estate is. It's not very far from here. I'm thinking that it might be where they have your father. Either there or at Castle Glanach. But Castle Glanach isn't much more than a pile of ruins on the other side of Loch Stenness, so . . ."

Jesus. The parchment slipped from my fingers and fluttered to the bed. With every new bit of information, about a zillion more questions sprung to mind. But for some reason, the only one I could think to ask was, "What's a red fish?"

"A funny fish," Aileen replied.

"A what?"

Aileen shook her head, perturbed.

"What's the matter?"

She grabbed my knapsack off the floor and yanked out my sketch pad and a pencil, then scribbled something down and shoved the sketch pad into my hands.

SALMON

"It's bad luck to say the word out loud," she whispered. She fiddled with her hair. "No smart Scot would ever say that word."

I wanted to believe her. I did. She was pleading with me with her hopeful, anxious expression; she was appealing to my own superstitions and compulsiveness. She was saying *Trust me.* Wasn't she? Somehow, though, I *couldn't* believe her. No smart Scot would say the word "salmon"?

On the other hand, I wasn't really in a position to argue.

"We'll need all the luck we can get, Carlton," she said. "The Forbas have issued a fatwa against your clan. It's a good thing I'm here."

"They issued a . . . what?"

"A fatwa, mate. You don't know what that means? Maybe you Yanks really *don't* know about anything except MTV!" She giggled, then stopped, quickly covering her mouth. "I'm teasing you. I do that when I'm nervous. 'Fatwa' is an Arabic word that means 'religious edict.' In the West, it's become synonymous with 'death sentence.' I'm trying not to use so many Scottish phrases around you, Carlton. They confuse you."

I nodded. She was certainly right about that. Right now, I was very, very confused—to the point of being unable to think. Which was good. Yes, right now, it would be wise to do some bullet-point *non*-thinking, so I wouldn't have to remember:

- DAD, IMPRISONED ON THIS HELLISH ISLAND SOMEWHERE, "IN NO CONDITION TO LIE"
- OLIVIA SOBBING THOUSANDS OF MILES AWAY, AND MARTHA TRYING TO REASSURE HER
- THE INNKEEPERS DOWNSTAIRS IN CAHOOTS WITH THE FORBAS (OR MACCLOUGHS)
- MY DEATH SENTENCE
- THE EXTREMELY UNNERVING COMBINATION OF AILEEN'S INSANITY AND BEAUTY

"How can I find the proof?" I whispered. "I don't even know what it is. I don't even know where to start looking. I just— How am I going to save my dad?"

"Don't worry," Aileen began. "I wouldn't worry."

I almost laughed. Great! Aileen wouldn't worry! Boy, what a relief. Good thing I had my *Magnus, Robot Fighter,* escape pod—my sketch pad—because it was time to separate from the mother ship. Yes, it was time for a very long commercial break. No more memory from this point forward . . . just smiley, happy, toothpaste-commercial-type stuff. It was time to retreat into my mental prison, my superstition as religion.

Aileen kept talking.

At least I think she did. Maybe it was even about how to rescue Dad. I couldn't be sure, though. Like my cell phone, I was out of range. My pencil had struck paper.

Three . . . two . . . one . . . ignition . . .

54

BERE BANNOCKS

As it turned out—

The innkeepers exempted us from our morning chores. Aileen convinced them to do so by promising them an extra thirty pounds apiece for our overnight stay. She offered this generous sum out of my pocket. She did more than that, too. Apparently, she'd overcome her anxiety about the Forbas or the MacCloughs or whoever, and she'd spent the night eating bere bannocks[47] and drinking whiskey with these two grizzled toothless hog farmers long after I'd fallen asleep over my sketch pad upstairs.

They'd all had a marvelous time. Or so she told me.

The funny part? I didn't learn any of this until I was back in the *Deux Chevaux* the next morning, chugging through the mist toward the MacClough red fish factory.

[47] There are many recipes for baking the Scottish cakes known as bere bannocks, but in Orkney it's:
    2 cups of beremeal (barley meal)
    1 cup of all-purpose flour
    1 teaspoon baking soda
    1 teaspoon cream of tartar
    Salt (if desired)
Mix dry ingredients thoroughly. Add enough milk, water, or buttermilk to make a stiff but soft dough. Roll out flat pancakes on a floured (mixture of flour and beremeal) board to form the bannocks. This will make 2 or 3. Then cook on a hot griddle 5 minutes or so each side until both sides are browned and the middle is cooked. Spread with butter.

55

FRAIDY CAT

"Nice inn, aye?" Aileen asked as she drove. Her green eyes were puffy and bloodshot. She worked the gearshift, her bracelets jangling away like church bells. "Lovely old couple. But they do like to knock a few back, know what I mean?"

"That lovely old couple is in cahoots with the Forbas," I growled.

They were the first words I'd uttered since I'd woken up. My voice was hoarse. But I would have growled, anyway. I was in a growling mood.

Aileen burst into laughter.

"I'm glad you think it's funny." I stared out at a barren, fog-shrouded moor. Amazing—the hideous landscape matched my state of mind perfectly. "Those twisted old freaks could have slit my throat last night while you were getting plowed. Didn't you say you wanted to protect me? So you can get on *Cops*?"

Aileen fought back a few giggles. "I'm sorry. I don't mean to mock you. And I'm sorry for putting the drinks and our rooms on your tab.

But why do you think they're in cahoots with the Forbas?"

"Somebody snuck that parchment into my room, Aileen!" I practically shouted. "How do you think they got in there? My door was *locked*! Who else could have had the key? Jesus!" I shook my head. "*You're* the wannabe police officer. It doesn't take a genius to put two and two together!"

"Relax, Carlton," Aileen soothed. "Anybody with half a brain could have picked that lock. Do you want to hear me theory?"

I didn't answer.

"It's like this," she continued. "The Forbas tried to scare you in Edinburgh. I don't think they meant to kill you. I reckon they wanted to make you think your life was in danger. They never intended to run you down with that van."

"Oh, they didn't? Well, you might want to rethink that, considering that you dove out into the middle of the street and tackled me to the ground to save my life."

"Carlton, I'm serious!"

"About what?"

"About me theory! Listen, mate, all the Forbas want is for your dad to disclose the dagger's location. Aye? And they think he's holding out on them. They know *you* don't have it. So they're using you as both bait and bargain. If your dad thinks *your* life is in danger, he'll give up the dagger's location to protect you. That's what they're banking on. That's why they tricked you into coming here. Understand?"

I reviewed what she'd jabbered. Then I reviewed it again. I kept coming back with a big fat: *Nope, I do not understand.* Something was missing here (beside the dagger itself, that is), and I didn't know what. The compounding mystery just made me feel smaller and dumber and angrier. But at least I figured something out. I figured where a lot of that anger was coming from. Sad to say: It was jealousy.

I was jealous Aileen had stayed up and had fun without me with those two evil geezers in that awful place. It's true. As ridiculous and shallow as it sounds, I felt cheated. We'd shared a bonding moment in that room, over that parchment. Hadn't we?

"Look, mate, don't worry about the innkeepers," she added quietly. "I've known those 'twisted old freaks,' as you say, since I was a wee little girl. They would never sell me out. But you're in Orkney now. The Forbas—the MacCloughs—they're everywhere. They're probably following us right now."

"*What?*" I twisted around in the tiny little seat, squinting out the back window, but I couldn't see a goddamn thing through the fog. "Why didn't you tell me?"

"I didn't want to scare you. You seem like a fraidy-cat." She winked and patted my knee. "Teasing again! Nervous tic. Trust me: Your enemies won't try anything. They just want to keep an eye on you until Thursday. You're the bait and bargain."

I glared at her, my heart pounding. "How can you be so sure?"

"Well, they need something from your dad, right? Basic logic. If you're dead, they can't get it. Like I said, it's greed, pure and simple. Besides, you're with me. I've been accepted at Tulliallan. Crooks always think twice before hurting a cop."

I found myself wishing I'd followed my first instinct and stayed put at CM. Who would have thought that I'd wax nostalgic for a swirlie at the hands of Bryce Perry? Who would have thought I'd dream of attending classes like biology and precalculus? Who would have— Actually, I couldn't travel too far down the *who-would-have-thought* road. I'd be asking myself questions for days. Though I did have one more question for Aileen: If the MacCloughs were so powerful and omniscient, then why *were* we going to their red fish factory? If they knew I didn't have the dagger, what purpose would confronting them even *serve*? I yawned, suddenly worn out. Odd; I'd just woken up. Maybe it was just a surge of fraidy-cat fear.

"What are you thinking?" Aileen asked me.

"That I'm hungry," I lied. "I missed the bere bannocks last night, remember?"

Aileen grinned wryly in spite of the cheap shot. "I know. Gantin's wantin'."

"Sorry?"

"People who yawn are always hungry," she explained. "Don't you know that? Gantin's wantin'. It's an old Scottish saying. Anyhoo, I'm taking you to get some porridge. I feel bad about drinkin' the night away without ya. It's the best porridge in all of Orkney." She sighed. "Give this isle a chance, Carlton. If your life wasn't complete shite, I'm sure you'd think it was a lovely place."

56

WAY TOO GROWN-UP, AND WAY TOO CHILDISH

To Aileen's credit, the inn where she took me for breakfast wasn't another hog farm. It was pretty nice. It had a real dining room, at least, complete with tablecloths. She didn't use any more "old Scottish sayings" for the next hour, either. And the famous porridge—an over-sugared, milky-white sludge—was actually a lot tastier than I would have expected. (True, I hadn't eaten any solid food in nearly thirty hours.) I wolfed it down like a hog at the hog trough.

"Mind if I ask you something?" Aileen asked.

"Sure," I said, shoveling spoonfuls of the mush into my mouth. I did my best to avoid looking her in the eye.

"What are American boarding schools like?"

I lifted the bowl and dumped what remained into my throat. Then I thought for a moment. "They're like this thing called Bentham's Panopticon," I said, once I'd managed to gulp it all down.

Aileen's face lit up. "Brilliant!" she cried. She leaned toward me. "I imagine you hate Bentham, too, eh?"

"You know what Bentham's Panopticon *is?*" I asked.

"Of course I do." She wrinkled her nose. "Everybody in the UK knows about Bentham's Panopticon. Everybody studies it in school. We're not just a bunch of haggis-eating cretins up here. And maybe there's something *you* don't know, Carlton: The majority of people imprisoned in Bentham's time were Scots. Unjustly accused Scots.[48] That's why we don't like him."

I wiped my mouth with my napkin. "I'm sorry. I didn't know."

"How could you? It's neither fish nor flesh," she mumbled under her breath.

Way to go, I told myself grimly. *You offended her again. Nice work!*

I noticed she was staring at me.

"What?" I asked.

She laughed. "You're an odd one, Carlton," she said.

"I am? What about you? What about these old Scottish sayings of yours?"

"Ye'll no draw a strae across my nose," she said with a deliberate smile.

I tried to not smile back. I couldn't help myself. "Okay, you win. Tell me: What does *that* mean?"

"It means I won't let you pick a fight with me," she said. "You're a grump, and you're in the mood for a fight. But I want you to answer my question. What's an American boarding school *really* like? I mean, what are the kids like? Are they all like you?"

Now it was my turn to laugh. "Um . . . I don't think so." I thought about Bryce Perry and Kyle Moffat. "Basically the kids are a weird mix. They're a cross between being way too grown-up for their own good and way too childish for their own good. And I don't blame them. I think that's what happens when you don't live with

---

[48] I'm not sure if this is true or not—the "majority" part, at least—but many Scots *were* unjustly imprisoned under British rule for many centuries.

your parents. You sort of compensate in either direction."

She nodded, her smile fading. "I wish I'd gone to boarding school," she said. She gazed at my empty porridge bowl with that same distant look that she'd had at the airport when she'd reminded me of Signy.

"Boarding school isn't really all *that* great," I said, mostly to fill the silence.

She tugged once at her hair, and then stopped. "No, it's just that . . . Like, I went on holiday in Edinburgh, you know? Then I came back to Stromness to celebrate my acceptance into Tulliallan with me dad. But my pledge to protect you makes contacting me dad impossible. *You're* in danger, so I don't want to put *him* in danger. But in the end, that's fine, because my dad's a ponce, anyway. So maybe by agreeing to protect you, I was looking for a way out. I'm just saying, you know, maybe I wanted to avoid seeing me dad . . . like, subconsciously."

I swallowed.

There was something in her tone I hadn't heard before, something raw and honest, and I almost felt like reaching across the table and taking her hand. And with that feeling came a rush of others: the urge to tell her to forget about taking care of me, to go home and fix things with her dad before it was too late—or just to tell her to go straight to Scottish Police Forces or Tulliallan or whatever the hell it was, and tell *them* the truth: If the Forbas were indeed the MacCloughs, they'd admitted to kidnapping my father.

But I didn't tell her any of that.

Instead I said clumsily, "I know what it's like to have a lousy dad. Or . . . you know, a dad who acts lousy."

She looked up at me. Our eyes met for an instant. Then she turned away. "Ah, bollocks," she moaned. "Let's have a look at the MacClough factory, shall we?"

57

NOT THE DISNEYLAND CASTLE

Back in the little car, Aileen's mood seemed to brighten. "I've got a plan," she said, as we bounced up a hill through the mist. She had to shout to be heard over the struggling engine. "I think the best thing to do is just to confront the MacCloughs head-on, you know? We march right into their factory, and we show them the parchment, and we say, 'We know you're the Forbas. You've confessed to kidnapping this man's father. Now hand him over.' We could even stop in Stromness so you can buy me a video camera. I'd love to get this on tape, so we can send it to *Cops*. I mean, I can see the whole episode, you know? I can see the commercial: '*Cops* goes to Scotland!'" she cried, imitating an American accent. "'Police student saves kidnapping victim and rescues victim's helpless son! Exposes the MacCloughs . . .'"

Good Lord. My ears turned off.

Who was this girl? Yes, I had a hard time getting a bead on *any* human being (even myself sometimes), but Aileen was totally unreadable. One second, she was a kindred spirit in ways she didn't even realize. The next she was blabbering about being on *Cops*. Her plan was pretty far from brilliant, too. The brilliant thing to do would be to go to the police first (the *real* police) and *then* go to the fishery to confront the MacCloughs. That wouldn't even be brilliant. It would just be common sense.

"So what do you think?" she said.

"I don't know," I muttered.

She slapped my arm, laughing. "Not about the plan, you ponce. I was talking about the view." She tapped the windshield.

"Oh."

We were just cresting the top of the hill.

The morning mist had finally started to burn off. Far below, I could see a vast, rocky coastline—and plunk in the middle of it, a tiny walled town . . . as picturesque as Brookfield, complete with its own church steeple, but centuries older. Pointed rooftops and chimneys jutted from medieval row houses along the narrow, cobbled streets. A forbidding stone keep stood nearby to the west, even more ancient than the town. Its rough-hewn walls were crumbling—and there were hardly any windows, just narrow slits here and there; you could imagine archers behind them. Flying from one of its towers was a huge white banner, featuring a smiling red fish. There was something printed on it, too, but we were too far away.

I squinted at it as we drew closer.

"That's the factory," Aileen said. "It isn't the Disneyland castle, is it?"

I laughed. "No. I was just going to say, that banner looks a little out of place. How old is it? It looks like it's as old as the whole stupid feud my family and the MacCloughs have gotten mixed up in the first—"

SCREEEECH!!!

My forehead smacked against the windshield.

"Ouch," I muttered.

That really *hurt*.

I rubbed the bruise with my fingers. I wasn't quite sure what was going on. Aileen had slammed on the brakes. She was practically standing on them. We were skidding to a dead stop in the middle of a deserted road—with Aileen staring out the window at something, stricken, as if she had just seen Agricola's dagger itself.

58

WHAT YOU MUST DO WHEN YOU SPOT A LONE MAGPIE

"What? What is it, Aileen?"

Her face was pale. She rolled down her window—gasping for breath, her arm furiously pumping—and then thrust a shaky finger toward the sky.

I leaned over her, struggling to see what the hell she was pointing at. But all I saw was a large black-and-white bird, circling overhead.

"Good morning, captain," she whispered under her breath.

"Aileen, please."

"Shhh!" she hissed, her eyes pinned to the bird.

A few moments later, the bird flapped away. Aileen flopped back in her seat.

"Whew," she murmured. "That was a lone magpie, Carlton."

"A lone magpie?"

She nodded and turned toward me. She was still white as a ghost. "A lone magpie is the worst luck ever. I've never seen one. *That's* how bad it is. Magpies always come in pairs. Always. We can't go to the factory. Me mum told me, before she died, if you ever spot a lone magpie, you must say: 'Good morning, captain.' That's what you must say, Carlton. And then you must make an about-face."

"An about-face?"

"Yes! I'm so sorry, Carlton. I am so, so sorry."

"So . . . what does that mean exactly? We go back to the hog farm?"

She shook her head and started up the car again. "No. We go to Stromness. I know a pub there. I just need a pint or two to calm down. Then I'll be okay."

59

BACK IN A JIFF!

I wasn't sure what to say after that.

Her skin had turned the color of glue. She kept her eyes on the road for once. Five minutes later, we passed through town's gates. I caught a glimpse of a clock in a shop window. 11:45. It wasn't even noon.

It was Monday morning, and Aileen needed "a pint or two to calm down" after seeing a lone magpie.

I have to ditch Aileen.

I'm not sure where the decision came from, but there it was. It swooped down with the same frightening intensity as the lone magpie. Yet I knew right then it would be the one decision I would stick to, no matter what.

This girl was beautiful; this girl was training to be a police officer, but she was far too strange and fragile to be of any help. She was fearless in the face of murderous kidnappers but shaken beyond words in the face of a circling bird. And I didn't fault her for it. How could I?

She'd *volunteered* to help me—a perfect stranger, a wimp—out of the kindness of her heart. (Plus a desire to advance her career and to star on *Cops* and to avoid her father, but still.) The point being: I was just as much of a mess as she was, if not more so. This wasn't her problem. It was mine. I knew that now. I'd have to save Dad on my own. If I were both "bait and bargain," I couldn't allow her to be, as well.

So—

After Aileen had drunk her pints, I would thank her. Profusely. And then I would offer her a big fat stack of pound notes. I'd give her anything she wanted, plus a little extra for all her kindness and trouble. And then I would go withdraw those pounds from an ATM (even a town like Stromness had to have an ATM, right?), and then we would say our good-byes and hopefully hug and exchange e-mail addresses. And then I would report to the nearest police station and tell them everything, and they would deal with it, the way professional law enforcement officials *can* deal with such things.

Besides, Aileen isn't even a trainee yet, I told myself as she parked on one of the narrow little streets in front of a pub.[49] *She hasn't even started at Tulliallan or whatever it is. She's just very eager and very generous.*

She shut off the engine and stuck the key in her pocket. "Do you want a pint?"

"I'm not a big drinker," I said.

"Aye, but you never had a home-brewed Scottish lager, have you?" she asked. She tried to smile, but she was still out of sorts from the magpie.

I clutched my knapsack as I crawled out of the car. "No, I guess not."

Together we pushed the door open into a tiny, smoke-filled bar. It was packed with about a dozen haggard men. They looked like broth-

---

[49] I knew it was a pub because there was a big wooden sign hanging over the door that said *PUB*. From what I could see, Stromness was a town built only of pubs. Pubs and gift shops. And the occasional butcher. Mostly pubs, however.

ers. Maybe they were. They all had pudgy faces, short-cropped hair, and guts—and all were staring at an expensive flat-screen TV, perched above the bottles of liquor arrayed behind the counter.

There was a soccer game on.

I wondered for a second if anyone in this town actually had jobs. It was a Monday, after all. Shouldn't these guys be at work?

I glanced around. Various tartans hung on the oak-paneled walls, side by side with framed black-and-white photographs of uniformed soccer players. There was also a large photograph of a urinal. Maybe a photo of a urinal was good luck in Scotland? I'd have to ask Aileen before I said good-bye. (Or not.) Aside from the TV, these furnishings were at least as old as the airplane we'd flown over in, if not older.

The barkeep turned to us. He might have been a brother, too.

"Table?" he asked, his expression flat.

I assumed he was referring to the table by the front window. It was the only table I could see. It was completely covered in ashtrays. Many of the cigarettes were still burning. Then I realized why: There was no room for ashtrays on the bar counter. There was only room enough for the hundred or so glass steins that sat upon it, most of which were empty.

"We'll take it," Aileen said. "And we'll have two pints. Just gotta run to the loo. He'll pay!" She jerked her head at me. "Back in a jiff!"

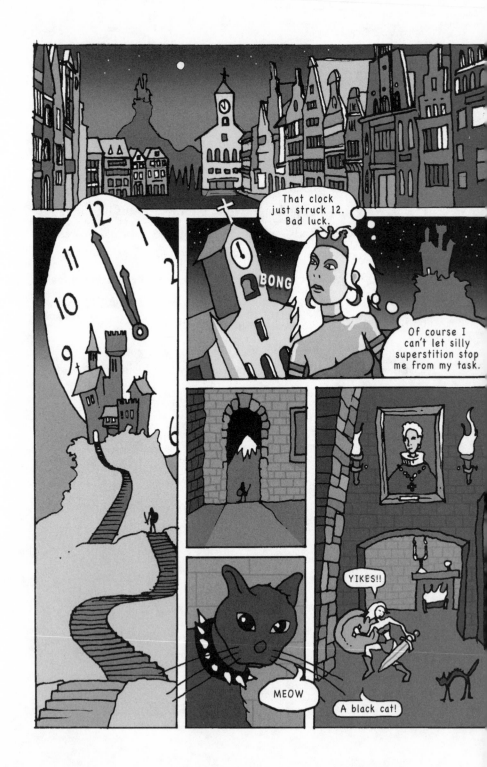

60

ART IS SHORT FOR ARTHUR

"B-U-U-U-R-P!"

I glanced up from the sketch pad.

"Pardon," Aileen said with a giggle. She covered her mouth.

Amazing: for a while there, I'd managed to forget that I was in a bar in a strange country on a Monday morning, surrounded by ash-trays and soccer thugs—across from a photo of a urinal—when I should have been trying say good-bye to Aileen, thanking her, and then getting the hell on with trying to rescue my dad.

Aileen had finished one of the beers. She was working on the second. For some reason, I had assumed she'd ordered the second one for me. Oh, well.

"Can I see what you're drawing?" she asked.

"I'll show you later."

As soon as she's done with that second beer, I'm going to say good-bye, I promised myself. *I won't procrastinate or be influenced by her beauty or by the way she's staring at me with those distant green eyes. That would be pitiful and corny, and I am not like that. I am a* *misanthrope. I act alone. Hey, that's a nice comic-book catchphrase!* *"I act alone." I wish I could think of another comic-book catchphrase* *right now, because I'll need to use it when I leave her.*

She reached forward and clasped my forearm. "Listen, I'm sorry if I went a bit mad back on the road," she said. "But a lone magpie is a very bad omen."

My pulse ticked up a notch. I was frozen again, unable to do anything but stare at her fingers. They were surprisingly soft and delicate.

She let me go and leaned back in the chair.

"You think I'm mad, don't you?" she groaned. She took a swig of beer and glanced at the TV.

"I just don't get what you're scared of," I said quietly. "You're not scared of jumping in front of a van to save a complete stranger's life. You're not scared of flying on an unsafe airplane or criminals or kidnappers . . ." I was having a hard time formulating my thoughts. I regretted opening my mouth. I could still feel her hand on my arm, even though it wasn't there. "And you're scared of a—a bird?" I finally sputtered.

"Carlton!" Aileen slammed her mug down, as if *I* were the lunatic. "That was a lone magpie!"

"I know. But that's all it was."

"Oh, well all right, then," she muttered. She rolled her eyes and upended the mug, draining it. "If you're so smart, then why are you scared of *everything?*"

An instant before, my brain had been full of hot steam, unable to see a clear picture. But now I could feel the temperature up there dropping, getting colder and colder, an *arctic* cold. I could feel it turning to Scottish fog, then liquefying into beer, then turning to ice, then plummeting until it was so deathly frozen that it would burn my fingers if I touched it . . . minus 103 degrees Fahrenheit—a Fortress of Eternal Life™ outer-space deep freeze that could be melted only by cryogenic technicians.

"What?" Aileen demanded.

"I'm only scared of what I don't know," I said. "Like where my dad is."

She belched again. "Carlton, that's nonsense. You should be scared of what you *know*. Like seeing a lone magpie. I *know* that's bad luck. Anyway, who are you to say what's real and what isn't? Look at you, drawing away. Those drawings are probably more real to you than your own reality. I bet you even think they're art." She lurched out of her seat and grinned crookedly. "I need to go to the loo. But you should remember what Keith Richards once said when someone told him his songwriting was great art."[50]

"What did Keith Richards once say?"

"He said, 'As far as I'm concerned, Art is short for Arthur!' Ha!"

---

[50] Keith Richards was born in 1943. In addition to being the guitarist for the Rolling Stones, he is also an unrepentant smoker and boozehound. He looks like an old-timey pirate.

61

WATER SEEKS ITS OWN LEVEL

The exact memory of what happened next is still a little fuzzy. I remember I stuck my tongue out at her behind her back. I also remembered I stuffed a big fat wad of pounds into her empty beer stein, over 400 pounds, to be exact: payment for her services, plus a hefty gratuity—just as I'd vowed—and that's pretty much it.

Then I ran.

"Oi!" the barkeep yelled. "Come back here, you wanker!"

The door slammed.

It didn't take me long to find the police station. It was at the end of the block.[51] I would have preferred if it had taken me a little longer, actually. I would have preferred it to be on the other side of town, so I could put more distance between Aileen and myself.

I hesitated in front of the police station door, anxiously fiddling with the straps of my knapsack. The gray sky grew even grayer.

I shouldn't have just ditched Aileen.

Nah . . . forget it. Good-byes were not my specialty. I figured she'd

---

[51] I knew it was the police station because there was a big wooden sign hanging over the door that said: POLICE STATION. Other than that, the building was indistinguishable from the pub I'd just left.

appreciate the bluntness of the gesture. Besides, I'd settled our account. (She could deal with the bartender, too.) Although, leaving without even saying good-bye or thank you *was* cold . . . but I wouldn't second-guess myself. Dad had three days left to live. I'd done the right thing. I'd *needed* to do it. Aileen was sweet in her own way, and well meaning, but she was too much of a freak—and, to be perfectly honest, too good-looking for me to be able to concentrate on what mattered.

Yes. It was time to contact the authorities.

Steeling my nerves, I took a deep breath, and I marched through the police station door, ready to wade into yet another ocean of mankind.

62

TINY BELL

A tiny bell rang as the door slammed behind me.

I glanced over my shoulder. The bell was attached to the knob with a fuzzy piece of yarn. Call me nuts, but if your entry is heralded by the tinkling of a little bell—a bell that hangs by a fuzzy piece of yarn, no less, in a picturesque Scottish town—wouldn't you expect to enter someplace warm and cozy? I would have thought so.

Instead I found myself in a claustrophobic hovel—smaller and smokier than the pub I'd just fled. I also found myself surrounded by pretty much the same pub crowd: pale men with flabby faces and sagging stomachs. The only difference was everyone here wore ill-fitting blue uniforms and pointy blue hats. If the thugs back at the pub were brothers, then these were their cousins. Or a rival gang? I couldn't quite believe they were cops.

Six pairs of cold, rheumy eyes stared back at me.

Nobody spoke. I sensed a palpable thirst for violence, as if they'd all been sitting around for hours, just waiting for an excuse to start pummeling somebody, *anybody*. And here I was! Too bad there wasn't a flat-screen TV soccer game to divert their attention. Nope. There was plenty of beer, though. Or there had been. The hovel was littered with empty bottles, lots of papers and maps and rotary phones—and a single archaic computer, bright yellow, the kind that you might see in a toy store or a made-for-TV movie from the eighties. For all I knew, they'd been drinking and playing low-tech video games all night. Now they were grouchy and aggressive.

"Aye?" one of them asked.

"Is this the police station?" I heard myself reply.

He burst into an evil, beery laugh.

I whirled around, fumbling with the door.

"No, wait, lad!" another voice bellowed.

Before I could escape, a large hand clamped down on my shoulder.

My blood ran cold. "What?" I choked out in a panic. For a second I wondered if the barkeep had phoned them because I'd just bolted—

"Keep yer breath tae cuil yer parritch!"

Oh, please. I stiffened, paralyzed at yet ANOTHER outburst of incomprehensible blather. Still, I almost had to laugh. Because it wasn't until then that I finally figured out why Aileen wanted to be a cop. In the brief time I'd known her, she'd always struck me as slightly criminal (the drinking, the offers to pay people with *my* money without asking me first, etcetera) . . . but I realized that in Scotland, there was no difference. Aileen wanted to be a cop for the same reason Dad wanted to be frozen with all those rich wackos. *Water seeks its own level*, as the blather went. That was the great thing about Scotland: All of life could be boiled down to a few concise aphorisms.

The problem was I couldn't understand any of them.

63

SOME DIZZY AMERICAN BIRD

The cop spun me around and pinned me against the door.

"Calm down, lad," he said. "What's the matter?"

Rage bubbled up, temporarily burying my fear. "Gee, I don't know, officer. Maybe because you're seizing me in a viselike grip? And you and your fellow hooligans just laughed in my face?"

He eased up.

"Pardon, mate. We don't mean to offend. We just don't get too many walk-ins on a Monday, you know? The last was some dizzy American bird about your age who was looking for Castle Fraser."

I blinked at him.

"Castle Fraser is on the mainland," he explained. "It's funny."

I blinked at him again.

He tried to smile. He looked almost as uncomfortable as I felt. "Well, maybe it's not so funny for a Yank. Never ye mind about that, lad. Ye've come to the right place. How can we be of service?"

"Are you serious?"

"Aye." He waved a hand at his fellow officers. "We're cops."

I glanced around the room. They all nodded eagerly. Their rheumy eyes had softened.

Suddenly, I felt like an idiot. These guys weren't thugs. They were just weirdos, like me, like *everybody*. I shouldn't have been scared of them. They were gruff and incomprehensible and probably hungover, sure, but even I should have been able to tell that they weren't *threatening*. It was ridiculous. It was shameful.

Unfortunately, this profound realization didn't help much. It just made me feel a lot guiltier about Aileen.

Again, I felt that uncontrollable urge to confess: about how the Forbas or MacCloughs had kidnapped my father, about how I was supposed to meet them at some place called Castle Glanach in about forty-eight hours, about how I'd just ditched the one other person who'd offered to help me . . .

But I didn't. I held it together. I kept my cool. The kidnappers had warned me not to get the cops involved. So I knew that telling these kindly-if-flaccid Scotsmen the truth would put them in danger, too. And, no offense to the Stromness police, but judging from the number of empty beer bottles in plain sight, they didn't exactly seem to be equipped to deal with a ruthless, deadly, powerful foe. They didn't even have any guns. Not a one. They just carried batons on their belts.

"You know, actually," I said, "if I could just check my e-mail, and maybe make a few phone calls, that would be great." I pulled my unusable cell phone out of my pocket. "This doesn't get reception here."

My eyes fell to the computer.

"What's the matter, lad?" one of the cops asked.

"Does that computer send and receive e-mails?"

They burst out laughing again.

Oh, brother.

"Pardon, mate!" another one barked. "That's just what the American bird asked, too. She said it looked like a karaoke machine!"

The next thing I knew, they were swarming over me, easing me into a soft swivel chair, and booting up the computer.[52] The modem was so ancient that they had to use one of the rotary phones to connect to the Internet. They placed the mouthpiece over a funny looking plastic device. It looked like an upside-down bra. Then one of the cops passed a plastic basket of cold leftover French fries to me.

"Chips, in case you get hungry, lad," he offered.

"Uh . . . thanks."

I managed a smile. I'd never been so fussed over in my life. And as the computer whirred and beeped and squawked, I renewed my silent pledge to leave these cops out of my own personal horror show. I would not endanger them. I would check my e-mail, then check in with Martha. I would let her and Olivia know that I was all right. And then I would lie low, until it was time to go to Castle Glanach, wherever *that* was. Maybe the cops could tell me how to get there. Asking them directions wouldn't put them in danger. It might even make them feel helpful, right? Sure.

Maybe they could even recommend an inn in town: some place quiet and out of the way, a place with a bathroom and electricity.

And maybe the kidnappers had already sent me an e-mail or a voice-mail message, apologizing for the misunderstanding—as they knew now that I had no possible clue as to how to meet any of their demands by dawn Thursday.

Maybe they'd even let Dad go.

I could always hope for another pleasant surprise.

---

[52] It was a Commodore 8032-SK, which I later discovered went out of production in 1983. It's equipped with a cassette drive, as opposed to a disk drive. It does not come equipped with a mouse, either; you have to work the arrow keys to move the cursor around the screen. Apparently, it was also the first Commodore computer to have a single keyboard; hence the initials "SK."

64

THE TWO E-MAILS I RECEIVED, PLUS THE FIVE I NEVER SENT

Without thinking, I checked the *Signy the Superbad* fan site first.

To this day, I honestly don't know why, although I guess it might have had to do with a vague hope of connecting with someone who *knew* me, with whom I felt close, and yet who didn't know a thing about any of my problems.

Or maybe I was just more self-absorbed than I would like to admit.

I am an artist, after all, a graphic novelist, no less. Art is *not* just short for Arthur, in my opinion. Sometimes what you call yourself is all you have to go on, no matter how lame or grandiose or straight up false it sounds.

There was only one message waiting for me.

> carlton dude hey is everything ok? hit me back and
> let me know what's up. I mean I know we're not

friends and like we've never met in real life . . . ok i'll just come out and tell you . . . i go to CM. i know who you are. everybody here is freaking out because you disappeared. it's like this big scandal, I mean things are pretty crazy here. you know how fast and loose rumors spread. mr. herzog is all making a big stink, talking about how mr. watts should be fired for dereliction of duty since he never bothers to check up on you, but actually i know that he does . . . cuz when you snuck out a while back to go to comic expo, I know that you had someone cover for you. i saw someone climb through your window. who was it? can you tell me? not a big deal if you can't . . . but seriously let me know you're all right. and if you're gone for good, i totally dig it. I'd run away from this place in a second.

☺—Night Mare

I sat there for a second, my eyes fixed on the screen.

I reread the message.

I read it again.

Horror took hold. I could sense the cops waiting for me to react in some way. I tried to act calm. I tried to pretend that I was just some dizzy American bloke, checking his e-mail because he was lost in Scotland. *Ah, he'll be fine,* I wanted the cops to think, for their own good. Surprisingly, the ruse was easy. All I had to do was sit and eat more cold chips. More surprisingly, for some twisted reason, I felt a weird sort of fleeting happiness, in spite of the horror. On some level, this letter *did* cheer me up.

People were sneaking into my room? Mr. Herzog was making a stink? Night Mare went to CM? Was she hot? Why the hell hadn't she introduced herself to me? My brain fizzled and crackled with these asinine questions (while avoiding the vital ones), then it pretty much shut down, just as it had after reading Dad's Final Testament.

It was another case of information overload. There was no way to process it.

Magnus, Robot Fighter = unequipped to deal.

I clicked off the fan site and onto my own personal e-mail, furiously punching the arrow keys. The computer whirred and beeped and squawked. Once again, there was only one message waiting for me, this one from Roger Lovejoy:

> Hi, Carlton! I'm trying to figure out what the hell you're up to! It's a little hard, seeing as you haven't returned any of my calls in the last two days! ☹!!! First you send me five straight e-mails one night, then nothing. Maybe you lost your cell phone? I know you artistic types are pretty psycho, but throw me a bone here! If you haven't gotten my messages: It looks like SIGNY is going to be syndicated! Like I said, your last strip blew everyone away! WE LOVE IT!!! Miso Horny and Chef Slimeball have serious marketing potential! I sent it to Jessica James and she's going to talk to her agent about running it with the next Horny & Single. (We can do a "horny" tie-in. The possibilities are endless. Miso Horny should be hotter, btw.) Big things are in the works, my friend! I can almost forgive you for sending your son in

your place to COMIC EXPO! I'll work the babysitting charge into our new deal! And, remember: I own all the merchandising rights!

All best, Roger

My hands began to shake as they hovered over the keyboard.

Theoretically, this e-mail should have cheered me up, too. It looked like my comic strip was going to be syndicated in edgy urban magazines, next to a "literary" comic. There would even be some cross-marketing and merchandising.

Neat.

Too bad I was probably going to die. All I could think was: *Five straight e-mails in one night?* My fingers grew clammy as I tapped the arrow keys, up to my Sent items. I pressed Return.

Holy—

Roger hadn't been kidding. Five of the last six messages in the outbox had been sent in a thirty-minute period, all to him, between 7:30 and 8 P.M. on Thursday, September 9 . . . *the exact same time I'd been fidgeting in that cab on the way to Meriden.*

I clicked on the first.

Dear Roger, Please keep an eye on my son, Carlton. He is attending this COMIC EXPO at the Meriden Ramada in my stead. Something has come up. I had to travel on business.

If there's an emergency, I may be contacted at 011-440-1249-75005.

I nearly vomited. That contact number was located in Scotland. I *knew* this, because it was only a few digits off from the police station's number, printed in plain sight on the rotary phone beside me. And Dad sure as hell couldn't have sent this e-mail. I clicked on the second message. It said the exact same thing. Then I clicked on the third. Same thing again. *What the—*

Another hand clamped down on my shoulder.

"I'm sorry, officer," I said, my voice quavering. "I won't be much longer."

"CARLTON!!!"

65

UNDERSTANDING

My plan for ditching Aileen didn't turn out quite as I'd hoped.

She'd managed to find me, and fairly easily, too. Looking back, I guess it wasn't so difficult. The town itself was barely larger than the Meriden Ramada. Besides, where else would I have gone? Another pub? Although that might not have been a bad idea, considering that now, for the first time ever, I wished I *were* drunk. At least then I would have had an easier time dealing with how she swiveled me around in the chair, yanked me up, and frothed at the mouth, all to the delight of the cops.

"Just like a Yank to land a possessive blond!" one of them hooted.

"Ya got yourself a real bird, haven't ye, lad!" another yelled.

"Aileen," I mumbled. "Please, stop, okay?"

"SHADDAP!" she yelled, her green eyes flashing.

She dragged me out the door. The little bell tinkled behind us. I didn't even get a chance to turn off the computer, much less thank the cops for their help, much less figure out who the hell had snuck into my room at CM and sent those five same messages to Roger Lovejoy.

"What were you thinking, you ponce?" she snarled. She jerked to a stop in the street. Her fingers dug into my bicep.

"Aileen. You're hurting me."

"What do you think you did to *me?*"

"I . . ." I didn't finish. Under the darkening overcast sky, Aileen's face looked bleaker than ever. But then I realized something. Those green eyes weren't flashing. They were welling with tears. "How did I hurt you?"

She turned away. "You had me worried to death. The kidnappers said not to go to the cops."

"I'm sorry, okay?" I said. I reached for her and then hesitated. "I didn't mean to worry you or bum you out or anything. I just thought . . . you know."

"No, I don't know," she said, sniffing and rubbing her eyes. She let out a sad little laugh. "You're like the cat that wad fain eat fish but widnae weet her feet," she said.

"What's that mean?"

"You don't get it, do you, Carlton?"

"No, I don't. That's what I'm trying to tell you. I don't get *anything* that you say, even the stuff I *do* understand."

"Not *that,* Carlton," she interrupted. "You don't get why I'm doing this. It's because I swore an oath to protect you. A true Scot never breaks her oath." She dug her hand into her pocket and shoved the crumpled mass of beer-stained pounds back at me. "I don't want or need your money. I'll pay my own way. Besides—" Her voice cracked. She bowed her head. Her long blond curls fell in her face. "Besides, I thought we were becoming friends," she finished.

I swallowed. Now *I* felt like I was about to cry. She thought we were becoming friends? Was that what friendship meant in Scotland?

Teasing, bickering, drinking beer at noon, spitting out incomprehensible aphorisms? Maybe it did. Really, the more I thought about it, I didn't know what *anything* meant in this country.

"Giffgaff mak's guid freends," Aileen whispered.

"Aileen, right now, I really need you to speak normal English— like the kind they speak on *Cops*, so I can understand it. Okay?"

She brushed her hair out of her face and looked up with a wistful smile. Her eyes were still red. "I know. I said that on purpose. It was a joke. Understanding friendship isn't easy to come by."

"No kidding."

"But ya see, Carlton, I thought we *did* understand each other. And that's why I'm so upset. I thought we could quarrel and shout and the lot of it, and that it was all right. That's the giffgaff. The back and forth."

"The giffgaff," I repeated.

Aileen's eyes sparkled. "Aye, the giffgaff."

"Thanks for clearing that up," I said. "Thanks for clearing up the meaning of 'understanding,' too. Now I understand."

"Aye" she said dryly. "You know sometimes words have two meanings."

"Another one of your mysterious Scottish phrases?"

"No, you ponce. It's a line from 'Stairway to Heaven.' And you call yourself a Zeppelin fan?"

I finally managed a smile. "These days, I call myself a ponce. So what now?"

She shrugged. "Now we go back to the inn and regroup. We'll come up with a plan, together. That way it'll be a good plan, for once." She paused, looking away, then glanced back up at me shyly. "That is, if you'll still have me around."

I stuck my tongue out at her. I stuck it out straight to her face, this time, too, and it was all the answer I needed to give. Which was a good thing, because if I'd opened my mouth to form actual words, regardless of their meanings, I would have made even more of a jackass out of myself. But we had an understanding now, Aileen and me.

66

IF YOU'VE EVER SEEN A HOUSE BURNING DOWN

If you've ever seen a house burning down—I mean, in real life, as opposed to in comic books—then you know it doesn't quite look the way you might expect. For one thing, there aren't that many flames. Sure, there are a few, licking at cracked windows and doorframes, but mostly there's just a lot of smoke. It isn't like campfire smoke, either. It's thick, black, and ugly, and it fades to a suffocating haze the further you get away from it and finally to a gauzy white mist.

I first began to notice that gauzy white mist about a half mile from the inn.

I didn't pay much attention at first. I thought it was the rain, the drizzle that had kicked up right after Aileen and I crawled back into the *Deux Chevaux*. What did I know about Scottish weather?[53] If I *hadn't* seen mist, I might have sensed a cause for alarm.

But then I began to notice a weird sort of stink. It was like a cross between burnt rubber and a wet wool blanket.

Aileen sniffed. "You smell that?"

---

[53] Scotland has nearly the same rate of annual precipitation as the Pacific Northwest.

"Yeah," I said, wrinkling my nose. "Is your car overheating?"

She shook her head, sniffing again. She pursed her lips. "Ugh. I don't think so." She turned off her windshield wipers for a second. The stink only got worse. The mist grew thicker, too. She turned wipers back on again. "So it's not *that*—"

I peered through the windshield.

Far across the moor, I could see a shapeless black cloud rising up from behind the trees on the other side.

Several hogs appeared out of the mist on either side of us—ghostly apparitions, milling around in the scrub.

Hogs?

I felt that safety pin prickling in my stomach again.

"Blast!" Aileen hissed. She jammed her foot on the accelerator. In seconds, the mist thickened into that suffocating haze, and the stench grew a hundred times more powerful. I coughed, cupping my hands around my mouth and nose. Aileen slammed on the brakes, nearly veering off the road. *SCREECH!!*

The next thing I knew, she was rolling her window down. What was she thinking, letting in rain *and* toxic smog? But before I could protest, the faces of the innkeepers swam into view.

"You better run, lass," the old man said.

"Who did this to you?" Aileen asked.

The old man cast an anguished glance back toward the cloud of black smoke, hugging his wife against him. "It was an accident," he whispered.

"An accident?" Aileen repeated.

"Aye. But there's nothing we can do now. He started screamin' and—"

"*Who* started screaming?" Aileen interrupted.

"Gregor MacClough."

Aileen went white. "Are you sure it was Gregor MacClough?"

"He said as much!" the wife whimpered. "He's looking for you two! He said you were traitors and that nobody would dare cross the most powerful clan on the isle! And then the fire . . . ya see, lass, he left the door open, and while he was screamin', well one of the hogs wandered in—I believe it was Nelly—and kicked over one of the lanterns, and old Gregor MacClough just laughed and said it was justice."

Not surprisingly, a volume switch got thrown off inside my head.

I couldn't hear a word. But this went beyond my usual listening problem. Everything became a distorted mishmash of coughing and brogue and pattering rain and the idling engine. My eyes bounced between the old man and woman, their toothless mouths chattering in despair, their gray hair matted in the drizzle. Part of me wanted Aileen to slam on that goddamn accelerator again and just leave them behind (the pitiful, cowardly part). But another part started whispering to me—and for some reason this part had the voice of Bryce Perry: "*Hello? Butt munch? These people are NOT in cahoots with the Forbas/MacCloughs! And they lost everything, thanks to you! If there was ever time for you to receive the swirlie to end all swirlies, now is it!*"

" . . . just take it," Aileen was saying.

I blinked and rubbed my stinging eyes, fighting to hear her over the din.

She hopped out of the car. "Take it and go to the Stromness Police. Tell them everything. They'll take care of you." She turned to me. "Aye, Carlton?"

My jaw hung open in a stupor. I could hardly breathe. The smog had thickened.

"Huh?" I managed, hoarsely.

"I'm tellin' 'em to take me car! We don't need it! All we need are the hills!" She waved a hand behind her, toward a gray wall of nothingness. "Come on!"

All we need are the hills?

"We need to make ourselves scarce, Carlton. Now!"

The rest was a blur.

Aileen dashed around to my side of the car and yanked me out, then sent me running across the moor.

I thought I might have heard that tiny little engine start up.

I hoped I did. The old couple deserved that car. They deserved a hell of a lot more than that car. They deserved to have their inn and hog farm back. They deserved their *life* back.

Too bad I couldn't say the same for myself.

67

A MILLION DOLLARS IN A WHISKEY BARREL

Aileen didn't stop running. I staggered and stumbled along behind her—up and up and up, with branches lashing my skin and rain stinging my eyes, trying to follow her wiry legs . . . and all I remembered thinking was: *Does she work out?* Sure: The StairMaster, the treadmill, the rowing machine . . . typical cop stuff. (And the beer-drinking, too.)

Whenever I paused to pass out or moan she simply grabbed me again.

My shins ached. My lungs burned. My knees turned to Play-Doh. Only when the rain stopped and the sky began to clear did she agree to take a break. The sun was low.

"Look," she gasped. She pointed through a little clearing in the foliage.

Far below, I saw the road to Stromness. From where we stood, it looked like a circus-freak snake, twisting and turning through the hills and moors, bulging in unexpected places. And beside a little bend in the road, maybe a mile away, I saw the inn. Or rather, I saw what was left of it beneath a plume of black smoke, tiny flames licking at the shutters and wooden doorframes. The building itself was hardly recognizable. It had been reduced to a heap of glowing coals and burning cinders.

This is my fault, I realized, overcome with sickening guilt. *True, Nelly the hog kicked over the lantern, Mrs. O'Leary's cow style[54], but I ruined the lives of that old man and woman.*

Aileen laid a muddy, rain-soaked hand on my shoulder. "I'm sure they have fire insurance," she breathed, as if reading my mind.

"Great. What'll they get? A hundred quid?"

"They'll get more than that," Aileen said in a distant voice. "I'll make sure of it."

I turned to her. "What do you mean?"

"Nothing. I'm just saying . . . the fire insurance in the UK is top-notch. Everybody gets a great settlement. And anyhoo, when this is over, I'll help you find those two, and you'll make it up to them. You'll leave them a million dollars in a whiskey barrel. And then you'll run. That's the way you do things. You're a generous soul, Carlton. You just haven't the faintest idea of how to deal with people."

Something in her voice struck me as odd, as if she were holding something back. But I ignored it. I ignored it because, in spite of every horrible thing I'd done, in spite of everything that had gone wrong, it helped to hear her say that I was a generous soul. I wasn't sure if I believed it myself yet, but it helped. A lot.

---

[54] This is a reference to the Great Chicago Fire of 1871; Mrs. O'Leary's cow started the fire the same way.

68

MORE WORTHWHILE THAN DRAWING

Aileen very graciously left me alone until sundown. Maybe she felt as guilty about the inn as I did. She steered clear of me as I sketched, constructing a makeshift lean-to over a dry patch of dirt in the woods nearby. Then she built a fire in the clearing. She accomplished this miraculous feat with only a lighter and Swiss army knife. Of course, she'd lived in the boondocks on an accursed island in the middle of Mordor for all her life, so outdoor skills were probably a necessity.

"Finished drawing, eh?" she finally asked. She stoked the blaze with some twigs.

"I guess." I stuffed my sketch pad back into my knapsack, then stood and stretched, shivering. The heat of the fire felt very nice against my wet clothes. "Do you need any help?" I asked.

"Nah." Her lips curled in a sly smile. "Carlton, you *do* always draw when you wish you were somewhere else, don't you?"

"Yeah. I guess I do."

She sighed, gazing into the crackling flames. "I wish I had something like that. You know, a hobby." She looked at me. "Other than arguing and drinking pints, that is."

I laughed. "You do have other hobbies. You brush your teeth compulsively, right? Plus, you rescue helpless strangers."

She turned away. "That's not a hobby," she muttered.

"But at least it's more worthwhile than drawing," I pointed out. I felt bad for trying to make a joke. "At least you have to be around other people."

"Aye, but it's nice to escape other people, too. Did your Dad teach you to draw? Or did you inherit your talent?"

"Did I . . . ?" The question caught me off guard. Did she really think drawing had something to do with talent? Talent meant Art. Art meant short for Arthur. Her question also had the unfortunate effect of lodging another painful lump in my throat. Here I was, sitting on a hilltop in a forest—with no food, no water, and no ideas—but I still knew I was better off than Dad. He was imprisoned down *there* somewhere.

I peered through the clearing toward the horizon.

The sun had just slipped beneath the hills.

Now, of all times, the isle of Orkney really *was* beautiful—spread out below us like a rumpled green quilt, the clouds pulled thin like cotton, lit in dazzling strokes of violet and orange, and beyond that infinity and space: the sky in a deep, Magic Marker, twilight blue, the kind of sky you only see in comic books, in *Peanuts* or in *MAD*.

"I'm sorry, Carlton," Aileen murmured. "I didn't mean to upset you."

"No, no, it's all right." I sat down on the other side of the fire. "I'm glad you brought up my dad. We need to make a plan."

"Aye," she said. "Aye, we do."

69

FOLLOW MY EARS

Aileen didn't say a word for the next two hours.

Not that I was upset. I was in no condition to make a plan, either.

Occasionally, Aileen hopped up to feed the fire. Other than that, we sat in silence under the starriest sky I'd ever seen. The moon was nearly full—beautiful to the point where I should have cared—but I was too busy thinking about my own agony. My joints had moved to a realm of pain beyond mere aching. Every time I shifted or stretched, I triggered another excruciating twinge or spasm. Also, my mouth felt like a car seat that had recently been occupied by a pro wrestler: grossly warm and fetid.

"What are we going to do for water?" I croaked.

"There's a stream nearby, down the hill a ways," Aileen said. "I heard it."

"Maybe I can just get a quick sip."

"Sure," she said. "So what were you doing on that computer back at the police station, anyhoo? Trying to come up with a plan?"

I licked my cracked lips. "I was checking my e-mail."

"Any news?"

I wasn't sure what she was talking about. My head swam with exhaustion and hunger and thirst. "Uh . . . well, I found out that my comic strip is about to get syndicated."

She scrunched her dirty eyebrows together. "What?"

"Nothing," I mumbled. "I also found out that somebody has been watching me at boarding school. Somebody Scottish. They snuck into my room and hacked into my e-mail and a bunch of other creepy stuff."

Aileen suddenly straightened. "Really?" she gasped, staring at me through the flames. "How do you know? I mean, how do you know it was somebody Scottish?"

"They left a phone number," I said. "It was almost exactly the same as the phone number at the police station."

She nodded, fiddling with her curls, seemingly distressed. "Oh. Right. It was probably Gregor MacClough. I told you he was powerful, didn't I?"

"Who *is* Gregor MacClough, anyway? What the hell is his problem? I mean, I'm sorry if one of my ancestors took something from him, but it's not my dad's fault."

Aileen shook her head, distracted. "I—I'm sorry. I'm too tired to talk anymore, Carlton. Look, if you want, you can go get a drink. The creek is to the east, just down the hill a ways. If you listen closely, you can hear it. Just follow your ears."

I tried to swallow. My throat was too parched. "Follow my ears?"

"Aye. And take a torch." She jerked her head toward the fire. "If you get lost, stay where you are and start yelling. I'll hear you. Don't move. Let me come to you."

I swayed unsteadily. "Which way's east?" I asked.

She pointed in what seemed a completely random direction.

"Thataway. I'll join you in a moment."

"Oh. Okay."

It seemed pretty obvious she wanted to be alone, for whatever reason. As a misanthrope, I could certainly relate. I grabbed a crooked branch nearby and stuck it into the flames. Sparks leaped and flew. Over half the stick was burning.

In a panic, I shrieked and dropped it.

"Carlton?" Aileen asked, still staring at the blaze as if hypnotized. "You okay?"

"I'm fine. No problem."

"Are you sure?"

"Yeah," I said, with fake confidence.

Hmm. Maybe I could find the creek without the torch. Sure. My eyes would adjust to the darkness, right? The moon was pretty bright. Plus, I'd done this a few times back at the house in Fenwick, just to get away from Dad after those infrequent miserable dinners we'd shared. I'd dashed away from the table after another of his rants about the feud, and then I'd roved the woods by myself until the rage and confusion subsided (or at least until I was too cold or hungry or wet or whatever to care). I simply had to do the same thing now. I had to turn away from the fire and face the blackness of the forest. I knew that, instinctively, as a human being, this would be difficult—because instinctively, humans are attracted to fire. They seek it. They ritualize it. They *sanctify* it.

Or so I'd read.[55]

---

[55] I'd read this in the same book I'd read that the ancient Egyptians loaded their tombs with snacks and gold coins and extra clothing.

70

USELESS

After about five minutes of staring into that forest, my eyes did indeed adjust. The night wasn't so black anymore. It was more a colorless, shadowy gray. I could see pretty well, or at least well enough not to bump into any trees.

Whatever. I was dying of thirst. I marched forward.

The firelight grew dimmer and dimmer. The air grew colder. The crackling flames faded to silence. Pretty soon, all I could hear was the sound of my footsteps . . . until I heard the gurgling of a stream.

My heart soared. *Yes! Aileen, you champ!*

I stumbled ahead. The gurgling grew louder, and then, as if in a dream, I found myself falling to my knees in front of a narrow brook. It was eerily blue in the moonlight, flowing over rocks and moss, and I began slurping up handfuls of water. It dripped from my chin as I splashed and laughed aloud. It was crisp! It was ice cold! It was salvation! I collapsed back into the dirt, my lungs heaving. I stared up at the sky. There were even more stars out here than in the woods in

Fenwick. I blinked a few times and wiped my mouth with my sleeve. And the joy receded. I closed my eyes.

Aileen was back there, tending our fire. She hadn't eaten or drunk a drop of water, either. She was making sure we would live another day. She was being responsible—for both of us. I, on the other hand, was looking out for myself.

If it weren't for Aileen, I wouldn't even be alive right now. And even if I survived until Thursday, Mr. Forba or Gregor MacClough or whoever would probably just kill me at the ruins of Castle Glanach and then toss my body into Loch Stenness. This running around in the woods . . . he'd probably *engineered* it. He was a freaking criminal *genius*. For all I knew, Night Mare was a MacClough. Why the hell not? To hear Aileen tell it, anyone could be. They were that powerful. Even if they *were* broke. But maybe that was a lie, too. Maybe they were rich beyond belief. Who knew?

The key is to expose them for who they really are, I said to myself.

Right. It came back to the same old conundrum: The key was to prove that the Forbas were the MacCloughs and that they'd kidnapped my father. But if everyone around here already *knew* that the Forbas were the MacCloughs, it should be easy. Maybe they thought an ignorant American wouldn't be able to figure it out—or that a misanthropic American would be too scared to fight back. But they didn't count on the fact that I'd have help from a true Scot. And like Aileen said, true Scots were fighters.

71

GOOD MORNING, CARLTON

I awoke with a start. I wasn't quite sure where I was. There were trees and bugs and mud . . . *Wait!* I was in Scotland. But there weren't any stars overhead. The sky was that Magic Marker blue again, except that birds were chirping.

The sun was coming up.

Bad idea to have fallen asleep.

Fear crept over me. My neck was stiff. My back was sore. My muscles felt as if they'd been weighed down with lead, what with all the hiking and running. I leaned over the brook and rubbed my eyes, then splashed some water in my face.

"Aileen?" I tried to yell. It wasn't much more than a gasp. I took a deep breath. "Aileen?" I managed, a little more loudly. I spun around—

And found myself face to face with a smelly, slimy, dripping wet fish.

It was about a foot long. It was also dead. I knew it was dead because it was dangling from a few slender fingers. One of its big eyes stared right at me.

"So whaddya think, Carlton?" Aileen bellowed. "Breakfast trout!" She grinned down at me, waving the fish in my face, her green eyes twinkling. Her clothes were soaked through. "There's so much trout in this stream you can just reach in and grab 'em! They're not as good as funny fish, but they make a good breakfast."

I nodded. I teetered on the edge of the creek bank for a hallucinatory, shimmering instant, with Aileen and that fish staring back at me—and then I lost my balance, tumbling backward into the icy water. *Splash!*

Now I was awake.

72

DELICIOUS BREAKFAST

After I crawled out of the brook, Aileen filleted the fish. I'll spare you the messy details. I will say this: Fresh trout cooked over an open fire is delicious—particularly if you haven't eaten anything but a bowl of sugary mush and cold French fries in the last three days. I began to feel better. The longer I sat there in the dirt, stuffing my face, the more the pain melted away.

"So, Carlton?" Aileen asked, trying to sound cheery, maybe for the both of us. "Do you know how to brush your teeth and shower in the wood?"

"Can't say that I do," I said.

She furrowed her brow. "Carlton, what's wrong?"

I stared back at her. Her hair was so matted it had begun to knot into dreadlocks. Her wet bracelets and jeans and sweater were stained with dirt and charcoal and grease. She was more beautiful and mysterious than ever.

"*I'm* what's wrong," I said.

"Ah, bollocks," she groaned. "Stop feeling so sorry for yourself. That's the sort of tripe you hear from the perps on *Cops*.[56] I'm in as much of a mess as you are, in case you don't remember. And *I* don't have me toothbrush. At least *you* have your sketch pad. Now, do you want to learn how to brush your teeth and shower in the wood or not?"

"I guess I do."

"Come on, then," she said. She grabbed my wrist and yanked me to my feet, dragging me back down the hill toward the creek.

"Aileen, please."

"Hush. First we're going to brush our teeth." She plunged into the woods, pulling me behind her, and stopped in front of a dead tree. "Here we go! Perfect." She stood on her tiptoes and snapped off a branch—then began chewing it.[57] She raised her eyebrows. "What are you waiting for, a formal declaration?" she asked, garbling her words with the twig. "Start brushing!"

"I don't know . . ."

"Why?"

"It's an old American superstition," I said flatly. "Never brush your teeth with a branch from a dead tree."

She rolled her eyes. "Very funny." She tossed the branch aside and seized my wrist again. "Suit yourself. But at the very least, you'll have to dry your clothes and bathe yourself. You're soaking wet!"

I staggered after her. "What do you mean, dry my clothes?"

Aileen didn't answer. She dashed ahead to the creek. Morning sunlight streamed through the forest, glistening off the water in a thousand bright sparkles. I squinted at her in the glare. I smiled dubiously. I wasn't quite sure what she had in mind—

I stopped smiling.

Aileen peeled off her sweater and bra, and then began to remove

---

[56] "Perp" is cop speak, short for "perpetrator."

[57] As I later discovered, Aileen also learned this tooth-brushing trick from a short story she'd read as a child. Only she got it wrong. In the story, the protagonist (a boy, I might add) chews on a stick of a *living* tree, a green sapling, to clean his teeth. God only knows what chewing a dead twig did to her breath. I could never tell; she never let me near enough to find out.

her dripping jeans and underwear.

In less than five seconds, she was buck naked except for her bracelets.

What the— I turned away, my face on fire.

"Blast!" she cried. "Oww! It's frigid, aye? Come on in, Carlton!"

"No." I shook my head furiously, gazing up the hill toward the smoldering fire. "I'm not going in there."

"Why not?"

"You're *naked*!" I shouted, with my back turned to her.

She giggled. "So what? Just come in! The water's not that bad once you get used to it."

There was another splash.

"I can't," I said. I wasn't even sure if I said it audibly. It was all too goddamn confusing. I trudged up through the forest. My skull pounded. I felt sick. I felt more than sick; I felt a sudden dire need for my sketch pad.

"Don't take such a puerile attitude!" she called after me.

Puerile? I picked up my pace. Was that another Arabic word? I thought I had a decent vocabulary, but apparently not. I'd have to look that one up when this whole horrid ordeal was over.[58] Then again, I might be dead within the next few days.

Aileen couldn't seem to stop giggling. "Don't you want to prove yourself, Carlton?" she yelled. "Isn't that why you're feeling sorry for yourself?"

Jesus. I broke into a sprint. How perfect. This was the exact same question Bryce Perry had asked me back at the Who-Would-You-Bang Forum, only four days ago. (Was it only four days? I couldn't even tell anymore.) It was another case of déjà vu . . . another case of fate— just like with the Zeppelin connection.

The difference was that *this* time, I'd also asked the question of myself.

---

[58] **pu·er·ile** \pyooeril\ *adj.* **1.** Childish or immature. **2.** Trivial.

The other difference was that I didn't know how to answer. Not even close.

All I knew for sure was: If Bryce Perry were here, he'd be splashing around buck naked with Aileen, too. He'd have his clothes off in a jiff. No doubt about it.

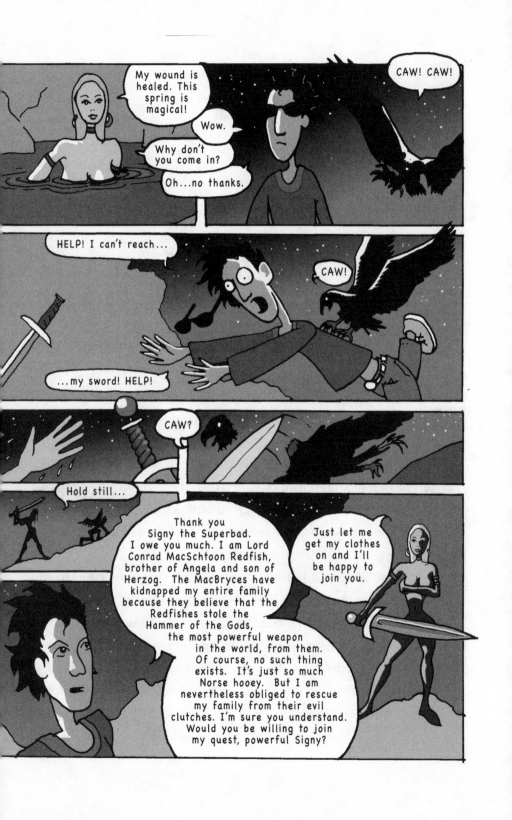

73

WILD MINT

Aileen must have taken pity on me then. As soon as she'd finished bathing, she got dressed again and sat me down by the fire and laid her hand on my arm.

"Sorry to tease you back there, mate," she said. "Honestly. I was just having fun. Have you been thinking of a plan?"

"Sort of," I said—even though that was only maybe half true, at best. "I just think the key to solving this whole mess is . . . flipping it."

"Flipping it? What do you mean?"

"Well, Mr. Forba kidnapped my dad. He's made no effort to conceal that fact. And as you said, everybody in Orkney knows that the MacCloughs are the Forbas. So Gregor MacClough must be Mr. Forba, right? So he must have kidnapped my dad. The key is just to prove that to the cops. We have to get *that* proof from *him*"—I sighed—"because I'm pretty sure we won't be able to find Agricola's dagger by dawn Thursday."

She withdrew her hand and nodded, staring into the fire.

"Aye. That we won't."

"But I'm not sure if storming into their factory is the best idea."

"Aye. It's not. The magpie showed us."

"Right. So—"

"Listen, Carlton." Aileen turned away from me, struggling to pull the knots from her damp curls. "I grew up around here. I know this wood very well. I wasn't going to tell you this because I didn't want to put any crazy notions in your head, but . . ." She shook her head and walked to the edge of the clearing, staring out at the rolling green quilt below us.

"But what?" I asked.

"Nothing."

"Aileen, come on," I pleaded. "This is my dad's life we're talking about. He has a four-year-old daughter back home. Whatever it is you want to tell me, just go ahead. I can handle it. I can keep it together. I promise."

She nodded. She kept running her fingers through her hair, with her back turned toward me. "I know where the MacCloughs live. There's a way to get to their land through this wood. If we stick to the right route, we'll end up at their property."

I stared at her. "So you're saying we should go there?"

"Aye," she breathed. "They might even have your dad in that place."

I hopped up and slung my knapsack over my shoulder. "Let's do it, then."

She shook her head, still unwilling to face me. "Look, Carlton, I know you want to prove to me that you can be brave and helpful. I know you feel obliged to me for saving your life. But it might be better if I go it alone once we get there—" She broke off.

"What?"

She whirled around, grinning excitedly. "Look at that! Wild mint!"

My forehead crinkled. "Wild . . . mint?"

She scurried toward the edge of the clearing, plucked some frail, anemic-looking weeds from the dirt, and stuffed them right into her mouth.

"Wild mint!" she said as she chewed. "It's good luck!"

I tried not to gag. "Is that another Scottish superstition?"

"Nah, it's just me *own* superstition." She reached down and yanked up some more, thrusting them toward me. "Want some? It's great for your breath. Even greater than a stick from a dead tree."

"Uh . . . no thanks," I said. Until she'd mentioned it, I hadn't even thought about my breath. "Can I ask you something, though? Why do you think you should go it alone once we get there? Shouldn't I be the one to confront the MacCloughs? Especially if that's where they're holding my dad?"

She glanced at me, then down at the earth, embarrassed. "I just—"

"You thought I'd be too scared?" I asked quietly.

"I . . ." Her hair hung in her face. I couldn't tell if she'd said "I," or "aye." It didn't really matter, though, either way.

"Well, you're right," I said. "I am scared. And that's why there's no way I'd let you go in there alone."

She laughed and looked up. "That's daft, Carlton."

"Yeah, I know," I said. I eyed her crumbling fistful of weeds. "But I don't think you're really in a position to talk about what's daft and what isn't. We have a plan now."

74

MAYBE A LITTLE TOO CHATTY

It seemed that Aileen was in a position to talk about lots of other things, though.

She grew pretty chatty as she gathered up some leftover fish and stuffed it into her satchel. The journey would take us well into the night, she said.

I was happy about that. Or not so much happy as relieved, because I needed the time to summon whatever courage I'd pretended to reveal just now.

Then we were off, plowing through the forest toward the MacCloughs. And maybe it was the wild mint, but Aileen talked a blue streak as she hacked away at the brush with her Swiss army knife. She asked me a lot of questions. She asked again about the kids at boarding school. I told her the boys were all misogynists, and the girls were all ditzes. She asked about my mom. I told her I missed her. I told her I missed my stepmom, too, even though she was alive. I even told her I missed her maybe more than my *real* mom, because I didn't even really remember my real mom. I mentioned I missed my half sister, as well.

Then Aileen asked me if I'd ever had a girlfriend.

75

AILEEN AS LUCY, THE PEANUTS IN-HOUSE SHRINK

I swatted a fly out of my face, pausing for a second. "Excuse me?"

"Have you ever had a girlfriend?" she repeated.

Good thing she was up front. I started blushing. "No."

"Really?"

"Yeah, *really*," I said.

She glanced over her shoulder. "Why not?" she asked matter-of-factly.

I scowled. "I don't know."

"I'm afraid that won't do," she said in a dry voice. "We're in the middle of the wood, Carlton. We've got a full day's hike. You might as well talk. We've got nothing else to keep us busy. Tell me: Why have you never had a girlfriend?"

Why? I slowed to an ambling trudge, making certain to keep at least ten paces behind her. *Maybe because girls terrify me even more than the rest of human society. Maybe because the girls at Carnegie Mansion all go for guys like Bryce Perry and Kyle Moffat. Maybe because the one girl who might ever possibly be interested in me hasn't even introduced herself to me face-to-face, and goes by the e-mail handle of Night Mare.*

"Do you have trouble meeting girls?" Aileen asked.

"That's part of it, I guess," I said. "I mean, right before this all happened, I actually did meet these two girls—these two *women*, really—at a comic book convention. One was sexy in a sleazy sort of way. The other was cute in an angry sort of way. They were both psychos. So I haven't had the best of luck."

Aileen laughed.

"What's so funny?" I asked.

"You're a misogynist, too, Carlton," she scoffed. "You just told me that all the girls at your school are ditzes. And then that these two women you met are psychos. You think *all* women are trouble."

"That's not true!"

She spun around. "Then why did you leave me without even saying good-bye, back in town?" she demanded, raising her eyebrows.

I stopped in my tracks. "I—well, that's . . . I'm sorry," I stammered.

"I'm sorry, too. That was unfair." Her expression softened, even though she waved the knife around for emphasis. "You've led a sheltered life, Carlton."

I nodded. She was right. But for a moment, I was conscious only of the knife and of her staring at me—and the birds squawking high above us, the bugs buzzing around us, and the cool breeze rustling in the leaves and the dirt caked on my clothes and hands. I wished my life were sheltered right *now*.

"It always used to bother me when people said that," I said.

Aileen just laughed again. She turned and resumed hacking away at the brush.

"You know what I don't get?" I added. "You've become so cheerful again. How do you do it? Like I said, I'm scared out of my mind."

"Well, if it makes ye feel better, I'm scared out of my mind, too," she said.

"So you've been putting on an act. Good. That, I can relate to."

"You know what you're *really* scared of, though? You're scared of *losing* people. You lost your mother. You're worried about losing your stepmother and half sister. And in all your talk of your worry, you hardly ever mentioned your dad."

I frowned. "Your point being?"

"*That's* why you don't have a girlfriend," she told me. "You never made the effort to get close to a girl, because you were too worried that if you did, you'd lose her. You'd get hurt." She paused. "It's why you're a misogynist, too, I reckon."

"Are you giving me therapy?" I asked.

"Aye." She chuckled gently. "Maybe I am."

"Well, let me tell you something, Aileen. That's very kind of you. And I appreciate it. But as a great man once said: 'Therapy is for whiners.'"

76

TIME TRAVEL TO
THE LATE RENAISSANCE

As it turned out—

Aileen overestimated how long it would take us to reach the MacClough's estate.

We made it by sundown, scampering up a rocky incline to a narrow precipice that overlooked their "lands," as Aileen put it. I understood now why she described them that way, because she knew we would suddenly time travel to the late Renaissance. I swear, that's what it felt like.

The house was more of a castle, built of the same rough-hewn stone as the factory, but definitely much more Disneyland. It looked a little like the Admissions Hall at Carnegie Mansion, in fact: a stately jumble of ivy, Gothic arches, chimneys, and tiny windowpanes glinting in the afternoon sunshine. There was even a hedge maze near the swimming pool, as well as a massive satellite dish that looked as if it could receive messages from Pluto. And next to that was a construction site, hidden by a tall wooden fence. I stood on my tiptoes. I saw something, a flash of dull concrete, but that was it.

Maybe they were building a pool house. *Jeez.*

These people definitely weren't broke. And they definitely *were* powerful.

"Isn't it a wonderful isle?" I heard myself joke.

Aileen didn't reply.

She was crying.

77

THE MOST WONDERFUL SURPRISE OF MY LIFE

"Aileen, what's the matter?" I whispered, overcome with worry.

"Carlton." She shook her head and trembled. She wiped her eyes. "I—I—"

"What?" I asked. "What is it?"

She swept me into her arms and started kissing me.

78

BACK IN CELL PHONE RANGE

Okay. If you haven't already guessed: I'd never been kissed before.

So, yes, my heart was pounding and all the rest of that crap. But I tried not to fight it. I tried to enjoy it. I closed my eyes, figuring that's what I was supposed to do. I tried to concentrate on the magical sensation of her lips against mine, of her hands draped around my waist, of the tinkling of her bracelets in the wind. But I couldn't. For some freakish reason, all I could think was: *She's taller than I am. Also, her breath really isn't that bad. I was expecting the breath of that guy from the bookstore who told me* Peanuts *was crap. Then again, she's been chewing wild mint.*

But that's what happens when you receive the most wonderful surprise of your life. Because it's so wholly unexpected, you don't know how to react. Your brain turns to the ridiculous and inane, because that's what your brain is used to—

And then it was over.

She pulled away. She looked down, her eyelids fluttering.

"I'm sorry," she breathed.

"Don't be," I said.

She glanced down at the MacCloughs' estate. "I don't want you to go down there, Carlton. It's too dangerous. I have to do it alone."

I shook my head—rattled, dumbfounded, flabbergasted. "Aileen, I don't get it. Is there something you've been trying to tell me?"

"No!" she interrupted. She hugged me again, burying her face in the crook of my skinny neck. I could feel the moisture of her tears; I could feel her heart pounding right next to mine. "I just don't want you to get hurt," she said. "I just—"

Bee-bee-beep! Bee-bee-beep!

Something vibrated in my front pocket. Aileen withdrew, frowning. My eyes widened. I couldn't believe it. My cell phone was ringing. Somehow, *here* of all places, I was in range again. Could that big satellite dish have had something to do with it? I dug the phone out of my pocket. My hands shook. I gaped at the caller ID.

It was a number from the States.

I pressed the answer button. "Hello?" I whispered.

"Carlton! Roger Lovejoy here!"

I glanced at Aileen. She was still dewey-eyed. Her cheeks were rosy.

Right then, I had a vivid fantasy of hurling my cell phone over the precipice—so far and fast it would smash right through one of those storybook windows and knock the evil patriarch of Clan MacClough/Forba flat on his Scottish ass.

79

REGARDS FROM OLIVIA'S CONFIDANTE

Roger Lovejoy sniffed. The signal crackled. "Carlton? You there?"

"Yeah," I managed. "Hi, Roger. You know, this really isn't the best time—"

"Where are you right now?" he interrupted. "You sound like you're in *Italia*. Look, before we get to *Signy*, I know you have a crisis on your hands. One of your son's teachers called me. So I know Carlton Junior ran away from school. I don't know any of the details, but I imagine this situation has got you more screwed up than usual. Sorry."

I squinted into space. "One of my son's teachers . . . called you?"

"Yeah. A friend of mine. A cat named Nelson Herzog."

"A . . . cat?"

Roger Lovejoy chuckled. "What, you gotta bust my chops? I like to say 'cat.' I know you're upset and"—there was a hiss of static; his voice suddenly dipped in volume—"but the sense I got, when I met Carlton Junior there at COMIC EXPO, was that he's a good kid. A little quiet, maybe, a little on the creepy side, but smart, you know?" He sniffed again. "The point is he'll come back. Kids always come back."

Aileen tapped my shoulder. "Who's that?" she mouthed silently.

I shook my head. There was no easy answer to that question.

"So here's the deal, *capiche?*" Roger Lovejoy continued. "I don't know if you've been checking your e-mails, but Jessica James is very interested in licensing the Miso Horny character for merchandising. You know, what with the whole *Horny & Single,* it's a very obvious fit. She's even thinking Bee A. Vixen can model for it. And if this connection pans out—"

Click.

My thumb smothered the End button.

"Who's that?" Aileen asked again.

"That was . . . " I racked my brain. "That was a guy I know," I said. A feeble response, but it was the best I could do. It was *true,* at least. Before she could ask another question, I hurriedly dialed up my unheard messages.

There was only one.

"Message one, received Sunday, ten forty-three A.M.," the automated female voice announced—then suddenly Martha's hysterical wail blared into my eardrum. "Oh, my God, Carlton! Where are you? You went to Scotland, didn't you? The police called and said that somebody broke into your father's apartment! Just please call me, okay? Wait. Olivia wants to say something."

There was some fiddling, and then Olivia's tiny voice came on the line: "Carlton, I just want you to know that Conrad MacSchtoon sends his regards—"

The cell phone went dead, as mysteriously as it had come to life.

80

POWER NEXUS AND
THE AUTUMNAL EQUINOX

Aileen let me cry for a while, which was kind.

Maybe I shouldn't have cried at all. Maybe now she wouldn't want to kiss me again. Maybe it wouldn't matter, though. I'd cried in front of her plenty already.

Maybe, maybe, maybe. I hated that word.

When I finally gathered my wits, she offered her theory as to why the cell phone had flickered on and off.

"We're at a power nexus, Carlton," she said solemnly.

"I see," I said.

"Do you?"

"No. No, I don't. As usual, I have no idea what you're talking about."

"You're a ponce," she said.

"Aye, I am a ponce," I said.

She laughed. "Don't talk like that. You sound like an ass."

"Agreed. So what's a power nexus?"

"It's a place that harnesses the energies of the earth, moon, and sun," she answered straight-faced, as if she were describing an auto repair shop. "This entire isle is a power nexus. That's why so many circles and tombs were built here."[59]

Under any other circumstances, I would have laughed. Or made up an excuse to leave. But I couldn't. This girl—this tall, brave, gorgeous, passionate, psychopathic girl—she had just *kissed* me, for Christ's sake. And from where I stood, she looked like an angel from a stained-glass window. The sunset framed the back of her head, tinting her curls with fiery red highlights. Her eyes glittered like pieces of jade.

"So what are you saying?" I asked.

"I'm saying we should maybe wait to enter the MacCloughs' estate. I think it might be wise of us to stand at the center of the Ring of Brodgar."

I paused, thinking of a delicate way to phrase the question I wanted to ask.

"What the matter?" she said.

"I'm sorry, Aileen, but why would we make a detour to some weird stone circle when we've just spent all day hiking through the woods to get here?" I replied, figuring honesty was the best policy. "You said yourself that my father might be inside. Right *here*."

She nodded, once again squinting at me as if *I* were the lunatic. "That's precisely why we need to go to Brodgar," she said.

"Why is that, again?"

"Because we *have* to," she answered without batting an eye. "Because it all fits. Because I didn't think of it before I got here. Because it'll give us the strength we need."

---

[59] The freaky thing is that there are more than a thousand prehistoric stone circles scattered across the UK and northern France, all of which were built between 3250 and 1500 B.C. Some are as tiny as nine feet in diameter (Keel Cross); others encircle entire towns (Avebury). The most famous is Stonehenge, for its astronomical alignments, but many others are astronomically aligned, as well—including the Ring of Brodgar. And the freakiest thing is that nobody knows who built them or why.

There were about a thousand more questions I wanted to ask. *It fits because you didn't think of it before you got here? Doesn't that mean it* doesn't *fit? Is there any way you can write up a user's guide to all your superstitions? And are you just using this mysterious stone circle as an excuse because you yourself are too frightened to break into the MacCloughs' home with me? Are you just as terrified as I am?*

The question that popped out, however, was: "How far is this stone circle?"

"Not far," she whispered. "Just on the other side of the ridge. We'll be there by nightfall." She stepped toward me. "You've never seen anything like this place. It's *magic*, real magic, Carlton. We'll light a fire, right in the center of the circle, and we'll feast under the light of the moon. And we'll be a conduit—a conduit of energy older than time or man—and we'll take it and use it to storm the stronghold of Clan MacClough . . ."

Good God.

I couldn't hear a thing she was saying. All I could hear was the voice in my head, like a gym coach, pleading: *Kiss her! Take her in your arms and kiss her, you moron! Kiss her the way she kissed you! Prove yourself!*

Of course, by the time this internal coaching was finished, she'd already hurried back into the forest.

81

MAYBE THERE REALLY IS MAGIC

The Ring of Brodgar stands on a flat peninsula with hills in the distance. It looks exactly the way you might expect an ancient stone circle to look: an array of monoliths, crudely carved. But to camp in the center of it at night, under the light of a full moon . . . to build a fire with no other human beings in sight but a lone companion (and the most beautiful girl you've ever seen, who's just kissed you!) . . .

You might think: Maybe there really *is* magic.

We arrived about two hours after the sun had gone down.

I thought I would be tired and hungry, but I wasn't. The ocean wind mussed our hair as we marched across the grass toward the massive stones. Some were short, nothing more than little boulders. Others were three times as tall as I was—dark shadows that towered over me, silhouetted against the starry sky.

"I'll gather the firewood," Aileen told me. "You go on in." She paused, then lurched forward and pecked me on the cheek. "Go on!"

I watched her go, her long hair streaming behind her.

I turned and stood at the edge of the ring.

It was so huge. I couldn't even tell how wide it was. As wide as the town of Stromness? Maybe. I remembered a passage from a Dylan Thomas story that I'd read at CM in third form English[60]: " . . . *my young body like an excited animal surrounding me, the torn knees bent, the bumping heart . . . the little balls of dirt between the toes, the eyes in the sockets . . . I was aware of me myself in the exact middle of a living story, and my body was my adventure and my name.*"

The air was silent, except for the soft rhythmic crashing of the waves nearby.

Maybe there really is magic, I said to myself again.

I broached the circle's edge and marched toward the circle's center. I almost expected a bolt of lightning to strike me down. I mean it. There was a purity and sanctity to this place that's hard to put into words. It evoked a kind of awe that I think only comes when you're in the presence of something truly mystifying, something so old and ancient and secret and wonderful . . .

Too bad Dad isn't here, I thought. *It would actually make a great site for the Fortress of Eternal Life.*™

I laughed to myself as I thought that. Then I realized my cheeks were wet.

But that was all right. I wiped the tears away and took a deep breath. And as I stood at the center of the circle, I felt closer to Dad than I'd ever felt.

Aileen and I *would* find him. We *would* rescue him. We would confront Mr. Forba or Gregor MacClough or whatever he called himself. And we would learn about *his* Enemy Within . . . and we would convince him to buy that old toothless couple a brand-new hog farm because

[60] Dylan Thomas lived from 1914 to 1953. He was a rake and a drunk, but he was an amazing writer, and probably one of the most famous modern British poets. The passage comes from a story he wrote called "The Peaches," from a collection *Portrait of the Artist as a Young Dog.* He wasn't much older than me when he wrote it. And I know this all sounds a little heavy and pretentious, like I'd entered another Dark Time . . . but I guess that's how it goes. Some things *are* pretty heavy, especially at the edge of an ancient stone circle under a full moon at the autumnal equinox.

Gregor probably wasn't all that evil, either. Because as human beings, we were all trapped in roles. We had to—

"Carlton, I'm knackered."

Aileen was back, already arranging a pile of sticks for a fire.

"Will you wake me up when I'm done here?" she asked. "After I build this fire, I'm going to take a wee nap."

"Do you need any help?"

She shook her head, setting the pile ablaze with her lighter. "No, it's all taken care of." She stuck the lighter back into her pocket. "You should get some rest, too. It's important to let the energy flow through you in a subconscious state. That's what the ancients did. It allowed their dream lives to meld with their real ones."

I gazed down at her as she curled up in front of the fire. Her face flickered with soft orange light. "Is that true?" I whispered, ready to believe anything.

She smirked, closing her eyes. "No. But it sounds good, doesn't it?"

A smile spread across my face. "It does," I said. I bent down beside her and kissed her on the cheek. "Good night, Aileen."

"Good night, Carlton."

I watched her for a while in the firelight. I wasn't tired at all, not the sleepy kind of tired, anyway. I knew I wouldn't be able to get any rest. So I watched over her—first as she squirmed to get comfortable, then as her breathing settled into an even rhythm, and finally until her lips parted and she began to snore.

I'd never seen her look more sweet or beautiful or vulnerable.

As quietly as I could, I pulled my sketch pad from my knapsack.

And I didn't pull it out because I wanted to be somewhere else. I didn't pull it out because I was desperate to escape reality.

I pulled it out for an entirely new reason.

I wanted to *embrace* reality.

PART III

82

AN ENTIRE IRRITABLE AND PETRIFIED CONVERSATION, SPOKEN IN A WHISPER

"Are you sure this is safe, Aileen?"

"Don't be a ponce, Carlton. Look at us. We're breaking into a villain's house in the dead of night. Of course it's not safe."

"No, that's not what I mean. I mean, do you think trying to open a random window and climbing through it is the safest plan? Don't they have alarms?"

"This is Orkney. Maybe the rest of Scotland has caught up with the twentieth century. I couldn't tell you."

"But Gregor MacClough has a satellite dish. It's right over there."

"Aye?"

"If he has a satellite dish, he might have alarms, too."

"Carlton, he's a Scot. He probably doesn't even know what an alarm *is*. If he has anything, it'll be broadswords and battle-axes and maces. And I don't mean those wee little cans of pepper spray. I mean those big wooden clubs with spiked iron balls at the top."

"Thanks. That makes me feel much safer, Aileen. What about guns?"

"I very much doubt if he has guns. True Scots only hunt with crossbows."

"I wasn't talking about for hunting. I was talking about for blowing away teenagers who break into their homes in the middle of the night."

"Carlton, either we open this window or we don't. And as far as feeling safe goes: Everybody in the States owns a gun, and there's, like, ten thousand murders a year in the States. Hardly anyone in Orkney owns a gun, and there were two murders on this island in the last decade.[61] So you probably *should* feel safe. The worst you'll get is your arms hacked off with a battle-axe. This isn't sophistry, Carlton."[62]

"This isn't what?"

"Never mind. Now remember: Walk like a cat."

---

[61] I was never able to verify this statistic.

[62] soph-ist-ry \sofistree\ *n*. Overclever or fallacious reasoning.

83

PHOTOS ON THE WALLS

I stared at my reflection in the darkened window. I looked very, very pale in the moonlight. I imagine I would have looked pale, anyway, even if the sun were shining brightly and I had a deep tan. Aileen pulled out her Swiss army knife. She offered a tentative smile, then grabbed the window and heaved it open—and without another word crawled into the darkness of the MacCloughs' mansion.

I felt sick. I had no choice but to follow. I climbed inside and tip-toed after her.

Even in near-perfect darkness, the house didn't look the way I would have expected. It was *modern,* for one thing—which only hammered home my certainty that it was armed with laser sensors and state-of-the art teenager neutralization devices. It must have been newly renovated, too, because I could smell paint. Also, the door-knobs weren't the circular kind. They were the *lever* kind—in other words, the kind you only find in newly renovated homes of the deadly, omniscient, and ultrapowerful.

On the plus side, Aileen did seem very confident.

She prowled into a long hallway in perfect silence. My own muddy sneakers squeaked and squished on the stone floor. She paused and frowned, pointing at her feet. Apparently, the trick to walking in perfect silence was *not* to tiptoe. It was to lay your feet perfectly flat on the floor with each step, and to peel them off from back to front, just the way a cat does with its paws.

I tried to imitate her.

I didn't have very much luck.

It didn't matter, though. Maybe spending the night at the Ring of Brodgar did in fact infuse her with some kind of magical psychic ability, because she glided stealthily to a random door and pushed the lever to open it.

A recessed light in the ceiling flickered on.

"Blast!" she whispered.

She closed the door behind us.

Oh, my God.

I staggered forward, nearly falling to my knees. The room looked a lot like the Stromness police station. There was the same, sloppy, working-headquarters sort of vibe: two desks, lots of papers, maps, empty beer bottles, photos taped to the walls, and a computer— though this one was recognizable, as it had been built in the last five years. But I didn't really pay much attention to the computer. Mostly, I paid attention to the photos on the walls.

All were black-and-white.

Most of them were of me.

84

A FEW QUICK QUESTIONS

I wasn't sure how to feel. Can *you* imagine what it would feel like to break into a stranger's house in a country you've never been to and discover an entire room smothered in candid 8 X 10-inch glossies taken of you at school? Some blurry, some in focus, some, eerily enough, with your eyes staring straight at the lens. Going to class. Entering the dining hall. Climbing out of your room on the way to COMIC EXPO.

Neither could I.

85

SHITE

"Shite," Aileen pronounced.

"You said it," I whispered back. I covered my eyes for a moment and then turned away. I couldn't stand to look at the photos.[63] Instead, I began snooping around the room, suddenly filled with righteous venom. If this old Gregor MacClough bastard and his henchmen wanted to spy on me, fine. But now it was my turn to spy back.

On one of the desks there was an old letter, crumpled and yellowed with age. It looked like a lot like the parchment they'd sent me.

I took a closer peek.

My heart skipped a beat.

I read out loud to Aileen, in as quiet a voice as I could:

"'The fourth of May, nineteen hundred and twelve . . .

"'To Clan Forba from Carlton Dunne . . .

"'We are off to the New World. I trust that if our ship does not sink, then you will receive this post. I trust that lady luck, in all her good graces, will side with us. Lady luck, or perhaps the fates with

---

[63] This wasn't just because I was horrified. As lame as it sounds, it was also because I can't stand the way I look in photographs. I look even skinnier and dorkier and more frazzled than I do when I look in the mirror.

their tangled webs, will grant us our redemption, because in spite of your ambush, victory was mine, was it not?

"'I may never know why you had murder in your heart, as it was my sole intention to bury the feud and the myth of Agricola in its rightful place, in the cave just right of the ruins of Castle Glanach. Aye, 'twas the very same cave where your ancestors poached the dagger from Agricola himself, or so the legend has it. I know your fortune has started to wither. You feel you've been cheated. And I pity you. But I feel no remorse. Your treachery was no match for my own, nor your cunning. Can you still see me, escaping across Loch Stenness in my canoe? Can you see me, waving the dagger in triumph, its blade of gold gleaming in the sun? Can you read its inscription—?'"

"Shhh!" Aileen hissed.

I gulped. I hadn't realized I was yelling, and had also added my own fake Scottish accent. "Sorry. I got a little carried away—"

"Shaddap!" She lunged forward, grabbing my arm. She raised a finger to her lips, her eyes wide. In the silence, I heard the slow thud of footsteps, directly overhead.

The color drained from my face. "Shite," I whispered.

86

A BIG FAT ONE-HUNDRED-EIGHTY-DEGREE NOSEDIVE

Aileen was already bolting out the door.

I was too stunned to follow. But it didn't matter. If luck had been on our side until that point, it decided to take a big fat one-hundred-eighty-degree nosedive: Aileen's bracelets got caught on the door lever. She didn't even notice—neither of us did—not until she'd run out into the hall and accidentally slammed the door behind her: *SMACK!*

I winced.

That slam was very loud.

Aileen lurched back into the room. Our eyes met again. Hers were wide and terrified. I can only guess how mine looked. She fumbled with her bracelets, and in a panic, she yanked her wrist free. The silver hoops hung from the door lever, jangling.

"Oi!" a raspy voice shouted from down the hall. "'Oo goes there?"

Oh, God, no. I knew that voice. It was the voice on the phone, the voice of the kidnapper, the voice of Mr. Forba/Gregor MacClough—

"I have to get my bracelets!" Aileen whispered. She tried to pull them off the lever, but her hands were too unsteady. They slipped from her fingers, bouncing to the floor and rolling across the room. She bent down, fumbling for them.

Now it was *my* turn to lunge.

"Are you crazy!" I breathed, pulling her up. "Leave them! We have to get out of here! Signy left her crown when she lost it in the castle!"

Aileen frowned at me. "*Who* left *what?*"

"Never mind." Not good. I was starting to get my fantasy life mixed up with the real one.

"Oi!" the voice shouted again, much closer this time.

Aileen shook free of me. In one deft maneuver, she crossed her arms in front of her face and sprinted across the room—diving straight through an open window. *Whoosh!!!* She somersaulted to her feet on the lawn outside, like some sort of martial arts expert. "Come on!" she hissed.

I gaped at her. Apparently, she *would* make a good cop. I also realized, with a strange clarity, that for the second time in five minutes I had to follow a madwoman through a window. *No time to second-guess, champ!* My inner coach exhorted. I put my best *Magnus, Robot Fighter*, face on and dove through after her, somersaulting across the grass myself. Not as courageously or athletically.

Aileen swept me up and ran.

It was only after we'd escaped back into the woods that I noticed my hands were bleeding, my neck was sore, and my back was killing me.

Still, it could have been worse. Much worse.

I had both my arms. They could have been hacked off with a battle-axe.

87

THE PRICELESS GIFT
OF FRESH BREATH

Once again, Aileen took pity on me. She promptly led us through the wilderness back to Stromness and escorted us to the first inn in town.[64]

We arrived just after daybreak.

The inn—Stromness Inn—was two blocks from the police station.

It was tidy and cozy, just nine rooms in all, and newly renovated, like the MacCloughs' estate. Not only were the sheets clean, they didn't smell like hog dung. There were phones and showers in every room. There was even a gift shop in the little lobby.

"Nice, eh?" Aileen asked.

Very nice, I thought. I didn't have the strength to form words.

I charged two adjoining rooms on the forbidden credit card. I figured another two hundred forty pounds on top of the almost two thousand dollars I'd already spent wouldn't make much difference at this point, especially if Dad and I were doomed to die in the next twenty-four hours. Aileen agreed to meet me in her room in a half hour or so, after we'd cleaned up a little.

---

[64] My sense of direction was completely shot, but Stromness, the Ring of Brodgar, and the MacCloughs' estate were all within a three-mile radius—give or take a quarter mile.

"Take your time," she told me.

I planned to.

Once alone and inside my cozy little chamber, I headed straight for the bathroom. Disregarding that brief peek in the MacCloughs' window, I hadn't actually looked in a mirror since I'd been at the airport, which was . . . *man*. Four days ago?

My stomach squeezed. My nerves still twitched from the various near-death experiences. I was more fatigued than I'd ever been in my life, yet not sleepy in the least. Every body part sent a contradictory message.

I was not cut out for a rescue mission.

My reflection agreed.

I looked like death.

It was almost funny. *Christ.* My hair stuck out in a thousand different directions. My cheekbones seemed extra hollow and sunken, too. But that might have just been all the dirt. It accented my features like poorly applied makeup. I spent five minutes washing my face, and then grabbed my toothbrush from my knapsack. Unfortunately, the bathroom did not come equipped with little tubes of toothpaste. I scoured the cabinets under the sink and behind the mirror. Nope, nothing.

But then I had a thought.

Aileen must have been desperate for toothpaste, too. Way more desperate than me. Of course she was! And even though it wouldn't be much, even though I owed her my life . . . wouldn't it be a nice surprise if I showed up at her room with a tube of Crest or Colgate or Aim? She'd lost her bracelets, after all. She could use a pick-me-up. Besides, sometimes little gestures like that could mean a lot. Sometimes little gestures could mean the *most*.

Anyway, selfishly, I needed to go to the gift shop. I had to buy a new T-shirt. All my clothes stank to high heaven. I *owed* it to her to change.

88

ANNABEL REDS

Fifteen minutes later, I arrived at Aileen's door—freshly showered, wielding a brand new tube of Colgate, and sporting a spanking new I GOT SMASHED IN STROMNESS sweatshirt.[65]

There was a note perched on top of the knob.

Come on in, the lock's open
Make yourself at home. I'll be done in a jiff.—A

I stuck the note into my pocket and pushed the door open.

"Hello?" I said cautiously. "Aileen?"

The shower was running.

My eyes scanned the room. Her beat-up leather satchel was on the bed. *Perfect!* I thought. I could stick the tube of toothpaste in there, and then when she looked through it later, she would find a little surprise. The best gifts were always surprises. I dashed over and opened it— *What the hell?*

There was food in here. Little individually wrapped packages of smoked fish. And not just *any* smoked fish: MacClough-brand

---

[65] Total cost of the toothpaste and sweatshirt = 68 pounds. Not that I cared . . . but still. Where do little inns in tiny towns get off jacking up the prices like that?

smoked salmon. Yup, there it was, printed right there on the plastic wrap, complete with the little smiley-faced fish logo. The slices were called Annabel Reds. Even in my exhausted, frightful, freaked state, I still didn't get it. If she had food this whole time, why did she lie to me in the woods? Why catch the fish if she already *had* fish? Couldn't we have just eaten *this*? I mean, sure, yes, the MacCloughs were bad people, but still, if they made decent food—

The bathroom door flew open.

Aileen stood wrapped in a towel, dripping wet. Her hair hung in her face. She looked enraged.

I gaped at her, clutching the packet of smoked fish in one hand and the tube of toothpaste in the other.

"What are you *doing?*" she shouted.

"I was uh—um, I just wanted to surprise you . . ."

"By snooping through me stuff?" she snapped.

I shook my head. "The note on your door said—"

"I don't care what the note said!" she interrupted. "That's me bag! It's mine!"

My heart pounded. *Jesus.* I supposed I should have known better than to trust any generous instincts, right? I supposed I knew better than to try to figure out what the hell would make Aileen happy, too.

I dropped the fish and the tube of toothpaste and fled.

89

MY GRAND MASTER PLAN FOR VICTORY

Just my luck; before I even got a chance to settle down in my room with my sketch pad, there was a knock on the door.

"Yeah?" I groaned.

"It's Aileen. Carlton, I'm so sorry. May I come in?"

I sighed, tossing the pad aside. "Sure," I mumbled.

She opened up. Her hair was still dripping. She hadn't even put on her shoes yet. She offered a shaky smile from behind her curls.

"Carlton, I apologize for all that," she said softly, closing the door and leaning against it. "I just didn't want you to find me red fish. You see, I was ashamed. I knew from the moment we found that envelope Sunday night that the MacCloughs were behind this. And . . . I didn't want you to think *I* was in cahoots with the enemy. You know, the way you thought the innkeepers were . . . and if you found the red fish, you might think . . . you know, the brand association . . . " She stared down at her bare toes, chastened.

"Couldn't you have just *told* me all that?" I asked. "I don't get it."

"You don't get what?"

"If you had the food, you should have shared it. I was hungry out there." I yawned. "I'm hungry right now."

She nodded. "I know. I know. But it was the MacCloughs. I was . . . scared."

All at once, I felt terrible.

I could *stand* to be a little hungry every now and then. It wasn't the end of the world. Besides, she didn't want to share the food with me because it was MacClough-brand food. She also knew she'd be able to fend for us both in the woods—which was a hell of a lot more than I could say. I hadn't helped in the least.

"Carlton, listen, I've been thinking," Aileen said. She sat down next to me on the bed. "We've known all along that Gregor MacClough has your father. We've *proved* it. But now we've created a bit of a mess, because we broke into *their* home. My bracelets are still there! They have something on *us* now. Anyhoo, most of the local police are on their payroll, anyway."

"The local police?" I cried, my voice rising to Zeppelin-concert decibel level.

"Shh," she said, laying a hand on my knee. "Let me finish. I was thinking: Something about that letter we found last night wasn't quite right."

I shook my head, at a loss. "What do you mean?"

"It said that Agricola's dagger was made of gold. But in the letter the Forbas dropped off at the inn, they said the dagger was made of silver."

"Oh." I took a deep breath. "It also said there was an inscription, right?"

She nodded.

"Aileen, this may sound crazy but . . ." I fought to ignore my accelerating pulse. "Brass is sort of the same color as gold, right?"

She shrugged. "Aye. I reckon."

"See, my dad has this letter opener. It's a piece of crap. But he always kept it hidden, and he always treated it like it was the most valuable thing in the world. And I'm thinking, maybe he did that for a *reason*. Maybe he knew that the MacCloughs were always watching him, so he wanted to convince them that he still had Agricola's dagger. Because I'm thinking maybe his grandfather Carlton Dunne the first— the one who wrote that letter—maybe he switched the daggers, because he knew he'd be walking into an ambush at Castle Glanach back in nineteen twelve."

Aileen raised her eyebrows. "Carlton, you sound a bit daft. Maybe you should eat something. I'll go get the red fish—"

"No!" I grabbed her arm. "Aileen, I'm serious. Maybe the *real* dagger was buried in the cave to the right of the ruins of Castle Glanach that day—like it says in the letter. Maybe my great-grandfather tricked the Forbas, as only a wily Scot could. Maybe *that's* the proof: the dagger itself, buried in that cave for almost a century. And if we go there, and we find the dagger, then we win. You see? The MacCloughs are due to meet us there at dawn tomorrow. Don't you get it?"

Aileen frowned at me. "Really, Carlton," she said. "I can get the fish."

"No, come on!" I cried. "If we *do* find the dagger there, nobody has to get hurt. The MacCloughs will be at the ruins at dawn tomorrow, right? That's what they said. So what if we're waiting there with the dagger? We can just make an even exchange: My dad for the dagger. We can do better than that. We can make them promise to buy that old couple a new hog farm."

"Carlton, please—"

"Aileen, I mean it. This is our only hope. This is the only way we can possibly save my dad. And I have this feeling—call it a hunch, call it superstition, call it whatever you want—I just *know* that dagger is buried in the cave to the right of Castle Glanach."

Aileen clasped her hand over mine. She didn't say anything for a long time.

At last, she nodded. "All right. I'll take you to Castle Glanach. And we'll look for the dagger. But you have to promise me one thing. We wait till tonight to go. You spend the rest of today sleeping. You need the rest. Then we eat a nice dinner. Agreed?"

"Agreed," I said.

She stood and walked to the door. "Promise me you'll sleep?"

"I promise."

"Good." She hesitated, and then smiled shyly. "Good night, then."

"Good night," I replied.

She closed the door behind her.

As soon as she did, I grabbed my sketch pad. I knew I wasn't going to be able to sleep. Besides, it wasn't even night. It was ten in the morning.

90

A BIGGER VERSION OF A KICKED-IN LEGO FORT

As it turned out—

The ruins of Castle Glanach were nothing to write home about.

I'd been expecting something huge and terrible and magical, like the Ring of Brodgar. But Castle Glanach wasn't much more than a pile of rocks, perched upon a little inlet, wedged into a bunch of rocky cliffs. It was approachable only from one direction, off the road from Stromness. The shattered remnants of a few walls stood here and there, but not much more. It sort of reminded me of the LEGO forts I used to build as a kid, the kind I never put much thought into, the kind I kicked down as soon as dinner was ready.

Not that this matters. Not really.

No. Because as it turned out—

Agricola's dagger was *not* buried in the cave to the right of the ruins. Not unless my great-grandfather was the size of a kitten. There was only one cave to the right of Castle Glanach, and it was about six inches wide. Aileen couldn't even stick her head inside. She managed to stick her lighter in, but that was it. The cave floor was solid rock.

In other words: My grand master plan for victory turned out to be a big fat wash.

91

ONE WAY IN, ONE WAY OUT

"I don't get it," I said, shambling away from the tiny cave in a funk. "We were so close, so sure of ourselves . . . where did we go wrong?"

Aileen didn't answer. There *was* no answer.

I stared out at Loch Stenness. The waters were as flat and stagnant as those of a giant toilet bowl. I could see the moon's reflection in it, a perfect mirror image.

I was exhausted: exhausted from having drawn all day instead of slept, exhausted from the walk here—another three-hour hike through hills and moors—exhausted from the endless movement that led nowhere, the endless frustration.

I'd screwed up.

"In the letter," I mumbled, struggling to think. "In the letter . . . "

"Aye?"

"In the letter, Carlton Dunne hinted that he buried the dagger in the cave to the right of the castle. And then he was ambushed."

Aileen shrugged, standing in the rocky shoals by the water's edge.

"But he *couldn't* have buried the dagger in the cave to the right," I said.

"Aye," she concurred.

"So we must be missing something."

"Carlton, he also said that he took the dagger with him," she groaned.

Hmm. That was true. On the other hand, his description of the dagger matched Dad's letter opener perfectly. The blade was gold, not silver. So the dagger he'd waved over his head *had* to be the letter opener. So he must have ditched the real one around here somewhere . . .

I backed up a few paces, trying to get some distance, some perspective on the whole site. Maybe if he'd approached the castle from another direction . . . but no. That was impossible. Not unless he'd scaled down the cliffs that surrounded it on three sides or swam the loch. It was approachable only from the rocky, muddy beach where we stood. That's what made it such a great place for an ambush. There was one way in and one way out. And as we'd seen, there was only a single cave to the right of the ruins.

Could the dagger be buried somewhere *in* the castle, then?

I stepped through a gap in the walls, prowling over the uneven stone floor. Nope. Doubtful that the dagger was in here. It was weird . . . in a floor this old, I would have expected more deterioration—with weeds poking up through cracks and holes. But the surface was solid and unbroken. It was even more solid than the cave floor. It looked like glazed ceramic, slick and glassy, glittering with starlight and moonlight.[66] There was no *way* the dagger could be buried in here. Not unless Carlton Dunne had brought a jackhammer with him.

I shook my head and trudged back out onto the beach.

Think, think, think, my sleep-deprived brain pleaded.

---

[66] The term for this sort of rock is "vitrified" rock. It's another mystery of ancient Scotland—and equally as perplexing as the stone circles. There are at least sixty vitrified forts or castles scattered across the country, but nobody can say for certain how they were built. To vitrify rock, you need to melt it. It's essentially cooled lava. In other words, you need to build a fire as hot as a volcano. This requires serious science and technology. So how did ancient Scots build fires that hot? Like the stone circles, there are plenty of wacky theories—most of them having to do with UFOs or black magic or something known as a "power nexus."

The MacCloughs would be here at dawn. We had less than five hours. But for all I knew, *they* had found the dagger long ago. Maybe they'd already killed Dad. Maybe they were just planning to ambush us here, as they'd ambushed my great-grandfather. I almost wished I *had* tried to smuggle Dad's stupid letter opener aboard the plane, so I could at least try to pull off another scam . . .

Wait a second.

The letter had mentioned an inscription, as well.

"Aileen?" I called.

"Aye?"

"What does 'michts no aye richt' mean?"

She laughed, turning toward me. "Why do you ask?"

"That's what the inscription on my dad's letter opener says."

"Really? That's a laugh."

I frowned. "It is?"

"Well, not a *laugh* . . . but you know—as you can probably figure out, it means: 'Might does not make right.' But it has a double meaning, too, at least among Scots. It also means 'Might can come from where you'd least expect it.' Most people are right-handed, aye? The right side may seem stronger, but appearances can be deceiving."

The right side, I repeated to myself.

Once again, I felt that strange squirming sensation in my mind and gut, of racing down a hundred blind alleys toward a hundred dead ends yet, somehow, each dead end appeared more promising than the last.

"In other words, power can come from the *left,* not the right," I heard myself say.

She walked over and stood beside me. "You're talking to a lefty, so you know I agree with you," she said. "But what are you driving at?"

"It's like what you said about the word 'understanding.'

Remember? It can mean a bunch of different things—like the word 'right.' Right can mean right and wrong, or it can mean right and left. Or it can just mean yes. Right?"

She took my hand.

"Keep yer breath tae cuil yer parritch," she said. "Carlton, listen to yourself. You need to calm down. You've gone mad."

Maybe I had gone mad, but my gaze swept over the cliffs to the left of the ruins . . . and there at the bottom, where the cliffs met the wet sand, I spotted a cave entrance—a jagged black hole big enough to swallow up a person easily.

92

I'D SAY IT WAS GOOD

"Come on!" I cried.

I staggered across the beach, dragging her behind me.

"Carlton, wait." She paused outside the cave and ignited her lighter, creating a very tiny makeshift torch. "Let me go first. There may be snakes or vermin."

I swallowed, eyeing her as she ducked down and crept inside.

Whatever. If she wasn't scared enough to keep out, then neither was I.

My real life is exactly like the last comic I drew! I'm trailing behind a beautiful girl in a cave, about to uncover a hidden treasure! And there's just mud and sand under my feet, and I am trying to concentrate only on my feet, just like that first time I snuck out at CM to go to COMIC EXPO, so I won't lose it . . . but now that I think about it, the deeper we go, the drier the earth is, so something could definitely be buried here . . .

Aileen jerked to a halt. We'd reached the end. She held up her lighter.

Carved into the wall—sloppily, as if with a dagger—were these words:

MICHTS NO AYE RICHT
DUM MY WUNNAE LEE

"Oh my God," she gasped, trembling.

"What's that bottom part mean?" I whispered. I was trembling myself.

"It means—" Her voice caught. She gripped my arm. "It means, 'You need look no further for the proof,'" she choked out.

I didn't waste a second.

I plopped down on my hands and knees and started digging. I dug in a mad, mad, mad dash. Within seconds, I'd created a hole as deep as my wrist; within minutes, I was up to my shoulders. Dirt flew; my lungs labored—

"Ow!"

I stopped. My middle finger sliced against something sharp.

"Carlton, look!" Aileen shrieked. She bent down beside me.

There, at the bottom of the hole, was a silver blade, flashing in the lighter's flame.

It glistened with a lone drop of blood . . . *my* blood.

I went numb.

Carefully, cautiously, I seized the tip of the blade by my thumb and forefinger. I lifted it out of the dirt and sand.

It was heavy—way heavier than Dad's letter opener. It probably weighed twice as much. I shook it out once and wiped the blade on my shirt.

The silver shone clear and pure, like a mirror—as brightly as the day it was forged, as far as I imagined. The hilt was made of bronze and encrusted with tiny gemstones. They weren't fake, either. No pink glass here. Nope.

This was the real deal.

Suddenly I felt nauseated.

"I don't know if finding this was good or bad," I breathed.

"I don't know, either," Aileen said.

"I'd say it was good," a familiar voice rasped behind us.

93

THE ORIGIN OF THE SNACK PACKS MONIKER "ANNABEL REDS"

A tall, craggy old man stood at the mouth of the cave.

He had to stoop to fit inside. A long white beard hung from his chin. He was dressed in—of all things—a red-and-black-plaid kilt. And rubber boots. And a hunting jacket. He looked ridiculous. If I hadn't been so deathly afraid, I might have laughed. Unfortunately, he was pointing a double-barreled shotgun at us. This pretty much ruled out laughter. It also ruled out Aileen's theory that nobody on this island owned a gun.

The dagger slipped from my fingers.

"I was beginning to think you'd betrayed me," the man growled.

My heart pounded. Any shred of doubt vanished: This was Gregor MacClough. He had the same voice as the kidnapper.

"You've been out of touch, Annabel," he went on, smiling at Aileen. "You took much longer than expected. But I knew you'd come around when I went looking for you at the inn. When I went to send you a message. Too bad it burned down, aye? Pity that. Then you left your bracelets in the house. It was a sign. Wasn't it, deary?"

Aileen shook her head. "It . . . just— You knew . . . this—you knew that this whole business would take some time," she stammered.

I frowned, my eyes darting between them.

Do these two know each other?

"What may be done at any time will be done at no time, Annabel," the man said.

Annabel?

"Dad, please," she whispered.

Dad?

My mouth fell open. My eyes widened as I gaped at her. Realization upon realization exploded in slow horror, tumbling like dominoes through my brain—

"You're a MacClough," I whispered.

"Aye," the man said, even though I hadn't been talking to him. "I'm Gregor MacClough, mate." He slithered forward and plucked the dagger from the dirt. And with the same speed and athleticism as Aileen, he tossed her the gun and then bound my hands together with a rope. I was paralyzed. I could only stare at him. That is, until he tied a bandana around my eyes, blinding me.

Like father, like daughter, I thought.

94

WHAT'S HER FACE, A.K.A. WHO THE HELL KNOWS

Even if you haven't been played for a sucker in the worst way conceivable, being blindfolded isn't the most pleasant experience in the world. This goes double if you're a visually oriented person. All sense of balance and direction winds up circling the drain. Literally. You're a crumb adrift in a toilet-bowl current over which you have no control, swirling toward inexorable doom. So I didn't know where we were going. All I knew was: With the help of her father, Aileen (or should I say Annabel?) dragged me out of the cave and bundled me into a van. After bouncing around for who knows how long over what felt like an extreme dirt-bike course, the van stopped.

The back doors opened.

The MacClough father-and-daughter team dragged me out and stood me up. I could sense them on either side of me—but I couldn't tell who was who. Both their hands were equally rough. They both reeked of smoked salmon.

No wonder what's her face was so obsessed with brushing her teeth.

Ha-ha . . . ha.

"Ye've ta'en the wrang soo by the lug, Dad," Aileen said, whatever that meant.

"I widnae ca' the king ma casion," her dad replied, whatever that meant.

I may not have understood them, but at least I knew Aileen was standing to my left. *Michts No Aye Richt*, as the saying goes.

Ha-ha . . . ha.

Not so funny.

"He disnae ken a beef'ae a bull's fit!" Aileen shouted, her voice pleading.

"I'll be the judge of that!" her dad snapped.

I had the feeling they were talking about me. Not that it mattered much.

One of them yanked my blindfold off. I blinked a few times as my eyes adjusted to the glare of electric light—but I recognized instantly where I was. I'd been brought back to the old MacClough estate. No wonder Aileen (sorry, *Annabel*) had known there wouldn't be any alarms when we'd broken in. She'd grown up here. I suppose, in retrospect, that I should have felt lucky, too . . . I got a chance to see what the MacCloughs were in the process of constructing behind the wooden fence on their property. I got to see it from *inside* the wooden fence, no less.

It wasn't a pool house.

Nope. It was a miniature panopticon.

In the words of Aileen, a.k.a. Annabel, MacClough, I shite you not.

95

ONE-MAN ADMIRATION SOCIETY

Construction of the minipanopticon was nearly finished, in fact. Bravo. And to add further kudos, they'd done a very clever thing. I say clever, because I knew they had ripped off the idea directly from my father's design for the Fortress of Eternal Life™, and my dad is a very clever man.

What they'd done is this.

They'd installed rings upon rings of video cameras in the central tower: a hundred electronic eyes, all pointed at the cells that encircled them. They'd done so because the tower was too slender to fit any real *guards*; it was barely three feet across. The entire panopticon was only one story tall and maybe thirty feet in diameter, its barred cells no bigger than airplane restrooms.

And as I stood in front of one of those darkened cells—one of about twenty in the classic donut-shaped configuration of which I'd waxed so eloquently back in Mr. Herzog's class—I was struck with seven revelations, all in rapid bullet-point succession:

- I'D HAD IT PRETTY FREAKING GOOD AT CM.
- IRONY DIDN'T REALLY GET MUCH CRUELER OR MORE DEPRAVED THAN THIS.
- THE MACCLOUGHS HAD EMBLAZONED EVERY AVAILABLE SURFACE WITH THEIR CREST: A SERPENTINE DOUBLE HELIX.
- IT WAS THE SAME DESIGN I'D SEEN ON AILEEN'S BRACELETS.
- IT WAS THE SAME DESIGN I SHOULD HAVE *RECOGNIZED*—SEEING AS WHEN GREGOR MACCLOUGH CALLED ME ON THE TRAIN TO MANHATTAN, HE TOLD ME TO LOOK OUT FOR "THE CREST OF THE SERPENT" WHEN I ARRIVED IN EDINBURGH.
- AND WHAT DO YOU KNOW? I'D FOUND IT!
- OR RATHER, IT HAD FOUND *ME* . . .

All of which is a long way of saying that I had to admire the many levels of treachery. I had to admire Aileen or Annabel or whoever the hell she was. I had to admire her and her kilt-wearing dad as they tossed me into my cell—even after I'd put all my trust in her.

I *had* to, being the magnificently guileless poster boy for scams I'd always been.

How could I not?

96

A LAME ATTEMPT AT RECTIFICATION FROM A LIAR

Gregor MacClough slammed the bars behind me. *Clink!*

I lay flat on my back on the cold concrete floor. I had to scrunch up my knees just to fit. I closed my eyes. I would have preferred to have the blindfold back, actually.

"Dad?" I heard Aileen whisper.

"Aye?" Gregor MacClough growled.

"Can we leave Carlton's knapsack with him? He loves to draw."

"Mmm," he groaned.

She sniffled. It sounded like she was crying. Maybe she'd stubbed her toe or something. This was a construction site, after all. And if she had, I was glad. She *should* have stubbed her toe. She should have stubbed her toe on a cursed poisonous nail . . . yes, a nail that would infect her with a sudden terrible germ-warfare-style disease . . . one that melts a person from the inside out in a bubbling froth of viscous green fluid and dries into a hissing, puke-colored stain and leaves you there forgotten under the sneaker soles of every single person you've ever betrayed.

The door clinked.

One of them tossed the knapsack to the floor beside me. *Plop!*

The door clinked again.

"I'm going to sleep," Gregor MacClough proclaimed.

His booted footsteps faded out the door, and then into nothingness.

"Carlton?" Aileen whispered.

"Yes, *Annabel?*"

"Carlton, I am so sorry."

I sighed. "Well. If it's any consolation, so am I."

"Carlton, I—"

"Can I ask you something?" I squeezed my eyes shut as tightly as I could.

She sniffled again. "Of course."

"That whole thing outside the airport . . . you know, with the van almost running me over? Was that a setup?"

There was no answer.

"Aileen? Annabel? Whatever your name is? Hello?"

"Aye?" she said finally.

"Aye, hello—or aye, that was a setup?"

"Aye, both."

I frowned. Twenty-twenty hindsight was a remarkable thing. Especially blindfolded. Being blind made certain vision a lot clearer, in fact. I rolled over on my side, snuggling against my knapsack.

"Okay," I said. "That's all. You can go now."

"Carlton, let me explain," she whispered. "Please. I've been watching you for so long now. Don't you get it? Me dad sent me to America to spy on you. He wanted me to kidnap *you*. I watched you at school and at your house in Connecticut and your apartment in New York City . . . I'm the one who took those photos. And when you snuck out that night, to go to that comic book convention, I snuck into your room, hoping finally to find a clue toward the proof. *I'm* the one who hacked into your e-mail, Carlton! And when I saw all your drawings and read all your messages and figured out what was going on, I'm the one sent that weird bloke all those e-mails, making sure he watched you in me stead. I wanted you to be *safe*."

"Keep talking," I said dully. "This is a really great story. I'll have to work it into my next comic strip. Oh—but right. I'll be dead. Never mind."

"I'm telling the truth!" she wailed.

"Mm-hmm."

"Carlton, everything I've ever said to you is true!"

"Right. Like your name was Aileen?"

"That's not fair!" She wept.

I couldn't believe it. Hearing her bawl like this somehow made *me* feel bad. I almost hoped she and her dad would kill me sooner rather than later. I was too confused to go on living at this point.

"These last few days have been the most honest of me life," she croaked, her voice wracked with sobs. "Me dad sent me to spy on you. And watching you . . . I fell in love with you, Carlton. Don't you understand? You're me soul mate. We've lost our moms. We have no friends. You and I, we're trapped in these dumb lives of our forefathers' making, with our dumb dads calling the shots! And we just want to escape . . . and I saw that in your face the first time I laid eyes on you. I wanted to kiss you then, Carlton. I wanted to take care of you, to rescue you. But then me dad decided to kidnap your dad instead. He spent our last money on this whole silly, stupid opera-tion—sending me to the States and building this silly prison. So I snuck into your dad's apartment, to look for the proof, but then me dad found out and set up the business with the van—"

"SHADDAP!" I barked.

She sniffled again.

And then she ran, her footsteps fading from the panopticon, until the only sound I could hear was the sound of my own heart, flailing away.

97

THE SECOND HEAVY CHAT
OF THE NIGHT

I spent the next several hours in closed-eyed silence. Maybe it was
even longer than several hours. Maybe it was shorter. It was hard to
tell. In any case, I spent the time vowing never to trust another girl in
my life. I spent it vowing to break out and wreak horrible vengeance
upon everyone who had ever screwed me over, until—

I heard a little rustling in the cell next door.

"Hello?" I whispered anxiously. "Is somebody there?"

"Carlton?" a disembodied voice replied. "Is that you?"

I bolted upright, my eyes popping open. "Dad!"

"Yes, it's me," he said. "How are you, Carlton?"

"How . . . am I?" I laughed.

"Sorry. Stupid [#@%&*] question."

"Did you hear any of the stuff that happened a couple of hours
ago?"

"No. I was asleep. I think they drug the food in this place."

I heaved a shaky sigh of relief, even though I wasn't sure why.

"Oh. Good. So . . . how are you?"

"I'm alive."

"Amen."

"What's new?" he asked.

"Oh, you know. Same old, same old."

"Yeah. Me, too."

"I've been thinking a lot of the design of this place," I said. "I guess they got the idea from you, huh?"

"There are no original ideas, Carlton."

"And by using that old saying, you prove your own point, Dad."

"I guess so," he said.

"How's the constipation?" I asked.

"About the same. The train hasn't left the station in days. I feel like a school of jellyfish has made a cozy little home in my intestines."

"Nice imagery," I said.

"Yeah, well, you're not the only artist in the family." He cleared his throat. "Carlton, why didn't you ever tell me that you drew comics for a newspaper?"

I frowned. "How'd you find *that* out?"

"Gregor MacClough told me. He told me that his daughter was watching you. He told me that she snuck into your room at boarding school and that she hacked into your e-mail and that she engaged in a vigorous correspondence with your editor at some newspaper. You know what else he told me? I know you'll appreciate this . . ."

I swallowed. "What's that?" *Please don't let it be about how she kissed me.*

"Gregor MacClough was the one who first approached me about designing the Fortress of Eternal Life™. He used a straw man, some rich American quack friend of his, so I wouldn't suspect he was involved. His plan all along was to get me to design it. And once it was finished, his plan was to steal the design from me. But he never wanted to freeze people in it, the way all my other clients do. His plan all along was to freeze salmon in it. You know, so he can keep an eye on the salmon all the time."

98

DEEP, POETIC, AND ANNOYING

I suppose I should have been shocked.

I wasn't, though. It would have taken a lot to shock me at that point. To be honest, I was sort of relieved.

"Wow," I said.

"He definitely wants to freeze you and me in it, too, of course," Dad added, "but we'll be the only people. He told me so. Carlton, it looks like we'll be spending all eternity together, frozen and imprisoned in a building full of fish. Pretty gruesome."

"Could be worse," I said.

"Could be worse," he echoed.

"Dad, you know, before we *do* get frozen, I just want to ask you something."

"Shoot."

"Why the hell did you give me that coffee table book for my sixth birthday?"

He chuckled. "I wanted you to learn about your heritage."

"But we're from Scotland."

"The Vikings *conquered* Scotland from the Romans, Carlton. Why do you think our ancestors went around stealing ancient artifacts from their neighbors?"

Right. The answer made sense. It made as much sense as anything else, at least. No wonder I'd fantasized about smashing in heads with an ancient Nordic weapon. Viking violence was in my blood.

"Carlton, I'm proud of you," Dad announced out of nowhere.

"You are?"

"You came here to try to save me."

"Well, I'm not just here for you. I'm here for Olivia, too."

"Oh, my God." Dad gasped. "He took Olivia? That [#@%&*]—"

"No, no," I interrupted. "He didn't take her. She's fine. She wants her dad back. So I promised her I'd come get you. *That's* why I'm here."

Dad didn't say anything for a long time. I heard only the hum of the electronic cameras, pointing at us from the tower.

"Carlton . . . I—I know I haven't been a saint," he finally stammered. "Intimacy has never been my specialty. And the whole feud gave me a great excuse to avoid it. That's why I wanted to be frozen with the rest of my clients, you know? So I could escape—"

"It's okay, Dad," I interrupted, my throat tightening. "You don't need to tell me. You don't need to apologize. I know it all. I found your final testament."

"You did?"

"When I was looking for the proof," I said.

He drew in his breath. "Well, then, Carlton . . . I'm going to tell you something I've learned. I know now that the strongest things in the world are also the most porous and flexible. And that's the way I need to be. Like the atmosphere. You can see straight through to outer space, but you can't break through it without a rocket ship. And water? It slips right through your fingers, but if you get caught under even a centimeter of surface, you're dead. Human skin . . . it scabs and bleeds and sloughs off and *dies,* but nothing can penetrate it: neither atmosphere nor water. You see what I'm getting at?"

I laughed, wiping away a few tears. "No, Dad. Sounds like a load of deep, poetic, and annoying BS. Sounds like you've been stuck here for way too long."

He laughed again, too. "Well, hey, cut me some slack, kiddo. It's not every day you're locked up in a prison of your own making."

99

LOCK PICK

Something was wrong with my knapsack. The sketch pad wouldn't fit back in. I kept trying to shove it and shove it.

There was something poking out from down there, among all my dirty laundry.

I peered inside.

Good God.

It was Aileen's Swiss army knife. She must have left it in there by accident. I pulled it out. *Ha!* I thought. *Sucker!* A burst of tortured anguish shot through me, followed by rage and adrenaline. The karmic pendulum was swinging my way again. Yes! *This* served her right. Because now I would use her stupid knife to pick the stupid lock on these stupid bars, then I would use it to track her down and . . .

Best not to get too excited, though. She was probably watching me right now.

100

[#@%{*]-HEAD

"Carlton?" Dad asked. "What are you doing?"

"Busting us out of here," I grunted. I blindly reached through the bars and twisted my arms around, awkwardly struggling to insert one of the knife's little scissor blades into the keyhole. "I'm picking the lock . . ."

"Son?"

"Yes?"

"Don't be a [#@%&*] head."

I smirked. "Thanks for the tip, but I'm *not*. Believe me, you'll thank me when I'm done. I drew a comic about this once. I researched it. The way keys work is that they just push in a tiny little lever . . . the trick is to push that lever without having to navigate all the bumps and stuff in a keyhole. I can do this . . ."

"I don't doubt that you can," he said. "I'm talking about the surveillance. This is a panopticon. Remember? They're watching you right now. They're listening to me talk. And they're probably aiming a gun right at—"

"Dad, I know. I was just thinking the same thing, too. But, hey, maybe we'll get lucky. I mean, isn't the whole point of a panopticon really so the prison guards don't *have* to watch? For all we know, those cameras aren't even turned on."

The scissor slipped into a metal latch. I jammed it in as far as it would go. The cold metal bars dug into my wrists.

"I don't know," Dad said dubiously. "If they—"

CLACK!

The door swung open.

101

THAT MAKES TWO DOUBLE-BARRELED SHOTGUNS

"What did I tell you?" I whispered elatedly.

I dashed out and scrambled over to Dad's cell. He smiled at me through the bars. I suddenly realized I hadn't actually seen him since I'd left for school this summer. *Jesus.* He looked like he hadn't showered, shaved, or changed since then. His suit was torn and filthy. What little hair he had left was a mess. Stubbly whiskers covered his face in a shadow of unfinished beard growth.

My lips tightened as I crouched beside the lock. I was going to get back at the MacCloughs for doing this to him. Oh, yes, I was.

Hmm.

Picking this lock was a little trickier than the last. The little scissor blade wouldn't even fit into the keyhole.

"Um . . . how's it going there, Son?" Dad asked nervously, staring into the bank of video cameras.

"I don't get it," I muttered. "Maybe all the locks are different—"

"Oi!" a voice hissed.

The knife clattered to the floor.

A silhouette emerged from the shadows behind the tower.

Great, I thought, panicked.

It was Aileen. Or Annabel. Or whoever.

In addition to her battered leather satchel, she was carrying a shotgun. This gun was longer and more lethal looking than the one her dad had carried. Funny: It was also symbolic of yet another lie of hers—another to add to the list of thousands. Nobody she knew owned a gun in Orkney? Her whole freaking family owned guns.

Ha . . . Maybe it wasn't so funny.

"Hi," I mumbled. I raised my hands over my head.

She slung the rifle over her shoulder and glided in her silent cat-like way over to the cell door. "Put those down," she whispered, pulling a key from her pocket.

I stared at her. "What?"

She stuck the key into the cell door and swung it open, then reached in and dragged Dad out. "I was hoping you would find the knife I left you," she said in an oddly flat voice. "Now come on. We're getting out of here."

I glanced at Dad, baffled.

He gaped at her.

"Now!" she barked. "We don't have much time."

"What are you doing?" I struggled to my feet.

"Ending the feud once and for all. Me dad doesn't plan on letting you go, Carlton. He plans on wiping you out. The entire Dunne clan, too—including the wee one back in the States. I'll be damned if I let him get away with it. I should have known he'd go this far when he sent me to the States, when he took your father, when he let that inn be torched. He's gone mad. But a body kens best whaur their am shae nips."

Dad squinted at her. "What was that last part?"

I grabbed his other arm. "Don't ask," I grumbled. "Don't ask *anything*."

102

TIME

Time really does stand still when you're locked up in a prison. For some reason, I'd thought the sun had long since risen. But it was still dark as the three of us sprinted across the damp lawn back toward the wilderness and Loch Stenness. For some reason, I'd also assumed that Annabel had taken some rudimentary precaution to make sure we could escape safely, seeing as she'd made the effort to bust us out of the panopticon in the first place. But she hadn't. I was quite sure of this because her dad began shooting at us before we'd even made it past the swimming pool.

Ping!

The bullet bounced off the satellite dish.

If being imprisoned makes time stand still, then being shot at has the exact opposite effect. Time accelerated like a rocket, propelling us into a sweaty, manic, fevered chase. Gregor MacClough pursued us into the woods. He hollered and swore at us the whole way. Luckily, he only managed to get one more shot off. I'm not sure if that was because he couldn't reload and run at the same time, or if he was concerned about accidentally shooting his daughter. Somehow, I had a feeling it was the former.

And then the woods came to an end, as abruptly as they'd begun.

And the three of us nearly plunged right into the placid waters of Loch Stenness.

103

AN UNCEREMONIOUS SPLASH

"Heh!" Gregor MacClough snarled, bursting out of the woods seconds later. "Isn't this a case of history repeating itself?"

I gulped, glancing between the muzzle of his shotgun and the water's edge. This was it. This was *really* the moment of my death. That old ticking clock had finally expired. And I was definitely too young to die. This wasn't just cowardice or desperation talking, either. I mean, it *was*—but I was a seventeen-year-old comic book geek. It wasn't fair.

"Hand it over," he commanded.

The bad part: We were all panting too heavily to respond. But there was no need. There was nothing *to* hand over. I assumed he was talking about the dagger, and my dad and I certainly didn't have it.

At this same exact moment, we both turned to Aileen.

She pulled the dagger from her satchel.

Its silver blade flashed in the moonlight.

I turned back to Gregor MacClough, my heart thumping as loudly as a *Deux Chevaux* engine.

A smile spread across his face. His hard eyes locked with his daughter's. "You're a good girl," he said.

"No, I'm not," she said.

"Aye, you are."

"No, I'm not," she repeated. "But as Mum used to say, there's no use keeping a dog and barking yourself."

She gave him a long, sad smile, fiddling with her hair.

Then she spun around and hurled the dagger over the loch as far as she could.

The four of us watched it as it spun end over end in the night sky, glittering in a graceful arc, until it vanished beneath the water with an unceremonious splash.

104

NOTHING MORE

"Annabel!" Gregor MacClough wailed. "What have you done?"

"I've ended it," she answered simply. "I've ended it all. The dagger is gone. No more blood needs be shed. No more crimes need be committed. The Dunnes stole the dagger from us centuries ago, yes. But we kidnapped a man. We betrayed another. I betrayed him. I betrayed the man I love! It's shite! It's bollocks! We're no better than them. I say the crimes cancel each other out. I say we make peace. I say it's over and done with. I say, Michts no aye richt."

Her father dropped the gun and dashed to the water's edge, his lips quivering.

All of a sudden, he looked very frail and helpless.

All of a sudden, I almost felt sorry for him.

Annabel took my hand. "Now you can tell your little sister that her father is coming home," she whispered. "Good-bye, Carlton."

She kissed me once on the cheek—and gathered up her father and her gun and disappeared back into the woods.

That was it. There was nothing more.

It was . . .

It's hard to say what it was. I can only describe it viscerally: it was that fast, that shocking, that simple but dramatic.

In that moment, it was over: All five days' and eight hundred years' worth.

I watched her go.

105

ALL THE PEOPLE WHO HAVE WALKED OUT OF MY LIFE FOREVER

Dad sat down on the damp sand.

I sat down beside him.

We sat there next to each other, he and I, as the first light of sun began to glow at the horizon. I wondered what he was thinking. I hoped it was something along the lines of What a big fat relief.

He deserved to think that.

For my part, I was thinking about Annabel, of course. And that got me thinking about all the other people I'd watched walk out of my life forever.

- MOM, THROUGH NO FAULT OF HER OWN
- MARTHA AND OLIVIA, GRIMLY PACKING UP THEIR BELONGINGS LAST WINTER
- KYLE MOFFAT AND BRYCE PERRY, WORDLESSLY EXITING THE WHO-WOULD-YOU-BANG FORUM

And then, naturally, in bullet-point style, I thought about Mr. Herzog. True, he'd never walked out of my life. He'd showed me how to leave, though. He'd shown me the exit: *"If a person stays locked in that mental prison for too long, only a massive epiphany or a traumatic event can break a person free . . . Only that can stop a person from seeing the world as a two-dimensional conflict of Good versus Evil . . ."*

He was right.

That smart, groovy, tweed-wearing Good Guy was right.

So I guess I'd watched another person walk out of my life forever too: me.

I knew then that for once, my Enemy Within and I had an understanding. We weren't at odds. We'd made peace, the way all real comic book heroes do with themselves. I'd lost Annabel forever, but I'd *lived*. She'd given me something. She'd finally given me that key to the mental prison. She was the only one who could.

I put my arm around Dad's shoulder.

He put his arm around mine.

"Beautiful sunrise, isn't it?" he said.

"It is," I said. I opened my mouth to add something.

"What?" Dad asked.

"Nothing."

"No, tell me." He pulled me closer. "What were you going to say?"

"I was going to say: 'What—me worry?'"

EPILOGUE

106

SENSITIVE BUSINESS MATTERS

When I returned to Carnegie Mansion, four days later . . .

It was pretty bizarre.

For one thing, my whole dream pretty much *did* come true. People weren't frantic in their pajamas (it was afternoon), and the campus wasn't crawling with cops (it never had), but I sure as hell wasn't invisible anymore. I was "That Guy Who Ran Away for a Week." People didn't just smile at me; they *followed* me. They whispered about me. Perfect strangers[67], kids who had never once even said hi, suddenly approached me as I walked from the principal's office to my dorm room.

"Where have you been?" they wanted to know. "What happened to you?"

And this was all within the first two hours of being back.

It was a little overwhelming, to say the least.

So was the amount of schoolwork I had to make up.

Honestly, I'd half expected to be kicked out. But Dad—God bless

[67] By strangers, I mean girls, too.

him—not only sat down with the administration on my behalf in a fit of magnanimous weirdness but offered a donation in the six-figure range and swore I'd never run away again. Of course, he was in a great mood. Because two days earlier, upon our return to the States . . .

Martha and Olivia asked to move back in with him.

And he agreed but on one condition: that Olivia allowed him to have direct access to Conrad MacSchtoon. After all, if his daughter and her business partner were wheeling and dealing, then he wanted to be privy to inside information. He told her that he felt entitled, if only for having spawned such a genius. He buttered her up.

Olivia drove a hard bargain. She eventually acquiesced, however, provided that Dad talk to Conrad MacSchtoon only in her presence, so she could monitor their conversations. After all, certain business matters were particularly sensitive.

Dad agreed.

Olivia and Martha moved in immediately.

107

THE SWIRLIE THAT NEVER WAS

But back at school that first day, I had my own business to take care of. I was as single-mindedly focused as Olivia.

I had to plunge Bryce Perry's head into a toilet.

I'm not sure how or why this brilliant idea lodged itself in my brain. But sometime, somewhere on the journey back from Orkney to the States, I saw myself marching straight into Bryce's room, grabbing him, and giving him the swirlie of a lifetime. I figured I owed it to myself, as much as to him.

So that's what I did.

Well, the first part anyway. As soon as I got back to my dorm, I headed straight for his room. The door was unlocked. I threw it open.

Bryce was sitting at his computer. He jumped.

"Carlton!"

"Yes, Bryce. It's me. Time for a swirlie."

"You're back." He sighed. "Jesus, dude. You had me scared to death."

"I what?"

"When you didn't reply to my e-mails."

My eyes narrowed. "What e-mails?"

"I'm Night Mare, you idiot," he said. "I thought you would have figured that out by now. Who the hell else pays any attention to you?"

I blinked a couple of times.

A lot of questions arose. But the one I chose to ask—and I'm not sure why, maybe it was the shock, maybe it was the disbelief—was: "Um . . . you're not gay, are you?"

He laughed. "No, Carlton. I'm not gay."

"I mean, it's totally cool if you are. But I'm not, so—"

"I'm not gay, dude!" he barked. "Jesus. I like comics. But comics are freaking dorky. So I like to keep that private, you know? Anyway, last year, when I was borrowing your crap, I looked through your sketch pad. I never told you about it, because, you know, I was looking through your crap. But I saw a bunch of sketches of *Signy the Superbad*. And I mean, I'd already figured it was you—but this was proof. I was a fan already. So I thought I'd write in and say what a kick-ass job you were doing."

I slumped against the doorframe.

It took me a moment to process this all. I didn't know what to think. On some level, I was supremely disappointed—because my second order of business, after giving Bryce Perry a swirlie, was meeting Night Mare and sweeping her off her feet.

"Why didn't you just tell me?" I finally asked.

Bryce snickered. "Come on, dude. You can't tell anybody who you really are at this school. I mean . . . *you* know that better than anyone."

I nodded. I thought of Annabel.

"You're right," I said. "But I—"

Bee-bee-beep. Bee-bee-beep.

"Sorry, hold on a second." I pulled my cell phone out of my pocket. "Hello?"

"Carlton! Roger Lovejoy here!"

108

SOME LIMEY

I glanced at Bryce Perry, cupping my hand over the mouthpiece. "I gotta take this," I whispered. I hurried back to my room.

"Hello? Roger?"

"Carlton, let me just tell you: You did great. This serial is your best work. I love it. I love everything: Herzog, Angela, Conrad . . . these characters have some depth, you know? I can see this being a real story. A real graphic novel, as you like to say."

"Really?" I asked.

"Yeah! Just do me a favor. Never send your son to a convention in your place again. Don't get me wrong: I love the kid. He's just not *you*—know what I mean?"

I grinned. "Sure, Roger."

"So listen, where did you get the idea for the Hammer of the Gods?"

"Well . . ." I was about to tell him a lie. But I decided against it. If guys like Bryce Perry were coming clean, then why shouldn't I come clean, as well? "My dad and I are way into our Viking heritage," I admitted. "Also, we both love Led Zeppelin."[68]

There was a sniff.

"Your dad?" he asked.

"Yeah. It's a long story."

"You'll have to tell me some time."

"I will," I said. "When we meet face-to-face."

"I'd like to do that." He paused. "You know, Carlton, I have to be honest with you. You've really turned me around in these past couple of weeks. I didn't even want to hire you at first. The only reason I did was because somebody offered me a bunch of money. They sent me an anonymous check."

I laughed. "That's a good one, Roger. Have you heard the one about the one-legged dwarf?"

"No, I'm serious! I never found out her name. I only spoke to her once. She was some limey. She said she'd been watching you, and she loved your stuff. She said she overheard that first phone call. You know, when you had your son call me, last October?"

And all at once, his voice began to recede—as if he were speeding away down a long tunnel. . . .

And the only part of it I caught was: "By the way, you and your son sound a lot alike, you know that?"

---

[68] The most popular biography of Led Zeppelin is *Hammer of the Gods*, by Stephen Davis. My dad owns an autographed copy. Stephen Davis was born in 1947.

109

SOME SECRETS YOU JUST HAVE TO TAKE WITH YOU TO THE GRAVE

I spent the rest of the afternoon alone. It had nothing to do with misanthropy; I just needed some time to myself. I would have missed dinner and spent the entire night by myself, too, if it weren't for a knock on the door, around 7:15 P.M.

"Carlton, dude!" Bryce Perry hissed. "It's me and Kyle. Can we come in, bro?"

"Door's open," I replied.

They rushed in and sat down side by side on the edge of my bed. Both of them gazed at me, eyes and smiles wide.

"So?" they said.

I laughed. "So . . . what?"

"So who was that chick who snuck into your room that night, dude?" Kyle yelled.

"Dude, you can't keep secrets from us," Bryce said, winking at me. "Why do you think we forced you to host the Who-Would-You-Bang Forum? We know you've been banging some chick. We saw her sneak into your room the night you snuck out. Just tell us who she is. Is she the reason you ran away? She doesn't go to this school, right? Did you meet her at some comic book convention?"

Now I *really* had to laugh. "No, Bryce, I didn't meet her at a comic book convention."

"Where did you meet her, then?" Kyle asked.

"Uh, it's a long story. I don't even know where to start."

There was another knock on the door.

Oh, brother. I supposed I should get used to this. Everyone was watching me now. Then again, they always had been.

"How many other people did you invite here?" I groaned, opening up.

I froze.

It was Annabel.

She stood there before me, in a blue dress. I'd never seen her in a dress before. Her hair was clean and golden, flowing in wavy curls down her shoulders. She was smiling. She was a vision.

In her left hand, she held an electric toothbrush.

"Hallo," she said.

"How—what—how did you find me?" I gasped, instantly forgetting Bryce and Kyle. "What are you doing here?"

"I always wanted to come to the States to be a cop, remember?" she said. She waved the toothbrush at me. "Anyhoo, I used some of the money to fly over and to buy one of these gizmos, so I never have to worry about me red fish breath again."

I shook my head in shock. "Money? What money?"

"The money the Edinburgh museum gave me. Just a little token of their thanks for donating Agricola's dagger. I also used it to help get that old couple back on their feet . . ." She sighed. "Anyhoo, me dad is done with his dirty business. I threw the dagger into the loch on purpose. I threw it there because I knew that I would be the only one able to find it. I'm the only person in all Orkney who knows how to scuba dive!"

I stepped toward her.

I couldn't believe she was real.

I reached forward . . .

She looked down at her shoes. "The past is gone, Carlton," she murmured. "Period." She glanced up with a rueful grin. "And I knew that nobody in all of Orkney would think to scuba dive for a dagger. So here I am. I'm moving to Hartford. I'm applying for American citizenship, and I think I'll be able to get it. And as soon as I pass the test and get my card, I'm going to enroll in the police academy there. And maybe, just maybe, if I'm lucky . . ."

"You'll get to be on *Cops*," I finished.

She laughed. "Aye."

I took her free hand. "Annabel, I have to ask you something."

"Anything."

"How come you never told me that you knew about my comics? How come you never told me that you offered Roger Lovejoy money to hire me?"

She stepped closer. "Because that would mean telling you the truth, Carlton. That would mean telling you I'd spied on you. That would mean telling I'd fallen for you from afar, from before you could possibly realize it." She paused. "Besides," she whispered, "there are just some secrets you have to take with you to the grave."

"There are?"

"Aye."

"Bollocks," I whispered.

She smiled. "Bollocks," she whispered back.

I pulled her close and kissed her.